Fate was playing a trick on him...

Kendra Rutherford was a judge! He would have to be on his best behavior. If Kendra presided in Queenstown, and chances were fair that she did, she would hear his case. Actually, the less he saw of her, the better it would be for the both of them. He hadn't thought seriously about a woman for six long years, since his bitter divorce. Yet the minute he saw Kendra sprawled on the ground, relaxed and yielding, his dormant libido kicked to life with a vengeance.

His reaction to Kendra, a beautiful, intelligent woman, didn't really concern him much. After all, a man wanted to know that he could cut the mustard if he needed to. It did, however, bother him that Kendra seemed to know he wanted her. She'd known he desired her the minute their eyes met. And that made her and the desire she provoked in him hard to ignore.

Books by Gwynne Forster

Kimani Romance
Her Secret Life
One Night with You

GWYNNE FORSTER

is a national bestselling author of twenty-five romance novels and novellas, plus five novels and five novellas of general fiction. She has worked as a journalist, university professor and as a senior officer for the United Nations, Population Division, where she was chief of research in nonmedical aspects of fertility and family planning. In addition to her works published in the name of the United Nations Secretary-General, she has, under her own name, twenty-seven publications in the field of demography. For six years she served as chairperson of the International Programme Committee of the International Planned Parenthood Federation (London, England). This position took her to sixty-three developed and developing countries.

Gwynne holds B.A. and M.A. degrees in sociology and an M.A. in economics/demography. Nine of her novels have won national awards, including the Gold Pin Award, which she won in 2001 for her romance novel *Beyond Desire.*

Gwynne sings in her church choir, loves to entertain at dinner parties, and is a gourmet cook and avid gardener. She enjoys jazz, opera, classical music and blues, and she likes to visit museums and art galleries. She lives in New York City with her husband.

ONE NIGHT
WITH YOU

Gwynne FORSTER

KiMANI
ROMANCE

Acknowledgments

My sincere thanks to my editor, Mavis Allen,
who makes it a pleasure to write; to Carole Joy Smith,
who has known me longer than most people have and
whose friendship and never-ceasing encouragement are
among the true treasures of my life; and to my beloved
husband, my solid rock every day of our marriage.

 KIMANI PRESS™

ISBN-13: 978-0-373-86008-1
ISBN-10:   0-373-86008-0

ONE NIGHT WITH YOU

www.kimanipress.com

Printed in U.S.A.

Dear Reader,

Thank you for making *Her Secret Life,* one of the July 2006 launch books for the Kimani Romance line, such an overwhelming success. I have tremendously enjoyed and been greatly heartened by the letters I received about Jackie Parks and her sizzling romance with Warren Holcomb. To answer some of you, I don't have a sequel planned at this time. I enjoy writing romance, among other reasons, because I always leave my central characters satisfied and happy. Being a Libra, I love to have things balanced and beautiful.

For those of you who read *Naked Soul* years ago and wanted a story about Ossie, you will meet him as Reid Maguire in *One Night with You.* You will also meet Kendra Rutherford, Esq., a savvy sister with inches in all the right places, who makes Reid's life complete.

In addition to my Kimani Romance books, please don't forget that I also write for Kimani Arabesque. I think you'll love the strong hero, Sloan McNeil, in *McNeil's Match,* (released in September 2006), a man any woman would want.

Chapter 1

"I'm fed up. I deserve a life, and I'm going to have one," Kendra Rutherford said aloud minutes after she awoke that cold December morning. So resolute was she that, without waiting to brush her teeth, she wrote a letter to the Chowan County, North Carolina, court clerk.

> Dear Sir,
> For the last five years, I have gone once monthly to every hamlet in Chowan County to judge the cases awaiting trial. I am tired of it. I am bored with it. I want a change, and if you cannot assign me to a single, permanent jurisdiction, expect my resignation.
> Yours sincerely,
> Kendra Rutherford, JD, Esq.

She addressed, stamped and sealed an envelope, thinking, *I can always return to law practice. Arguing some of these petty disputes is less boring than judging them anyway.*

"But being a judge is an esteemed position," her sister, Claudine, said when they spoke later that day.

"Big deal," Kendra replied. "It's been so long since I had a date that I wouldn't know how to act on one. Nobody invites me to go anywhere. It's been a year since I was in anybody's home other than mine, excluding yours and our parents', of course. In the first place, people who know I'm a judge practically genuflect when they see me, and in the second, I don't stay any one place long enough to make friends with men or women. Half the time, my family has no idea where I am unless I telephone."

"Good grief, Kendra, I hadn't thought of it that way. Papa loves saying, 'My daughter Kendra, the judge.' He'll be unhappy if you quit."

"He'll be even more unhappy if I go nuts. Fourteen years after getting my law degree, I don't have a single thing to show for it. As a judge, I'm at the bottom of the pile. Socially, I'm not even *in* the pile. There'll be some changes made. And soon."

"It isn't like you to do anything rash, Kendra."

"That's the worst thing you could have said to me. Hell, Claudine, I don't even *remember* being a teenager. Work hard, study hard, please everybody! That's been my life since I remember it."

"Yeah? And it paid off, didn't it?"

"Depends who's looking at it. Look, sis, I'd better

pack," Kendra said. "I have to try cases in six towns before I get back home. Last time I was on this circuit, I ran out of stockings and underwear, so I have to concentrate on what I'm doing right now. Talk to you soon."

Reid Maguire propped his left foot on the bottom rung of a ladder that leaned against Philip Dickerson's stables and looked eye to eye at the owner of the largest agricultural enterprise in southeastern Maryland.

"It's time I left Dickerson Estates and got on with my life," Reid told Philip, the man who had saved his life and, in due course, become closer to him than his own brother. "I've saved enough to get started, and I have a job. I'll be an assistant architect in a noted firm, but after what Brown and Worley and that class-action suit did to my reputation, I'm fortunate to get that."

"It isn't going to be easy for you, Reid. You were one of the foremost architects in that part of Maryland, and you had your own firm. You were the one giving the orders. This will be a terrible comedown."

"I know, Philip. And I've reconciled myself to it. But by all logic, I should be dead, and if it hadn't been for you, I would be. It had to be a blessing that I stopped you on the street in Baltimore that day and asked you for a dollar and a half. I meant to buy a razor with it and finish myself off. One day I was on top financially and professionally, and, thanks to the biggest lie ever propagated in a court, a day later I was flat-broke and even my home and my car were taken from me. Worst of all, with my reputation destroyed, no one would hire me. I slept on the street, and lived off the kindness of strangers.

"If my beautiful wife had sold the jewelry I'd bought her or gotten a job and taken care of us until I could ride out the storm, it would have been different, but no. The lady walked. You didn't give me the money I asked you for, Philip. Instead, you offered me a job and a second chance. If you ever need me, just call. You will always know where I am."

"Thanks, friend," Philip said. "Just stay in close touch. I know you'll be back on top. If you need me, you know where to find me."

They embraced each other, and Reid gazed around him at the prosperity that was Dickerson Estates, cultivated land as far as he could see; fruit and nut orchards. He painted in his memory the big white Georgian mansion, stables, barns and the dormitory he had designed that allowed the eleven men who lived and worked on Dickerson Estates to have privacy within the context of communal living—men of different races, languages and religions whose lives Philip Dickerson had turned around when he gave them a second chance.

It had been his home for six years. Years during which he'd come to accept that the woman he'd loved, who'd sworn that she loved him and who bore his name, had divorced him because he could no longer care for her in the manner to which he had made her accustomed. He gripped Philip's shoulder and, for a moment, stared into the man's eyes, sky-blue eyes that he'd always seen as gentle and caring.

Without another word, he walked away. As he headed

down the lane to the big iron gate that bore the letters *DE,* Max, Philip's foreman, drove past him and stopped.

"Hop in, Reid. Where you headed?"

"The bus station. Trains and planes don't go to Queenstown, North Carolina, where I have a job."

"Never heard of it. What part of the state?" Max asked as he drove through the gate.

"It's over on the Albemarle Sound toward the border with Virginia."

"It won't be the same here without you, man. We'll all miss you. Good luck to you."

"Thanks, Max."

Two hours later, Reid sat on an interstate bus headed for the next chapter in his life.

Kendra drove through the sleet and slush to get to the post office. No matter how many times she asked the court clerk to send her mail to her home address, the man sent it to the post office box that she used only to prevent certain people from knowing where she lived. To her delight, she found the clerk's letter and opened it before she closed and locked her box. "Dear Judge Rutherford," he wrote.

I am happy to inform you that as of January eleventh, you will preside at criminal court in Queenstown. If I may be of any further assistance, please let me know.
Ethan Sparks, County Clerk

Hmmm. So she had only to ask. It was a lesson she did not plan to forget. Inasmuch as she'd had few reasons to spend her salary, apart from rent and a few personal items, she decided to buy a house. She packed her belongings, had them stored, drove to Queenstown and rented a room in a bed and breakfast, then began her search for a house. After a week, she settled on a town house in Albemarle Gates, a new, elegant Queenstown community on a hill overlooking the Sound and within walking distance of Courthouse Square where she would work. The back of the house afforded an unobstructed view of the Sound. Delighted with her choice, she signed and received the deed, had her furniture and other belongings moved to her new home and settled in at Number 37A Albemarle Heights, Albemarle Gates.

The second morning Kendra was in her new home, exhausted from moving and arranging furniture, the sound of drums, at least one bugle and a trumpet brought her to her second-floor window facing the street. She dropped the pillows she had been changing on the bed and raced down to the front door to see what she thought was some kind of ceremonial parade. Native Americans, some in full tribal regalia, danced along in traditional tribal steps, and as many African-Americans, including the bugler and the trumpeter, danced with them. When they stopped in front of Albemarle Gates, she was delighted, but when a neighbor standing nearby groaned, "Oh, Lord. Here they are again," she got a feeling of apprehension.

"What's the problem?" she asked the young woman.

The woman rolled her eyes and threw up her hands as if in exasperation. "Honey, you don't want to know."

"Oh, but I do."

"They're picketing the builders, Brown and Worley, because they built this community on top of sacred Indian burial grounds, and in this town, whatever riles the Indians upsets the blacks and vice versa. They stick together, and they get things done, but not this time. Nobody is going to tear down Albemarle Gates. Besides, I hear Brown and Worley are fixing to build another one of these communities over near the park. Where you been you don't know about this?"

"I've been in Queenstown exactly ten days." She turned to introduce herself, but the woman had left. *Hmmm. Nice to meet you.*

She went back into the house and sat down to contemplate what she'd just learned. How would the controversy affect her in her role as judge? Obviously, many local people would think that, by living there, she had taken sides with Brown and Worley. She didn't like it, but she'd signed the deed and taken the mortgage, and she didn't see a way out.

In the supermarket the next day, Kendra received a sample of small-town hospitality when she put her groceries on the check-out counter. "How are you today?" she asked the clerk. "Pretty cold out, isn't it?"

"Push your stuff forward. The belt's not working."

She scrutinized the woman, making certain that she was a sister. "Do you live here in Queenstown?" Kendra asked her.

The woman stopped work and gazed at her. "I live here. My mother and father live here, and so did my grandparents and great-grandparents. Anything else you need to know?"

Taken aback and angered at the woman's insulting tone, Kendra said, "Pardon me. I didn't expect a nasty response to my graciousness. I don't care where you live." She paid for the groceries and drove home. In front of her house, she took the bags of groceries out of the trunk of her car, closed the lid and lost her footing, slipping on the ice. Her packages fell to the ice, spilling the contents, and she struggled unsuccessfully to get enough traction to heave herself to her feet. Not certain whether to laugh or cry at the spectacle she suspected she was, she relaxed and lay there.

To her amazement and eternal thanks, two large hands gripped her shoulders and lifted her to her feet. A smile began to spread over her face as she looked up at her rescuer, but it ended around her lips, as she practically froze. She had never seen such eyes, mesmerizing grayish-brown eyes that seemed ready to sleep beneath their long curly lashes. Eyes that didn't seem compatible with the man's strong masculine presence. She stared at him. Poleaxed. Stupefied and unable to pull herself out of it.

"Are you all right now?" he asked her, his voice deep and lilting.

She thought she nodded. He bent down to pick up an orange and was suddenly chasing oranges and lemons across the ice, music pouring out of him as he did so, in what she figured was a laugh. As he managed to retrieve the fruit, he stashed it in the pockets of his thick leather jacket. He seemed to be having the time of his life as he chased and recovered the fruit. He got a head of cabbage, looked at it, shrugged and handed it to her. She put it in the grocery bag. He played the game until the grocery bags were almost full. Then he took the fruit from his pockets and put it in the bags.

"Where do you live?" he asked her. "I'd better carry this for you, because I'm not sure I'm up to sliding around to pick this stuff up again."

"I don't know how to thank you. I'd probably still be trying to get up."

"It was my pleasure. Best exercise I've had in a while."

She opened her front door, and he put the bags on the floor in the foyer beside the door. "I'm Kendra Rutherford, and I just moved here."

"I'm Reid Maguire, and I live in that apartment building across the street from here. Nice to meet you." He turned and left, and she realized that he had shown absolutely no interest in developing a friendship with her. What a letdown!

Reid Maguire didn't talk much, and he never spoke if silence would suffice. He didn't know Kendra Rutherford, and his reaction to her was none of her business. If he'd learned anything, it was the virtue of feeding a good-looking, sexy woman with a long-handled spoon, as it were, so as to keep as much distance as possible between him and her. Kendra Rutherford might not be an aggressive man-eater, but her reaction to him was the same as his to her, and that spelled trouble.

There might not be another woman on earth like

Myrna, his ex-wife, but he didn't intend to start testing that theory. He'd had it with women, and he didn't want one cluttering up his life pretending that she loved him, when she only loved what he could give her. At the moment when he had needed his wife most, she had walked out on him.

Tomorrow, he would begin work as an assistant with the architectural firm Marks and Connerly, Architects, Ltd. He didn't intend to spread information about his former status. If his new colleagues guessed or knew who he was, so be it; if not, he didn't care. He was back in his chosen field, and he meant to make the most of it.

But he was not to have the benefit of anonymity. "I've been doing some research on you, Reid," Jack Connerly, the senior partner, told him when they met, "and I think we hit the jackpot when we hired you. We've contracted to design an airport terminal in Caution Point, about thirty miles from here. Would you like the job?"

"I'm stunned. How many enemies in the firm will this get me?"

"Who knows? Do you want it?"

"Absolutely. I'd like to see the site, but I don't have a car."

"You can take a company car. Make a list of what you need to work with and give it to the supply clerk. Your expenses are covered up to three fifty per day, excluding transportation, and you can't put alcohol on your tab."

"Thanks. I'll give you two or three sketches."

"Great. It's good to have you with us. Your office is two doors down on the right."

Reid walked down to the end of the hall and back. There were sixteen offices, eight on each side of the corridor, and only one office separated his from that of the senior partner. So far, so good. They weren't paying him what he was worth, but when he finished the design of that airport terminal, they would.

In the drugstore about three blocks from his apartment, where he stopped in the hope of finding a felt-tipped pen, he bumped into Kendra, almost knocking her down.

"Hello," she said. "I'm not usually this clumsy."

"It was my fault. I hope I didn't hurt you." He allowed himself a smile, and headed for the aisle in which he'd previously found unlined tablets large enough for drawing, though he would have preferred bigger ones. Seeing no pens of any kind, he walked around until he'd satisfied himself that he wouldn't find them in that store, and that he'd have to wait till the supply clerk at Marks and Connerly filled his order. As he started for the door, he noticed Kendra struggling with a large container of liquid soap and a few other items. After counseling himself to pretend he didn't see her, because he didn't want any involvement with her, he walked over to her.

"Let me help you with that. I hope your car is around there in the parking lot."

"It is. Thank you."

He lifted the container of liquid soap. "Did you think you could carry this?"

"I was hoping that I could."

"Uh-huh. Come on."

* * *

Kendra's eyebrows shot up. The man's attitude was as masculine as his looks and aura. His "come on" was nothing short of a command. She walked with him to the car, not in obedience but in gratitude for not having to carry that heavy load.

"You're very kind to me, Mr. Maguire."

"It's the way I was raised. I'll ride home with you."

He made no effort to be ingratiating, she saw, and she appreciated that. It had begun to dawn on her that Reid Maguire knew who he was and didn't have a need to curry favor or to shine up to anyone. Well, neither did she.

She parked in front of her house, opened the trunk of her car and, unwilling to wait for him to do it, walked around to remove her purchases. When she got to the trunk, Reid Maguire stood beside it with both hands on his hips. She glanced up at him and felt as if she would shrink beneath the assault of his withering stare.

"If you'll go ahead and open your door, Ms. Rutherford, I'll bring these things in for you."

"Thanks, Mr. Maguire." She did as he suggested, feeling as if she'd had a parental tongue lashing. She was not used to his kind of man. Besides, she didn't expect men to do things for her just because she was a woman.

"Where do you keep this?" he asked, referring to the big container of liquid soap.

"In the laundry room, but that's down in the basement."

"Ms. Rutherford—"

She held up her hands, palms out. "All right. All right. On that shelf to your left, please."

He put the soap on the shelf, came back upstairs and headed for the front door without saying anything.

"Mr. Maguire!" She spoke sharply, and he stopped, turned and looked at her with an expression that questioned her impudence. "Sorry, but I wanted to get your attention. Thank you for helping me. You were raised to be gracious. So was I, and I'd appreciate it if you would at least accept a cup of coffee or tea, or a glass of milk, in case you don't drink tea or coffee."

He stared at her for nearly a minute, and when a half smile formed around his lips, she nearly grabbed the banister for support. What a mesmerizing man! "Thank you for a cup of coffee. I hope it isn't instant. I get that at home."

She took a deep breath, recovered her equilibrium and said, "You'll smell it in a minute."

To her surprise, he followed her to the kitchen and took a seat. He pointed to a loose board at the base of the radiator. "Why doesn't this surprise me?"

"What? Why doesn't what surprise you?"

"That board hanging loose down there in a brand-new house. This builder is known for his shoddy work. I'll bet if I went through this house, I'd find a dozen things wrong with it."

She got two plates, cut two thick slices of chocolate cake, got forks and napkins and put them on the table with the cake. "The coffee will be ready in a minute. What do you know about Brown and Worley?"

"Plenty."

She put the coffee in front of him. "Would you like milk and sugar?"

"Milk, please."

Something wasn't right, and she had to find a way to pry from him the information that he was obviously in no rush to provide.

"Did you buy a house from Brown and Worley?"

"This cake is delicious. Did you make it?"

"Yes, I did. You didn't answer my question. But if you'd rather not…"

"Brown and Worley built an apartment house that I designed."

She stopped eating the cake and looked at him. "So you're an architect. I gather they did a poor job. Tell me what happened."

"Part of the building collapsed, injuring a number of people. The builders swore in court that they followed my design to the letter and brought numerous witnesses who attested to their competence. One man could not stand up to some of the most exalted building firms in this part of the country, at least two of which were owned by Worley's cousins. I lost a class-action suit, my home, my wife and every dime I had."

"Especially not one black man," she said under her breath, but he heard her.

"That, too."

"How long ago was that?" she asked him.

"A little over six years."

"Did you know at the time that the witnesses were Worley's blood relatives?"

"No, and neither did my lawyer. I discovered it a

couple of months ago while surfing the Internet for anything that would help my case."

"Did you print out what you found?"

"Yeah. Of course I did."

"Then you can reopen the case, but you have to do it within a year of the date on that printout. You may claim the Discovery Rule, which says you may appeal on the basis of new and relevant information. If you were bankrupt when the statute of limitations applied, you may appeal as soon as you get funds."

"Thanks. That's good to know. Mind if I ask how you happen to have this information?"

"I'm a judge."

His whistle split the air. "Where do you preside?"

"Beginning Monday, I will be the presiding judge at the courthouse up the street. I'm looking forward to it. Would you like some more coffee? I made a full pot."

"Thanks." He drank the second cup quickly.

"I expected that, in a town this size, people would be friendlier," she said and related to him her experience with the store clerk who resented being asked if she lived in Queenstown.

"They're hospitable, Ms. Rutherford, but you walked into a problem."

"What do you mean?" she asked him, and at the memory of her neighbor's comment about the group that marched up to Albemarle Gates, its members beating drums and blowing a bugle and a trumpet, fear seemed to settle in her.

"This building is sitting on sacred Native American burial grounds, and sixty percent of the people in this town and the surrounding areas think you've sided with the builders who committed this sacrilege."

"What will I do? I didn't know anything about it."

"Be careful, especially when you're out at night."

She sank into her chair, unaccustomed to the feeling of defeat that pervaded her. With a deed and a mortgage, she couldn't walk away from the house. "Thanks for the warning. I've been here barely two weeks, and I'm in trouble. I don't like the sound of this. Tell me, what do you do now?" she asked him.

"I just got a job with Marks and Connerly, my first job as an architect since that debacle, and I'm lucky to have it. I'd better be going. Thanks for the coffee and cake. Both were delicious."

She wanted to detain him, but she knew instinctively that it would be the wrong move. Reid Maguire was a loner, and every sentence he uttered seemed to struggle out of him. Grudgingly. "Thanks for the company," she said as she walked to the door with him, "and for the help."

He glanced down at her from beneath his thick, curly lashes and smiled with seeming reluctance. "It was my pleasure."

He left without saying another word. Didn't he know how to say goodbye, or did he have some kind of superstition about it? Holding a conversation with him was as easy as getting a politician to tell a straightforward, uncoated, denuded truth.

She raised her right shoulder in a limp shrug. Damned if she was going to let him bamboozle her every time he rearranged his face into a provocation for female capitulation. She'd like to meet the woman who walked out on that man. She watched his lilting strut as he crossed the street on his way home. Maybe he wasn't sex personified, but, to her, he was a tantalizing tidbit. Or, perhaps she'd been working in the boondocks too long. However you sliced it, Reid Maguire looked to her the way upstream salmon looked to a hungry bear.

A judge! Was fate playing games with him, putting him on his honor? If Kendra Rutherford presided in Queenstown, chances were fair that she would hear his case against Brown and Worley, provided he managed to bring it to trial. She hadn't been reluctant to give him good advice, and he meant to follow it, but the less he saw of her, the better it would be for both of them. He'd spent six long years on Philip Dickerson's estate, during which time he hadn't wanted a woman and hadn't touched one. Before Myrna walked out of his life, he hadn't been celibate or even considered it since he was thirteen, but his disappointment in Myrna had so embittered him that he couldn't have made love with a woman if his life had depended on it. Yet, the minute he saw Kendra sprawled out on the ice, relaxed and yielding to her inability to get up, much like a dying man submitting to the inevitable, his libido had returned with a vengeance.

It wouldn't have concerned him too much—after all, a man wanted to know that he could cut the mustard if he wanted to, but she knew he was there, and she knew it the minute she looked at him. That made the nagging desire that afflicted him when he saw her more difficult to ignore. But he had a long way to go before he could consider tying up with a woman; he meant to clear his name and reestablish himself, both of which could take years. By that time, Kendra Rutherford would have long forgotten that Reid Maguire existed.

He walked into his bedroom, pulled off his jacket and hung it up. He wouldn't mind having some more of that wonderful coffee she'd made. "Oh, damn. I left my drawing pad in her house. Too bad. It'll just stay there. I'm not going to give her the impression that I left it as an excuse to go back there. I'll use some plain bond paper." He remembered that a former classmate had settled in Caution Point and telephoned him.

"Marcus, this is Reid Maguire."

"Great guns! How are you, Reid? It's been years. Are you in town?"

He explained where he was, where he'd been and the reason for his call. "I can't even begin work, because I know nothing about Caution Point. What kind of place is it?"

"We're right at the edge of the Albemarle Sound, a sleepy town that looks old. You wouldn't want to put anything like the Sydney Opera House here. New buildings are usually dark-red brick or cement, and almost none are glass-fronted. Trees everywhere, park benches and wide streets. The tallest building is around eight stories, and we have only a few of those. I'm glad to know you're back in business, man. When you come here, I'd like you to meet my family."

"I'll let you know. Thanks for your help, Marcus."

He hung up, satisfied that he could acquit himself

well. The structure shouldn't be ultramodern, but neither should it be standard. He decided to produce a design that resembled a huge multi-level private house with a glass-and-cement exterior. Trees would surround its front and sides, and every long walkway would have two-way moving walks with comfortable, built-in seating at strategic stops. He warmed up to the idea, and was still hard at work at two o'clock the following morning.

On Sunday morning, Kendra went to one of the churches nearest to Albemarle Gates, a big, white-brick Baptist church on the corner of Albemarle Heights and Atlantic Avenue. African-Americans made up the bulk of the worshipers, and the smaller fraction consisted of Latinos, Native Americans and a sprinkling of whites. She sat in an aisle seat about midway, and it stunned her that when the collection was taken, the usher moved the basket past her so quickly that she did not have a chance to put in the twenty-dollar bill she held in her hand. When he retrieved the basket, he lifted it above her head, so that she knew his action was deliberate, that he did not want her to contribute. Whoever heard of a Baptist church turning down money?

Still shocked by the usher's deliberate snub, at the end of the service she attended the coffee hour in the hope of meeting some of the parishioners. However, to her chagrin, no one spoke to her. She left and trudged up the hill, hunched over against the wind that whipped in from the Albemarle, blowing her breath upward to warm her face. Finally, she ran the last few steps to her house.

The phone rang shortly after she entered her house. "This is Kendra Rutherford," she answered and remembered that she'd better stop identifying herself when she answered the phone, for she was sure to encounter local hostility in the course of her work.

"Hi. This is Claudine. Where were you? I rang you a dozen times."

"I went to church."

"See any nice guys?"

"Don't make jokes. If I had, I doubt they would have spoken to me." She told her sister about her experience at church. "I won't be going back there."

"Maybe they take seriously that biblical passage that reads, 'Judge not, that ye be not judged.'"

"I wish I thought it. I'll have to find out what's behind this. It's not normal."

"Sure isn't normal for a church to reject money. Why don't you ask one of your neighbors about it?"

"Maybe I will."

Reid Maguire didn't care to be friendly, but she wasn't asking for friendship. Tomorrow morning, she would be a stranger, perhaps an alien, on display among a people who, so far, hadn't shown her civility, not to speak of graciousness, the only exception being a man who'd come to town two weeks before she did. She needed information, and if he didn't want to provide it, she was going to give him an opportunity to refuse. She wasn't timid, and she didn't know anyone who thought she was.

Kendra put on her storm coat over jeans and a red cashmere sweater and headed across the street. After checking the list of tenants on the board in the mailroom to find the number of his apartment, she walked down the hall to the garden apartment in the back of the building and rang the bell.

The door opened almost at once, and Reid peeped out at her. Both of his eyebrows shot up. Then he opened the door wide and stared at her. "Uh... Hi. What's up?"

"I know you're busy, and I know you don't want to be bothered, Mr. Maguire, but you're the only person I've seen in this town who seems willing to give me the time of day. I've been snubbed royally, and before I'm a sitting duck on that bench tomorrow morning, I want to know what's going on here."

He stepped back and opened the door a little wider. "Come on in and have a seat." He showed her to a comfortable and very masculine living room. "If you'll excuse me a minute, I'll be right back."

She glanced at his bare feet and the jeans rolled up to expose his ankles and well-shaped calves, and took a seat. Evidence that he might be less than peerless, and therefore accessible, was not something that she needed. The man was neat, she observed as she looked around, and he had good taste. He'd furnished his apartment well, and without spending a lot of money.

She'd surprised him, and he didn't try to hide it. Thoughts of what could have run through his mind when he saw her sent the blood rushing to her face. He returned wearing shoes, his jeans had been unrolled and a plaid, long-sleeved shirt had replaced the short-sleeved T-shirt.

"Sorry I can't offer you coffee, unless you'd settle for instant."

She disliked instant coffee. "It's not my favorite, but if you make it strong, it isn't too bad," she said, wanting to be gracious.

"I'll boil some water." He was back in a few minutes with two mugs of coffee. "If I remember, you drink yours straight. What's the problem?"

She told him of her experience in church that morning and reminded him of the supermarket clerk's rudeness.

"I see. Look, Ms. Rutherford. Out here, African-Americans stick with the Native Americans, and you're the only African-American who's bought a town house in Albemarle Gates. According to what I've learned, there's been contention about that place from the time Brown and Worley posted a sign stating the intent to build. For the last three years, there've been riots, fighting, sabotage, strikes and picketing about that place. The Native Americans went to court, but as usual, they lost. Nobody cares about Indian graves. In fact, this country has a sorry record in dealing with Native Americans. Period.

"It's too bad you're stuck in that mess, but I don't know how you'll get out of it. Around here, feelings run high about that site, and from what you've told me, the locals seem to feel that you've taken sides against them."

"This is quite a pill."

"It is, but I don't think you should explain to people that you were unaware of the controversy. Seems to me, they ought to know that."

"Well, I thank you. Now that I know what I'm up

against, I'm really worried. I'd better go before it gets dark."

"Don't be afraid. I'll walk you across the street."

She leaned toward him. "Succeeding in this post is so important to me, and here I am in the midst of a political battle. I asked for a change, and this is what I get."

"What were you doing before you came here?"

"There are a lot of little towns and hamlets whose populations aren't large enough to warrant a full-time judge. I traveled among the small towns and hamlets in two counties, visiting each at least once monthly to try the cases on the docket. As judges go, that's about the lowest job. After five years, I demanded a change, and this is what I got.

"Reid—I hope you don't mind if I call you Reid. And please call me Kendra. As I was saying, I didn't have a life. I had no friends of any kind, because I couldn't cultivate them. I rarely saw the inside of my apartment for two consecutive days. I decided I deserved better. I came here with arms open, ready to embrace the world and everybody in it, and I got my first dose of rejection."

He propped his left foot over his right knee. "I can easily imagine that. You seem very young for a judge."

"I'll be forty in a couple of days. I'd hoped that my sister would come up to be with me, but she's preparing for a show, and can't spare the time."

"Can't you go to be with her?"

"It's a thought. We could at least have dinner together." Each time she caught him looking directly at her, he shifted his gaze, except when he was talking to her.

"You had five wasted years," he said. "Oh, I know

you can rationalize that as years of learning, but I suspect you didn't need to learn what you experienced in country courtrooms."

"Not all of it, or even most of it, but I did learn that there's something beautiful about simple people who see life and themselves accurately and who don't shy away from the truth, not even when it reflects adversely upon them."

"I met a few such individuals working on an estate during the last few years."

"What did you do at that estate, Reid, if you don't mind saying?"

"Philip taught me to be a groom. I worked on his farm and in his orchards, but mostly with his horses. I couldn't have made it back this far, if I hadn't had refuge on Philip Dickerson's estate. The man literally saved my life, and then helped me back on my feet. He wanted a dormitory for the men he'd salvaged, so I designed one and supervised its construction. Those guys live in splendor now. Philip gave us bank books and deposited a high percentage of our salary in it weekly. Since we had no expenses, our savings added up quickly because he paid us standard wages. He had rules, but those rules helped to strengthen every one of the twelve men who worked for him."

"Does he make any profit?"

Reid's fondness for Philip Dickerson showed in the warmth of his smile. His face radiated pleasure, captivating her. "Absolutely. Every man there would go to the wall for Philip. He treated each of us as if we were his ood brother. He and I became really close. I miss him."

Reid caught her staring at him, and she glanced away. "I've…uh…ruined your Sunday afternoon, Reid. Thanks for being so nice. I'd better go."

He stood when she did. "You haven't ruined my afternoon and another thing, Kendra. I'm not all that helpful. I mind my business and stay out of trouble.

"Something tells me that if you want to win a case in this town, you might need some local friends. You never know what's in the back of a juror's mind." He held her coat for her, and she had to resist the urge to move away from him. The man's aura was getting to her. She'd never shied away from men, but whenever she was close to *this* one, she got the feeling that she was about to step into a pool of hot quicksand. She turned, buttoning her coat, and he remained there, inches from her. She sucked in her breath and he stepped away from her in a move that said he did not want to become involved.

"Did you see a white plastic bag at your place?" he asked her, as if she had imagined that tense moment.

"About like this?" She held out her hands to suggest a space of about fourteen inches wide.

He nodded. "That could be it."

"I think I saw it on the kitchen counter."

He put on his leather jacket and walked out with her. When they reached the curb, a caravan of motorcycle riders approached, and he grabbed her hand, restraining her. "Let's wait till the last one passes," he said. "Sometimes they'll observe this crosswalk, but usually they won't."

She prayed in silence, "Please turn loose my hand." The last motorcycle passed, and he released her hand, as unceremoniously as if he'd never touched it. She had an urge to smack him.

"I'll get your bag," she said as they entered the house.

"Thanks. I'll wait right here." She brought the bag that obviously contained a tablet of some kind. "Why didn't you come back for it?"

"I didn't want to disturb you. Thanks." He had his hand on the doorknob and a grin on his face when he said, "Good luck tomorrow, Your Honor," and treated her to a wink. As usual, he didn't waste his breath saying more, but turned and left.

"I wonder what a full dose of that man's charisma would be like," she said aloud, "but I am not anxious to find out."

Chapter 2

Kendra locked her front door and sat down on the sofa in her living room, contemplating the enigma that was Reid Maguire. He didn't want an involvement with her, and probably not with anyone else, but if, as she suspected, he hadn't had a woman in his life for a while, he'd be as tempted as she was. Those were not terms that she cared for.

"I've got two problems," she said aloud, "and I'll probably solve my relationship with this community before I get Reid Maguire out of my blood." It didn't help that he was starting over, as it were, struggling to reach the pinnacle of his profession. That meant that she would empathize with him because, in some respects, she was doing the same. She went up to her bedroom, took a black robe from the closet and examined it.

Deciding not to wear a lace collar with it, she chose a white satin open-collared dickey. Her eight-year-old black patent leather boots would have to do because she'd broken a heel on her more presentable ones. Where was that box of jelly beans? She found it in a kitchen drawer, filled a plastic sandwich bag with some of the beans, put them into her briefcase, and considered herself equipped for work. She seldom allowed herself to be without a bag of jelly beans.

She reread the background information that the clerk had sent her on the first case, the suit of a woman who had bought a diamond bracelet over the Internet, had had it appraised and been advised that it was worthless. Unfortunately for the woman, she'd paid heavily for it. Either the buyer or the seller would learn a lesson.

She awakened the next morning after a restful night, got ready for her first day at work, made coffee and her thoughts immediately went to Reid who, she knew, had to settle for a cup of instant. She walked up Albemarle Heights thinking that she was fortunate to have found a house so close to her work, and so her mood was bright and cheerful when she entered the courthouse and showed her badge to the guard. The man nodded, but she wasn't sure toward which direction.

"Where is chamber 6A?" she asked him, and he pointed to his left with his thumb much as one uses the thumb to hitch a ride.

She could feel her temper rising. "I am the judge in charge of this court," she told him, "and nobody who works here should be rude to me and expect to keep his or her job. If you've got your behind on your shoulder because I bought a house in Albemarle Gates, it tells me how foolish you are. I came here looking for a house, found one and bought it. Neither you nor anybody else in this town put an ad in the paper or a sign near that property advertising your objection to that housing. So show me your best face and tell all of your colleagues to do the same, or this courthouse will have a completely new slate of employees. And soon! Now, where is chamber 6A?"

She had never seen a colder stare. "Yes, ma'am. Right over here, ma'am," he said and walked with her to the elevator. "Sixth floor, and turn right."

"That wasn't difficult, was it?" she said and got on the elevator without waiting for his answer.

Fortunately, her clerk showed better judgment. "Good morning, Judge Rutherford. I'm Carl Running Moon Howard, your clerk. Court begins at ten, unless you'd like the time changed, and ends at three. We have an hour for lunch. Here are the keys to your chambers. How do you like your coffee?"

"Good morning, Carl. I'm delighted to meet you. That's the warmest greeting I've received since I came to Queenstown. I like it black without sugar. Thank you."

"I know, ma'am. It's too bad you didn't know about those burial grounds. It's gotten to be political, and people are taking sides. I hate this kind of thing, ma'am."

"So do I, Carl. I saw ads in the papers for the houses, came here and drove throughout the city looking to see what else was available, and that suited me best. I had no way of knowing what that builder had done. I'd give anything if I hadn't bought there, but I am there, and I've put my money in it. So I'm staying."

"People will soon know what kind of person you are, ma'am. I'll get you some coffee. Incidentally, the previous judge had a little microwave oven, mini-refrigerator and coffeepot in that little storage room over there. It came in handy I don't know how many times. Your cases for today are in that black incoming-mail box."

He brought the coffee, and she studied her morning cases until she'd satisfied herself that she understood them and the hoopla surrounding them. The clerk had included half a dozen newspaper clippings about the cases she would hear that morning.

The jury had already been selected, and the morning session began normally enough, but within the hour, she found it necessary to put the defendant's attorney in his place.

"Would counsel approach the bench," she said after he ignored her mild reprimand.

"What may I do for you?" he asked.

Shocked, she quoted to him a section of the law that specified the conditions under which a trial lawyer may be cited for contempt. "I won't hesitate to do it," she said. "In fact, I'd enjoy doing it. It's best not to play with me. Your client's in bad enough trouble as it is. Do I make myself clear?"

With his face flushed and his lower lip sagging, he said, "I'm sorry, Your Honor. Please accept my apology."

"I take it you told him what was what," Carl said to her after she adjourned the court for lunch. "He was the attorney for a builder who tried to get that Albemarle Gates property and failed."

"How did Brown and Worley get it?"

"They say it was bribery, ma'am, but who knows?"

The lawyer for the plaintiff brought four expert witnesses to prove that the diamonds in the bracelet were, in fact, zircons, and the jury's guilty verdict did not surprise her. She agreed with it.

She left the court longing to tell Reid how her first day went. But why should he care? She went home, turned up the heat, changed into jeans and a sweater and gave some thought to what she would cook for her dinner. She had never been the object of scorn, and knowing that she was made her want to reach out to someone who cared. Dumping her troubles on her sister didn't make sense, for Claudine would stagger beneath the burden of it as if the problem were her own.

She scrubbed a potato, dried it, patted it with olive oil, rolled it in a piece of paper towel and put it in the microwave oven. She was staring into the frozen food section of her refrigerator when the telephone rang. *Please, God, don't let that be a harasser.*

"Hello."

"This is Reid. How was your first day?"

"Reid! I wanted to call you… I mean, I wanted to tell you about it."

"Well, how'd it go?"

"Good and bad."

"You're going to explain that?"

Why was she so nervous? "Wait a minute and let me get a chair." She put the phone down, rushed to the kitchen for a swallow of water, dragged a chair to the console on which the phone rested and sat down. "I'm back. Well, first the guard was rude to me when I walked into the building, but a few choice words subdued him. I have a really nice and competent clerk, a Native American man, who's gracious and helpful. But I had to put the defendant's attorney in his place with the threat of contempt. Seems he was the attorney for a builder who tried unsuccessfully to get permission to build on the Albemarle Gates property. Have you heard that Brown and Worley bribed anyone to get that permit?"

"They've been accused of it, but the accusation didn't hold up. I suspect you've had all the problems you're going to have at court—news travels fast. All the same, it pays to watch your back."

"It's not a good feeling, Reid, knowing that people don't like you although you've done nothing to earn their dislike. Besides, I'm a people person. I smile at folks, and I expect them to smile back, but nobody's smiling at me here."

"Nobody?" She imagined that his eyebrows shot up. "I smiled."

"Yes, you did." She settled more comfortably in the chair. "At least once."

Laughter rumbled out of him, and she wished she could have been with him then to see those lights dancing in his eyes. "If I had another potato," she said, throwing prudence to the wind, "I'd ask if you wanted to share my supper."

"What goes with the one you've got?"

"Steak burger seasoned with onions, egg, mustard,

ketchup and Maggi sauce, fresh asparagus and a mesclun salad."

"I've got an Idaho potato, if that would persuade you to follow through with that idea. And I'm pretty good at cleaning up the kitchen."

"You wouldn't consider scrubbing that potato before you bring it over, would you?"

"You bet. Uh…what time would you like to have the potato?"

"About a quarter of seven."

"Great. By the way, does Her Honor drink wine with her steak burger?"

"Whenever she has it in the house."

"See you later. And thanks, Kendra."

She hung up and sat there for some minutes contemplating what she'd just done. For a woman who didn't want a relationship with the man, she had all but initiated one with that invitation. *Oh, I'm not going to exorcise myself about it. He's not married, and he's good company. Besides, he's interested or he wouldn't have called me.* She started down to the basement for some firewood in order to build a fire in the living-room fireplace and stopped. Suppose his case came before her! She shouldn't develop a relationship with Reid knowing that, if his plan succeeded, he'd have a case before her within the next ten months. *Oh, what the heck, I can recuse myself.*

She toyed with the idea of changing her clothes to look more respectable, but discarded it. She looked perfectly fine in her jeans and sweater, and if she put on anything sexy, he'd think she was coming on to him, and he'd be right. Still, she combed her hair down, put a pair of medium-sized gold hoops in her ears and set the dining-room table.

Her doorbell rang precisely at a quarter to seven and she wondered if he'd been standing at the door looking at his watch so that he could do that. She opened the door and got a sharply raised eyebrow from him.

"Hi. I'd have whistled, if I hadn't thought it would be rude. You look…like a pretty teenager."

"Oh. Thanks. You mean the jeans?"

His expression suggested that she was unreal. "I mean the whole package." He handed her the potato, scrubbed and unwrapped, and a bag containing a bottle of wine. "I hope you like Châteauneuf du Pape."

"I'm not an aficionado of fine wine, Reid. I go to the liquor store and ask for chardonnay if I want white or Chianti if I want red, so I'll look forward to this one."

"It's smooth. I think of it as a red that suits a lady."

"That's the second nice compliment you've given me in the ten minutes you've been here. After the bashing my ego's had in this town, I needed it. Now, come on in the kitchen with me and behave yourself."

"Whatta you mean by that?"

"I mean if you keep saying such nice things, you'll have me in such a stupor that you won't get any dinner."

"Now, you behave. Where do you want this potato?"

She held out her hand. "Whoops!" she said when she felt the electric static that passed between them.

He stared at her, and she turned away, went to the counter and began greasing the potato with olive oil.

She'd made an enormous mistake, and she had to spend the evening with it.

"What are you doing to that potato?" His voice was too close, so close that she didn't dare turn to the left or to the right. *Dear God, please don't let him touch me.*

"Just what it looks like. Here. Wrap it in a piece of paper towel and put it in that microwave oven."

"Where's the paper towel?"

"It's… Oh, I don't know."

"Turn around here." His hands gripped her shoulders, but they turned her gently. "Come here."

His grayish-brown eyes had become thunderheads heralding what she knew would be a violent storm. She didn't know what he saw in her eyes, but at that moment she wanted him. He pulled her close and lowered his head so slowly that she reached up and with her hand at his nape, guided his mouth to hers. His lips trembled as they crushed hers. His groans sent shivers throughout her body, sending her blood rushing to her vagina, exciting her, and when he rimmed the seam of her lips with his tongue, she opened her mouth and sucked him into her, pulling on him, sucking and feasting. Her nerve ends seemed afire. If only she could crawl into him. The heat in her vagina rose with the seconds, and something akin to an itch demanded friction. Oh, how she wanted him skin to skin, his chest to her breasts, and his penis buried deep inside her. She pulled his tongue and sucked it vigorously until he suddenly pushed her away.

As if he feared that he may have hurt her feelings, he brought her back to his embrace, but didn't let his body touch hers. "I've been celibate for a long time,

Kendra, and if anything ever happens between you and me, I want to be sure of the reason."

She wanted to tell him that nothing would happen between them, but after what she'd felt seconds earlier in his arms, she didn't believe it and she didn't feel like lying.

Instead she said, "I could say the same, Reid. Take care of that potato for me, will you?" He didn't move, so she glanced at him.

"Have I... Are you... Is everything all right with you and me?" he asked her.

She faced him. "Yes. You're straight with me. Now we know where we stand."

He didn't bat an eyelash. "We always knew, Kendra. Now we have to deal with it. Is that blue thing the microwave oven?"

She couldn't help laughing. He'd put demon desire in its proper place and expected that she would do the same. "Yes, that's it, and I'd be happy if it was any other color." Their simultaneous laughter cleared the air.

"You could grow on me," he said, and turned the kitchen chair around and straddled it.

"What does that mean?"

"Come now, Kendra."

"Reid, talking with you is like taking a true and false test. You don't explain anything unless I pull it out of you."

"When I was in my twenties, I didn't appreciate your type of woman. Accomplished, cut and dried. What you see is what you get, and if you don't like it, keep moving. You're as straight as the crow flies and beautiful to boot."

"And I assume that means you like women who are honest."

A smile formed around his eyes, and she looked the other way. Did that man know how attractive he was? "Right. And beautiful. Don't leave that out," he said.

She liked his sense of humor, and she was beginning to like him. "How do you like your burger? Medium or well done?"

"Well done. May I watch you mix it up?"

She agreed, and he stood beside her while she added the eggs, onions and seasoning to the ground beef, made three large patties, put a small amount of oil in the frying pan and set the meat to cooking. "That's reasonable," he said. "You put in them what we usually put on them after they're cooked." She turned on the microwave oven, raised the steam level under the asparagus, took the bowl of salad out of the refrigerator and put it on the table.

"That didn't take long, and you got everything ready at the same time. That's a trick."

"I did the work before you got here, but took about fifteen minutes."

"Say, wait a minute," he said. "Don't put that food in serving dishes. I can serve myself right from the pots and pans. Remember, I'm the one who's cleaning up."

"But—"

"But nothing. If I'm cleaning up, what I say goes."

She handed him a plate. "Two of those burgers are yours. I can only eat one. I'll peel the potatoes."

"You can peel yours. I eat the skin. All I need for this potato is some butter and black pepper."

"Butter is not good for you," she said, "so you're getting a substitute that tastes like butter and has no trans fats."

The expression on his face was that of one thwarted in the course of a satisfying act. "But—"

"But, as your hostess, I have the responsibility to protect your arteries, and that's what I intend to do."

He filled his plate and headed for the dining room. "I don't suppose I can argue with that. What did you do with the wine?"

It dawned on her that he behaved almost as if they had known each other for a long time, and save for the minutes she'd spent in his arms, she felt about the same. Or maybe he didn't put on airs. After she said grace, he opened the wine, tasted it and poured half a glass for her. "I hope you like it. Say, why don't we drink to…" He got up and walked over to her, hooked his right arm through hers and said, "Let's drink to us. What will be, will be." He sipped the wine as he gazed into her eyes. "You like it?"

"What?" she asked him, thoroughly discombobulated. "Oh, you mean the wine. Stop knocking me off balance. I never did that before. I love this wine."

He returned to his seat and his meal. "This is the first wine I've purchased in almost seven years. Philip always provided wine for the help on weekends, but not during the week. He didn't allow any alcohol on the estate except in his house, and I soon got out of the habit of washing my dinner down with the best wine I could find."

"I'm learning that you were very wealthy."

"I was, and if I ever get back there, I'm going to live differently. I'm going to keep the friends I've made during the last six years, people who care about me, not people who loved what I could do for them."

"Did any of them stick with you?"

"Naah. It's like Billie Holiday said in that song. 'Money, you got lots of friends hanging 'round your door, but when the spending ends, they don't come 'round no more.'"

"I've never had a lot of it," she said, "so I don't know, but I'm not surprised."

"This is the best burger I ever ate, and I love burgers. Kendra, this is a wonderful meal right down to my *butterless* potato." Her head went up sharply. "Just kidding."

"The dessert is simple," she said when she brought the sliced strawberries that had been marinating in a mixture of raspberry jam and cognac. "If I'd made this last night, it would be better, but I did it after we talked this afternoon."

He tasted it. "It's delicious. Sit down and eat yours." He was good at giving commands, a habit that he would have to unlearn if they were to be friends.

"I told you about my first day on the job, Reid. How was yours?"

"Thank you for asking. It went smoothly, without a wrinkle. I got my supplies, a company credit card, a key to one of the company station wagons and, most of all, a key to an office one place removed from the senior partner. I know that last part doesn't mean much, but eventually it will. I'm satisfied, so far."

"Does the management know your story?"

"Yeah. They know about the trial and who I was before that, and I'm glad they do. It's all in the open."

She reached over, patted his hand and immediately wished she hadn't done it, for the static electricity shot through her again. With a grudging smile, he transformed his face into the picture of sweetness. "Wondering what it would be like if we really touch has begun to boggle my mind," he said.

She wasn't about to comment on that. "I wonder if I can get away with walking down to the water," she asked him, as if he hadn't alluded to the possibility of their making love. "I haven't done that yet, and I love the water."

He seemed pensive for a moment. "Ordinarily, I'd say, why not? But all things considered... Look. I'll walk down there with you Saturday morning. It's very lonely, and you hardly ever meet anyone, so..."

"Okay. Will we go before or after I do my marketing?"

"After. It's cold out there early mornings. Let's say...about eleven."

She looked at him while he savored the dessert with obvious relish, and her gaze focused on his long and tapered fingers, smooth hands that seemed so strong when they held her. "Do you play the piano or any other string instrument, Reid?"

"Piano and guitar. How'd you happen to ask?"

"Your hands are perfect for both. Nice hands."

"Thanks."

He stopped eating and gazed at her until she said, "Would you like some more?"

"I don't have any more space, or I'd love more. It was delightful." He still looked at her as if he wanted to find something in her, something that he hoped was hidden there.

"You make it very comfortable for a man, and you do it without trying. Thanks for the dinner." He leaned back in his chair and focused upon her so intently that she squirmed. And he realized it because he said, "I'm sorry. I'd better go. See you Saturday morning at eleven." He wrote something on the label of the wine bottle and said, "Call if I can be of help."

He stood, patted his pockets for his keys and, as if he suddenly remembered, took the dessert dishes to the kitchen, and was soon heard moving around there and whistling as if he were at home. He didn't ask for help or information, and she didn't offer any. It appeared that an architect followed some logic in the kitchen and the arrangement of its contents, and well that was, because she didn't dare go in there. Both of them were sitting on kegs of sexual dynamite, starved for affection.

He came back in about twenty minutes. "It's good as new. See you Saturday." As usual, he left without saying goodbye, and one day she would ask him why.

Talking about quicksand, Reid said to himself as he raced across Albemarle Heights. He knew himself and he knew that if he touched her, he'd want it all. She thought she was dressing down when she put on those jeans, but in them, she was sex personified. She hadn't wanted to give him the wrong impression, but he couldn't change what happened to him when he first saw her.

She's between me and what Brown and Worley owe

me. If their attorney learns that she and I are friends or even close acquaintances, I'll lose that case before it starts. I think I'd better make myself useful around here and get the people of Queenstown on my side. Kendra's right, because this is the jury pool.

Who would call him at nine o'clock at night? Certainly it couldn't be Kendra. He didn't know what he would do if she even hinted that she wanted him to go back there. He shrugged and rushed to the phone. She wouldn't do it. The woman had strength as well as guts.

"Maguire speaking. Good evening."

"Hey, Reid. This is Philip. How's it going?"

"Philip!" He sat down in the nearest chair. "It's great to hear from you. How's your dad?"

"Dad's fine. We're anxious to know how it's going with Marks and Connerly."

"So far, so good." He gave Philip the same information that he had given Kendra a little earlier. "It's a chance. I'll see the location for the airport terminal tomorrow and adjust my sketches accordingly. I like what I've seen of Jack, and I think we'll get along."

"You don't know how much it pleases me to hear that. Do you think you can come down to the barbecue Easter Sunday? If so, we'll be glad to see you. I'll let them all know I've spoken with you."

Reid hung up, gathered his laundry and put it in his laundry bag. He would drop it off at Royal Laundry—half the establishments in Queenstown had either *royal* or *crown* as a part of their name. He'd wash his socks, but he would gladly pay someone else to do the rest of it.

He got up early the next morning, made a cup of instant coffee, showered, shaved and dressed in an Oxford-gray business suit. How good it felt to be going to work as an architect again. If he wasn't careful, he'd feel tears sliding down his face. He got into the station wagon, adjusted the seat to fit his height and headed for Caution Point. He'd driven twenty miles before the pangs in his belly reminded him that he hadn't ingested anything that morning but instant coffee.

He pulled into a roadside restaurant, had a breakfast of melon, waffles, country sausage and perked coffee, and continued his journey. Remembering that he'd promised Marcus Hickson to get in touch with him when he went to Caution Point, he took out the cellular phone that he had bought the previous weekend and telephoned his old friend.

"Hello, Marcus, this is Reid. I'll be in town today. Could we meet for lunch?"

"Yes, indeed. You don't know Caution Point, so why don't I pick you up at twelve-thirty? Where will you be?"

"At the corner of Bowder and Checkers."

"Great. I'm driving a silver-gray Mercedes."

"And I'll be in a brown Cadillac station wagon. See you then."

A gray Mercedes, eh? He hoped his friend hadn't turned into a "rich man," because he'd sworn to keep his feet on the ground and to associate only with people like himself. He remembered that women loved Marcus, but that Marcus had his eye on a tall lanky one who, in his opinion, was the epitome of frivolity. *Well, we both had lousy taste in women. I sure hope he got over that one.*

He loved the location for the terminal. With a minor adjustment, the terminal he'd sketched with a round dome above a square building would best fit the space and the environment. He sat in the office that Jack Marks had rented for him, and altered the sketch. Then, in case Jack preferred the structure that resembled a large private house or mansion, he made notes as to the necessary alterations, locked the office and went to meet Marcus.

When the big gray sedan drove up, Reid got out of his station wagon and walked across the street to meet the man he hadn't seen since he left graduate school. He'd been in the School of Architecture and Engineering, and Marcus had been in the School of Music. They'd roomed two doors from each other in the men's dormitory. He smiled when Marcus started toward him, and the years quickly vanished as they laid up high fives and then embraced each other, their old routine.

"You haven't gained a pound, man," Marcus said, "but I've put on sixteen."

"Sixteen pounds is nothing on a six-foot-four-inch frame. If you'd lived my life—at least my life the last seven years—you wouldn't weigh more, either. Where'll we eat?"

"I assume you're going to explain that, but if I remember properly, I'll find out what it means only after I pry and insist."

"Oh, I'm not that bad. Did you marry that tall, slim beauty?"

"Yes, but she split when the going got tough. I've got

a real gem of a woman now, and she is definitely not the willowy type."

They ate at a new Italian restaurant not far from the school where Marcus's wife, Amanda, was the principal. "You learned a lesson," Reid said when the conversation turned again to their pasts, "and I sure hope the hell I did." He told Marcus about the loss of his company, his wealth and his reputation, how he'd made it back to where he was.

"I feel you, man," Marcus said. "I came within a hair of losing my business, and if it hadn't been for my wife, I would have. Next time you're here, I want you to meet her and my three children. The oldest one is from my first wife, but if you see her with my wife, you'd never know it. I'm a lucky man."

"I'm on my way back, man," Reid said, "and it's a great feeling."

"Take it slow," Marcus advised. "Be patient. If you find a good woman, latch on. She'll make all the difference. Say, what's wrong with me? I'm sitting here talking with a first-rate architect. Reid, I told you that I repair fine musical instruments, string instruments, and that my factory is in Portsmouth. I'm planning to open a factory here in Caution Point, and eventually— maybe two or three years hence—I'll close the one in Portsmouth. I repair anything from a Steinway concert grand to a Stradivarius. Would you design a building for me? The place has to be humidity proof."

"I work for Marks and Connerly, and I'm not sure you'd want to pay their fare. I'm also not sure they'd let me do it on the side. I'm straight, Marcus, so I'd have to ask. I can tell the boss of our relationship and see if that will make a difference."

"Not being able to make your own decisions must go against your grain," Marcus said.

"Not right now, because I know I'm lucky to be working for a company of this caliber. If I'm fortunate, I'll be back on top and running my own company in a couple of years." He showed Marcus his sketches for the airport terminal.

"Either one of these would work there, but I especially like this one," Marcus said, pointing to the one with the round dome. "It's unique and fits the area."

"Thanks. That's the one I prefer, but it's a long road from this point to the laying of the corner stone."

"I'm sure. When will you let me know whether you can design that building for me?"

"Next Monday, I hope. See you then."

When they separated, Reid had the feeling that he was on his way. He didn't go back to the airport, but took the shortest route to Queenstown. He parked the station wagon in the company's parking lot, locked it and went to his office.

"You're back?" Jack Marks asked him when he answered the intercom. "Are you satisfied? I'm not asking for a report, but I'm anxious to know whether you're comfortable with what you've done so far."

"I am, indeed," Reid said. "I need to make a couple of very minor changes. We can meet tomorrow, if you'd like."

"You bet I'd like. How about lunch? Is twelve-thirty good?"

"Fine," Reid said. "That's my preferred lunchtime."

"I'll stop by for you," Jack told him.

It would be a memorable lunch. "I love this one," Jack said referring to the one with the round dome. "It's perfect. Maybe we can use this other one for something else. It's very imaginative." He snapped his fingers. "It would make a great golf clubhouse. Put it under lock and key. If I can close a deal I'm working on, you've got another job."

Reid told Jack about Marcus's request. "I told him that I wouldn't do it on the side without your permission and that if you didn't like that idea, I'd ask if we could lower the price for him."

Jack's thick fingers brushed back and forth across his chin. "It doesn't seem to be a huge job, does it?"

"The biggest problem will be to control the humidity. It's close to the Sound."

"Right. There're some materials you can install in addition to air conditioning. Tomorrow, I'll write you a letter giving permission. I don't have time today."

"Are you sure it's all right, Jack?"

"It isn't something we would normally do, and I want to encourage you to tackle unusual jobs. It's good experience. By the way, Connerly and I have decided to change your title from assistant architect to architect. It makes more sense."

"Does it carry more pay?"

"Sure. A lot more. I'll ask the accountant to send you a note, and you'll get a personnel action sheet in a day or so."

Reid thanked him. He didn't do it profusely, knew

he deserved the title and pay. Nonetheless, he had a better feeling of his worth as an architect and as a man. "You're a straight shooter, Jack, and I appreciate that."

"It's only just, Reid."

Reid thought for a minute, then changing to a light subject he said, "If I'm going to live here, I want to be a part of the community, but I can't seem to find a niche."

"We have a great theatrical group that's extremely popular. Ever do any acting?"

"Not since undergraduate school."

"They're all amateurs. I'll tell Iris to give you the address and telephone number. This has been a productive lunch, Reid. Let's do it again real soon. Oh, and what we've discussed here is between you, me and Connerly. My architects do everything to get an assignment, except fight duels."

"You bet." He pointed his right thumb to his chest. "What happens here stays here."

He didn't know how he got through the remainder of the afternoon, for it seemed that he would burst with happiness. At a quarter to four, a messenger brought him a letter from the company accountant. He tore it open and stared at its message until the words blurred before his eyes. That promotion nearly doubled his salary. After his first month's pay, he'd have the means to retain a lawyer, and he'd soon be able to buy a car.

All the wonderful things that happened to me today, and I don't have anyone with whom to share it, he thought as he walked home. But he could share it with Kendra, couldn't he? Doing so wouldn't imply anything. After all, hadn't she shared her news with him?

What the heck! It was too good to keep to himself. He walked into his apartment, kicked off his shoes and pants, loosened his tie, dropped himself on his bed and used his cell phone to dial her number.

"Hi, this is Reid. So much has happened today that I have to dump it on somebody, and I don't know anybody here but you."

At the next words in her low, sultry voice, he nearly jumped off the bed. "Hi. Hang up, Reid. Then call me and say, 'You wouldn't believe the day I had. Can we get together so I can tell you about it?'"

He lay back down and stretched out. "What's wrong with the way I put it?"

"You said it as if you'd tell somebody else, but you don't know anyone else in town."

"Well, that definitely is not what I meant."

"So, what did you mean?"

He sat up. "Don't ask me a question unless you want the answer. I want to see you."

"Uh…where?"

"In the middle of Albemarle Heights. I don't give a damn, Kendra. I'll put on a jacket and tie, and we can have dinner someplace, but that would be three whole hours from now."

"Well, since you haven't bought a car, let's ride in mine. I'll put on a pretty dress, you put on that tie, and you be over here in an hour. How's that?"

"Woman, you move fast, but that suits me to a T. I'll be there." He'd almost added that he wanted a kiss when he got there, and it surprised him that that was what he needed from her most of all. He wanted her to rejoice with him, but what he needed was to know that she thought him worth her affection.

He showered, dressed in the Oxford-gray suit with a white shirt and yellow tie. He put on his gray Chesterfield-style overcoat, a remainder from his affluent days, and gave thanks that, in his lowest moments, he hadn't sold it or exchanged it for a hot dog. He'd been wearing it when he'd met Philip. A glance at his watch told him he had thirty-two minutes. He made it to the florist in eleven minutes and cooled his heels while the florist chatted with a neighbor. Vexed, though he knew it was the way of life in a small town, he turned to leave, and the man asked if he could help him. He bought an American beauty rose, had it wrapped in cellophane and tied with a red velvet bow.

He felt like a teenager about to take his girl to his first prom. What had happened to his resolve to stay away from her, his concern that associating with her might jeopardize his case against Brown and Worley? *I can't help it,* he said to himself. *Right now, I need to be with her.*

If Reid was able to rationalize his way out of his dilemma about Kendra, she had no such success, but admitted her strong attraction to him and the trouble in which it would one day land her, and figured that she would have no choice but to take it on the chin when it came. She hoped he'd be worth the price she had to pay.

She looked through her closet and pushed aside the sedate business suits and tailored dresses she wore to work until she found the red silk sheath that fit snugly until it passed her hips and then flared out sassy and flirtatious. Its low-cut bodice promised a delicious tidbit if she let him get that far. She looked at herself in the mirror and frowned. What was she thinking when she bought that advertisement for sex? No wonder she'd never worn it.

What the heck? He wants me, and I want him. Might as well be an adult about it. She combed out her hair and brushed it until it curved under at her shoulder, put on a pair of gold hoops, dabbed perfume in strategic places and took a deep breath. Did she dare wear those spike-heel sandals in weather that was below freezing? And could she drive while wearing them? *I can kick off the right one,* she said to herself and slipped her feet into the shoes just as the doorbell rang.

She opened the door and, to her delight, his eyes lit up and his long, sharp whistle made her heart sing. He stepped inside, closed the door with his foot, and she'd never seen a happier look on a man's face than when he gazed down at her. She felt her tongue rim her lips, and then his big hands were on her seconds before he lowered his head and she rose on her toes to meet his mouth. He came down hard on her, but she didn't care because she felt his need of her.

"Open up to me, sweetheart. Let me feel myself inside you."

She parted her lips, took him into her mouth and as he began to dance and twirl inside her, one of his hands moved down to her hips and the other locked around her bare shoulders. Oh, the feel of his hands on her naked flesh. She sucked him deeper into her mouth, holding him, caressing him while her nerves began to riot and the blood sizzled in her veins as it raced to her vagina. She heard her moans, but didn't care. She wanted him as she'd never wanted anything in her life.

He stopped kissing her and looked down at her. "Sweetheart, if we don't cut this out, we'll never get anything to eat."

Frustrated and not bothering to hide it, she poked his chest. "You shouldn't have started it. I opened the door, and you didn't even say hi, just like you never bother to say goodbye to me." His grin settled around his eyes, and it was all she could do to stop herself from putting her arms around him and hugging him. "Would you mind driving? I don't think I should unless I take off these shoes."

He looked down at her feet. "No wonder you seem taller. I'll drive."

When he handed her a red rose, she kissed his cheek. "You're such a sweet man," she said and turned away, intending to get a vase and water for the rose, but he grabbed her arm.

"Do you think I'm sweet, or were you making small talk?"

"Yes, I think you're sweet, Reid, and I'd… We'd better leave it at that."

Chapter 3

"You haven't asked where we're going," Reid said as they headed out of Queenstown. "Aren't you concerned?"

"Not really. As long as I can eat when I get hungry, I'll be happy. Besides, a really sweet man will do whatever he can to make me comfortable."

"Let's see. You told me that you're almost forty. Haven't you ever misplaced your trust?"

"I did once, and thereafter I protected myself, but while I was protecting myself, life passed me by. Do you get my drift?"

"Yeah. Are you saying you're willing to take a chance with me?"

"If you want the truth, Reid, I have not let myself face that question. In fact, I have skated all around it, and very skillfully, I might say."

"That's two of us. There're a lot of reasons why we should avoid each other, and you know all of them. But that's what I think when I'm being logical. The rest of the time, I want what you gave me when I walked into your house this evening." He drove into a roadside restaurant, parked and turned to her: "I want that and more, and I know that wanting you has nothing to do with the number of women I'm acquainted with in Queenstown. I would want you if I lived in Baltimore, where I know a slew of people, male and female, or for that matter, if I lived in Paris."

This man was telling her that she should take him seriously; that he wanted her and was bold enough to go after what he wanted. Taken aback by his bluntness, she stammered, "Oh…I think you're ahead of me."

"And if I did what I want to do right now, I'd take you in my arms and kiss you until I'm drunker off you than I was forty minutes ago."

She wanted him as badly as he wanted her, but she didn't want that to be the basis of their relationship and she decided to tell him so. "Do you think you can slow down, Reid? I confess that I want you, but I am not going to allow that to be the basis of a relationship with you. I need more. I need friendship, companionship and…and…okay, I'll say it…and love. I need caring and affection, and I'm dying to give all that in return. I want to make love with you in the worst way, but I've learned how to deny myself, so…let's go eat."

He gazed at her until she began to wonder at his mood. Suddenly, he said, "I'll buy that." His face transformed itself into a smile, and she wondered whether she'd be able to handle him if she ever needed to. He held her hand as they walked into the restaurant, a large but cozy room with hanging chandeliers, upholstered chairs, tables spaced far apart and the sound of soft, easy-listening music flowing around them.

"It's beautiful, Reid. How did you find it?"

"I saw it when I drove to Caution Point this morning and noticed that it was used for wedding parties, so I figured it would be nice. I called and made a reservation."

"Yes, it's beautiful," she repeated, "and so are you. You clean up real good, as they say."

His smile told her that he appreciated her compliment, but he added, "Thank you, Kendra. I'm beginning to feel like my old self, but when I look at you, knowing who and what you are, I'm humbled. You are so beautiful. I love you in that dress."

She nearly lost her breath, although she knew there had to be more to that sentence. The maître d' seated them in a corner near a fireplace, one of several in the room. The place was bound to be expensive, but she didn't intend to insult him by suggesting that they split the bill. She ordered white wine, and he asked for a wine and club soda spritzer. "I'm driving," he told the sommelier when the man looked at him disparagingly.

A waiter took their order, and she noted the frown on Reid's face when the man allowed his gaze to linger on her cleavage.

Reid raised his glass. "Here's to the loveliest of women."

"And here's to the nicest, sweetest man I know."

"Okay," he said. "I won't push you. You don't have to say anything about my...er...charm and—"

"Then, I won't. Did you rent a car today?"

"My boss let me use a company car." He leaned forward. "Kendra, I have so much to tell you. The day got better by the hour." He told her about his visit with Marcus, of Marcus's request that he design a building for him, about his boss's agreement allowing him to do it.

"Kendra, Jack invited me to lunch. He loved the sketch I did for the airport terminal in Caution Point, and another one that he thinks he can use for a deal he's trying to make. But, Kendra, even before he saw my ideas for that airport terminal, he and Connerly, the junior partner, had decided to raise me from assistant to full architect with double the pay. Do you—"

She interrupted him. "I think I'm going to cry. I—"

"Cry? Why, for heaven's sake?"

"I'm so happy for you. I...I'm...excuse me." She stumbled from the table and rushed to the women's room, where the tears flowed. Now maybe there was a chance for them. He would be his own man, the company recognized his value and he didn't have to look up to anyone. She patted cold water on her face, dried it with a paper towel, buffed her skin and headed back to the table.

The maître d' intercepted her. "Is Madame all right?"

"Yes, indeed," she said, and looked up and saw that Reid stood by the table waiting for her. If she had been at home, she suspected that she would have run to him, but she remembered who and where she was, controlled the urge and let her smile communicate to him her feelings.

He walked to meet her. "What happened? Are you okay?"

"I'm fine, Reid. Forgive me for letting it get out of control."

He assisted her in sitting down and walked around to his own chair. "I'm glad you're fine, but I need to know what happened."

She took a deep breath. "Not since I met you have I seen you so...so full of...of hope, so happy, just bursting with *joie de vivre*. Seeing you that way, almost watching years fall away from you. I couldn't help it. I'm so happy for you. It's the first time I've ever cried because I was happy."

"You were crying for *me?*" He reached across the table and grasped her hand. She didn't answer him. Something was happening between them, and neither of them would be able to alter its course. He repeated the question.

"Yes. Silly, aren't I?"

His gaze—fiery, turbulent—bored into her, refusing to release her, and she couldn't glance away. "I guarantee you that if I had you alone and in a private place right now, I would make love with you, and I wouldn't stop until you were mine."

"Could I...may I have some more wine, please?"

"Of course you may. I see you haven't disagreed with me. We're going to be lovers, Kendra. Maybe not soon, but you can bet on it."

"I've never had a man talk like this to me, so I don't know what to say to you right now."

"You haven't told me that I'm out of line. Am I?"

"I don't…no. You aren't out of line, but it's best you don't push me. I can get stubborn, even against myself."

A smile lit up his face, and it seemed as if a spotlight shone on him. He squeezed her fingers. "I won't push you. I'm a patient man, or at least I have been in the past. I hope I'll be able to boast of my patience six months from now. Something tells me I've never been tested."

She leaned back in her chair and looked at him. "When we met, I had trouble getting you to utter a sentence that had more than six words. Now you're very expressive. You talk to me. I like the change. Now if I can just get you to tell me goodbye when you leave me."

"That day probably won't come, Kendra. My mother was the last person to whom I used those two words. She's been gone since I was sixteen."

She turned over her hand so that her palm caressed his. "I'm so sorry, Reid. Who raised you after that? I mean, who saw you through school?"

"My dad. He's gone now. It happened while I was fighting that class action suit."

She'd like to know what it was about the man that got to her so thoroughly. *I'm not in love with him, so what is it?*

"Would Madame care for dessert?" the waiter asked. "Our dessert chef is world famous, sir," he said to Reid, who ordered a floating island.

"I'll have raspberry and peach sorbet," she said, pleased with herself for having resisted the sour lime pie.

"If we were in Baltimore," Reid said as they left the

restaurant, "I would take you dancing. I don't know any nice place around here, and that's a pity. You look so lovely that I don't want to take you home yet."

"There'll be other nights, Reid. At least, I hope so."

"And there will be, if I have my way. Say, do you have a regional map in the glove compartment?" She opened it and removed an AAA map. He took her hand, walked over to the light and examined the map.

"We can be in Elizabeth City in twenty minutes to half an hour at only moderate speed. What do you say?"

She loved to dance; imagined dancing with him. "I'm for it."

Half a mile down the highway, he filled up the gas tank, got back into the car and drove off singing, "God Didn't Make Little Green Apples."

"Can you cook?" she asked him, though she didn't know why the thought had occurred.

"I'm a pretty good cook. I like to eat, so I taught myself to cook. Cooking is a special kind of chemistry," he said, warming up to the subject. "It's a matter of putting together the right flavors and avoiding combinations that will blow up in your face. Right?"

"I hadn't thought of it that way, but that's close enough. Did you like chemistry in school?"

"I tolerated it. I loved physics."

They talked of their likes and dislikes in music, art, dance, literature and hobbies, and they shared their dreams. By the time they reached Elizabeth City, nearly an hour had elapsed, but neither noticed. He drove into a gas station and asked the attendant if he knew where a man could take a lady dancing.

"This lady is a judge," he told the man, "so it has to be a clean and classy place." He held a ten-dollar bill in his hand where the attendant could see it.

The guy peeped in the car. "Man, she don't look like no judge to me. Uh, sorry, sir. No problem, sir. Check out the Skylight Roof on top of the Wright Hotel. You won't find any riffraff there. Go straight till you get to a circle, turn left, drive four blocks. You'll be there."

She laid her left hand on his forearm. "Thanks for thinking of the quality of the place, Reid. It's been so long since I went anywhere special that I didn't think of it."

"When you're with me, Kendra, I'll do everything I can to take care of you, and I know you'd do the same for me."

When they reached the hotel, Reid said to the doorman, "Do you have a band tonight?"

"Yes, sir. Every night, sir."

He looked the man in the eye. "My date is a judge. Is it all right for me to take her in there?"

"Yes, sir. We cater to only the most discriminating guests."

She loved the room. Pink chandeliers cast a soft glow over the white tables, each of which held three white calla lilies in a slender vase. "I don't want anything to drink," he said, "but I'll order something for you if you'd like."

"Thanks. I'd like a ginger ale on crushed ice."

"I think I'll have the same," he said and beckoned for the waiter.

"What kind of music do you prefer to dance to?" he asked her.

"I love jazz saxophone, but it doesn't matter. I'll enjoy it no matter what they play."

Why was he looking at her that way? She wished she knew him well enough to read him. The band leader announced a fox-trot, and Reid stood. Just before his arms went around her, he kissed her with his eyes, warmed her with his repressed desire and a riot of sensation sent tremors throughout her body.

"Easy, sweetheart," he whispered. "I'm already drowning in your aura, so don't pour it on too heavily."

He was drowning? "If we get into trouble, we'll save each other."

He missed a step. "Honesty and straightforwardness are among the things I like about you, but I'd appreciate it if you would choose your times to be candid."

The piece ended, and the orchestra leader announced "Solitude," a Duke Ellington song from the 1930s. She moved into him then. She couldn't help it, for the alto saxophone moaned and cried, haunting, harnessing the blues for posterity. She gripped his shoulders and swung to his rhythm as if she had danced with him from the moment of her birth. Soon, she didn't hear the orchestra, only the music of his body moving with hers. When at last the music stopped, she looked up at him.

"If I didn't know better," he said, "I'd swear we've danced together for years. It's uncanny. I've known you a little over a month, and I feel as if I've known you for years and years."

"Seems that way to me, too. I think we ought to start back. It'll be after midnight when we get home."

They didn't talk on the way home. Normally, she

loved silence, because it allowed her to think. But not this mocking quiet, so intense that it spoke with the power of thunder. At last, they reached her house, and he parked and handed her the keys.

"I want to spend the night with you, Kendra, but I know this isn't the time. My body feels as if it's in a prison, locked behind bars and rearing to get out, but in a way, it's a good feeling. I'm alive, and I couldn't have said that before I met you. Come on, I'll see you into your house."

"Wait here," he said when they entered her foyer, issuing orders as usual. "I'll take a look around." As if she didn't walk into that house alone almost every time she entered it. He came back to her. "All clear. I'll see you tomorrow at eleven, and we'll walk down to the Sound, that is if you still want to."

"I want to. I had a wonderful time tonight, Reid, and I… Thanks for sharing your good news with me."

"Being able to tell you about it means more to me than you can imagine. See you in the morning."

"Wait a minute here," she said. "You give me an evening like this one and you aren't going to kiss me goodnight? Not even a peck on the cheek?"

He stared down at her until she wondered if she should have kept the thought to herself. "You want me to kiss you?" he said.

She didn't plan it, but her fingers worked at the buttons on her coat, releasing them one by one. "Yes." It came out as a whisper.

His hands slid beneath her coat, bringing her body to his, and his mouth came down on hers, fierce and hungry. His ravenous lips and his hands on her body, more possessive now and more familiar, sent darts zinging through her. But as quickly, he softened the kiss, and she parted her lips, shamelessly asking for more of him. He stopped kissing her and hugged her to him as if she were precious.

"Something happened to us back there in that restaurant, Kendra, and if I don't get out of here, I'll louse it up."

She stroked his cheek with the back of her hand. "I don't want that to happen. I'm a judge, but you're far more sophisticated, more worldly and more accomplished than I am. Right now, I feel like a schoolgirl on her first big date, and I'm reluctant to end it. See you at eleven."

"I've seen more of the world and I've done more, perhaps, but I am not more accomplished than you are. I'm proud of you." He kissed her forehead and left.

At least now she knew why he never bothered to say goodbye.

What an evening! She wouldn't lie if she said she'd never had such a good time and certainly not such an elegant date in her whole life. And with that handsome man dressed to the nines. Tripping up the stairs to her bedroom, she stopped midway, sobered by the thought that hit her like a bolt of lightning. She was on the verge of falling for Reid Maguire, a man she barely knew. And yet, it seemed that she'd known him all of her life.

Reid jogged across Albemarle Heights to the building in which he lived, wishing that he was dressed to run miles. He needed to vent, to expel the emotion, the sexual energy coiled inside him like a fanged serpent, energy that had been dormant for years, but which sprang to life the minute he saw her. What a relief it would be if he could open his arms wide and let the wind take him wherever it would.

All that had happened to him that day, beginning with Marcus Hickson in Caution Point, had raised his hopes for his future. But when Kendra had cried for joy at his good news and then opened her arms to him, something had happened to him, something that he had never experienced before, not with Myrna or any other woman. Standing with Kendra in her foyer, he'd felt as if he belonged to her, and it was a strange feeling, indeed, for, even as a child, he had been his own person.

He opened his door, went inside and headed for the kitchen where he got a can of beer from the refrigerator and took it to the living room. After kicking off his shoes and getting rid of his jacket and tie, he popped the can of beer, flipped on the television set, leaned back and prepared to straighten out his head. In the past, that hadn't been difficult, but the only image he saw on the screen was a sexy red dress and a woman whose allure had the power to shackle him.

He flipped off the television, drained the can of beer and went to his bedroom. "If I'm in love with her, I'm sunk," he said aloud. He knew the danger of deep involvement with her, yet he couldn't seem to stay away from her. But he would have to. It would hurt, probably both of them, but he had to settle the score with Brown and Worley.

He slept fitfully, rose early and began drafting the details of his design for the Caution Point air terminal. He didn't know when he'd ever felt so good. At nine o'clock, he telephoned Marcus Hickson in Caution Point.

"The news is good," he said after he and Marcus greeted each other. "And I'm surprised. My boss said I can do the job independent of the company, and he's promised to send me a letter to that effect. I'll be over the first weekend after I get that letter, and you can tell me what you need and show me the space."

"Great. I'll expect your call."

"I can't advertise that I'm doing this, because Jack—he's my boss—said he'll have problems with his other architects if they know about it."

"I can appreciate that, and I'll keep it to myself."

At a few minutes before eleven, he dressed in warm clothing, put on his hooded storm jacket and dashed across the street to Kendra's house. She opened the door at once.

"Hi." She reached up and kissed him quickly on the mouth, then licked her lips, as if savoring a sweet and wicked thing.

"Hi," he said. "Do I smell coffee?"

"You do, and I made it for you, because I know you've had nothing but instant."

He followed her to the kitchen, pulled off his jacket and threw it across the back of a chair. She took a mug from one of the cabinets, put a small amount of milk in it, poured the coffee, handed it to him and turned back to pour one for herself.

"Kendra, you're precious. Are you aware that if we

continue this way, we're liable to be stuck with each other for life?"

She didn't turn around to look at him when she said, "Worse things could happen to me."

He should stay where he was, and he should let that pass, but he got up and walked to her and, standing behind her, gripped her shoulders. "Does that mean you could love me?"

"Of course I could love you," she said, her voice low and without inflection. "Now go back over there and finish your coffee."

"What's wrong?"

"What's wrong is I'm scared. This is moving so fast. I want to be with you every minute, but I don't even know who you are, and you don't know who I am. I don't know what hurts you, makes you sad, angry, happy. I wouldn't know how to comfort you if you were down and depressed. Do you play jokes on people, Reid.? What games do you like to play? Oh, Reid. Hold me!"

He turned her to face him, wrapped her in his arms and stroked the back of her head as she rested it against his shoulder. "We *are* moving fast, and I tell myself to slow down, but I don't really want to. When I'm not with you, I'm thinking about you. Do you want us to…to see less of each other?"

"We ought to, for your sake. I want you to win that case, and a liaison with me could prove to be an impediment. I'm not willing to sacrifice that, no matter how we feel about each other."

"I know what you're saying, and I've thought about

it, too. And then, we're together, and our being together, like now, is so natural and so fulfilling," he said to her. "How am I going to give up the pleasure of being with you?" He released her and lifted the mug of coffee. "Could you top this off, please?"

She poured some of the coffee out and refilled the cup. "Let's go down to the Sound. I'll get my jacket while you drink that."

They strolled down Albemarle Heights to Washington Avenue, the road that led them to the Sound. Although flowers bloomed, the wind from the ocean still chilled, and she folded her arms to warm herself against it. As they reached the bottom—as the locals called it—of Washington Street, Reid's arm went around her, pulling her to his side.

"It irks me that I can't even hold your hand when we're walking the streets."

"Let's give it a try, Reid. We can talk on the phone, have an occasional dinner together at your house or mine, or maybe not. I don't know. Anyhow, I'll always be there for you if you need me. So, let's not see each other, Reid. I'm afraid that if we get closer, it may hurt you. I won't be happy with that arrangement, but it's best."

Reid faced the wind and turned her so that she had her back to it. "What do you feel for me, Kendra? I care for you. It's deep, and I know it isn't going away. Tell me."

"I care deeply for you. This isn't a brush-off, and you know it."

He looked into the distance. "I'm going to hire a lawyer and get started on that suit. I'm going to try to keep my distance, but I don't promise not to call you, and I want you to promise to let me know whenever you need me. Will you do that?"

"If I need you, I'll let you know." Her voice broke.

"To hell with it, baby," he said and put his arms around her. "Come on, let's go back."

After the first court session Monday morning, Kendra asked Carl, her clerk, to come into her chambers. "Carl, I want to get involved in the community, but I don't quite know how to go about it. If I'm going to live here, I have to have a stake in the place."

"We have a great little theater group, Judge. I used to belong to it, but after the babies started coming, I dropped out. What free time I had, I use to relieve my wife and look after the children. They'll be glad to have you, and especially if you can act."

"Do they put on real plays?"

"Yes, ma'am. I played Joey in *On the Waterfront,* and I'm just a so-so actor."

"Are those people going to treat me the way that guard did?"

"No, ma'am. Theater people are more broadminded. Anyhow, if I remember, at least three of them will probably ask you if you knew about the problem when you bought the house. You'll have a chance to tell your side. I'd go for it if I were you."

She thought for a minute. "I think I will, Carl. Who do I telephone?"

He wrote the information on a piece of paper and handed it to her. "Mike Reinar will be glad to see you, ma'am. The locals love that theater, but not many of them join."

"Thank you, Carl. I'll call him now."

Carl left the office in his usual fashion, so quietly that she wouldn't have known she was alone if she hadn't seen him go out of the door and close it.

"Mr. Reinar, this is Judge Kendra Rutherford. I'd like to join the theater group, and Carl Running Moon Howard told me that you are the person to call."

"What a pleasure, Judge Rutherford. I heard that we were getting a lady judge. We certainly will welcome you. I'm just casting for a play written by a very good local playwright. Would you be interested in reading for the part of the mother of a teenaged girl who's a problem? We won't always have roles suitable for you, but this one is."

"Thank you. I haven't acted since my university days, but I wasn't bad at it back then. When and where should I go?"

He gave her the information. "May I look forward to seeing you here?"

"Yes, indeed. Till then."

Deciding to look as much as possible like the average forty-year-old woman, she dressed in a straight black skirt that barely skimmed her knees, a red turtleneck sweater and black loafers, put on her storm coat and headed for what she hoped would be the beginning of fun and friends.

As she read, she warmed up to the part until, by the end, she felt as if she *were* the mother of a sixteen-year-old girl hell-bent on ruining her life. She handed the script back to Mike Reinar and asked him, "Well, what do you think?"

"I can't believe it," he said. "It's plain damned eerie. You read it as if it were written for you. The part is yours. Do you think you can look a little more harassed? I mean no makeup, no earrings and straggly hair?"

"I'm not wearing any makeup, Mr. Reinar, and please, call me Kendra."

"I'm afraid we'll have to take a vote on that. For now, I'll call you Miss Kendra."

Later, at home, it required all of her willpower to resist calling Reid to tell him what she'd done. She studied the part with the theme music of *Peter Gunn* in the background, for it helped her to concentrate. When she went to bed, she wasn't happy, but at least she was doing something other than sitting at home morose and longing for a man she shouldn't have.

The following afternoon, she had no afternoon cases, so she went to the theater, and Reinar guided her in projecting her voice. "You're a natural," he told her after reading with her.

"What a trial lawyer does has many elements of acting," she told him. "I practiced law for five years."

"Interesting," he said. "Lawyers are usually a lot richer than judges."

"But face fewer hazards," she said and changed the subject. "When do you hope to present the play?"

"Late May at the earliest. Not all of my actors are as quick a study as you are. Meanwhile, some of us will be practicing for our summer play in the park. Folks come from all around to see that. This year, it will be

Cat on a Hot Tin Roof. Can you see yourself playing Big Daddy's wife? I can."

"Let's see how well I do in this one," she said.

The girl signed to play the leading role seemed flat and lackluster to Kendra, but she supposed Mike Reinar knew what he was doing. She made up her mind to immerse herself in her role, and to enjoy every minute that she was on stage.

"It's not working," Mike told her after a week of rehearsals. "That kid can't act. The writer is going to rewrite it so that it's a family drama, and she's a minor player."

She adjourned the court for the spring recess as the county clerk directed, and decided to visit her sister in New Bern. *I can't leave town without telling Reid. It's bad enough that I can't see him and be with him, but I'm not prepared to pretend he doesn't exist.* She stopped packing and dialed his number. *It's only eight-thirty,* she thought, *so a call shouldn't disturb him.* The phone rang several times, and she was about to hang up when she heard his voice.

"Maguire speaking. How may I help you?"

Instead of saying hello, she said, "Don't you have caller ID?"

"Yeah, but it's turned off. *Kendra!* My Lord! I was so deep in this thing that I almost didn't answer the telephone. What is it? What's up? Are you all right?"

"I'm fine, Reid. How are you?"

"I'm able to work, eat and sleep, and for that I am grateful."

"I, uh…called because I'm going to New Bern for a week to see my sister, Claudine, and I couldn't make myself leave town for that long without letting you know where I am."

His long silence unnerved her. Finally, he said, "Could we maybe meet somewhere for a coffee or something? Please. I want to see you, if only for a minute."

"But—"

"I know I agreed, but, baby, this is like a death sentence. I just want to see you."

It hadn't been easy on her, but if she told him what she'd been going through, he'd be over there in five minutes. If she had any sense, she'd say no. She didn't. "I…uh…I'll make you a cup of coffee."

"I'll be there as soon as I put on my shoes."

She raced to the bathroom, brushed her teeth and combed her hair. The doorbell rang before she could consider doing more, so, dressed in T-shirt, cropped stretch pants and sneakers, she raced down the stairs and flung open the door. He smiled, opened his arms, and she sped into them.

"Oh, sweetheart," he whispered. "I miss you as much as if we'd been together for years and years and I hadn't seen you for months."

She kissed his cheek and moved out of his arms, for she had already begun to feel as if she never wanted to leave him. "Okay, come on into the kitchen while I make the coffee, but…no clinches, please."

His laughter curled around her like a soft breeze on a summer night. "When are you coming back?"

"Saturday week." She made the coffee, put some milk in a mug, added the brew, gave it to him and poured a cup for herself. "Tell me how your work is going," she said.

"Great. I'm back to my old level, I guess you could call it. I'm enjoying my work, and Jack seems pleased. I've begun designing that factory for Marcus, and next weekend I'm taking what I've done to Caution Point to see if I need to alter anything. But I think I'm right on target."

"Have you hired a lawyer yet?"

"I'm negotiating with Dean Barker. You know him?"

"I've met him a few times, and I know his reputation. You couldn't find a more competent, more honest attorney."

"Then, I'll hire him. I wanted to ask you, but—"

"Reid, didn't I tell you to call me if you needed me?"

"Yeah, you did, but if I took you seriously, I'd call all the time. What's your sister's telephone number?" She gave it to him. He stood. "Thanks for the coffee. Walk me to the door."

She wondered if he'd forgotten saying that he would one day take her to bed.

When she put her hand on the doorknob, he said, "Let me feel you in my arms before I leave here. Kiss me. I need it."

She reached up, cradled his face with her hands, parted her lips for the sweet torture of his tongue, and he went into her, giving her the sweetness she longed for. He made the kiss brief and put some space between them, although he still held her. His eyes sparkled and a half smile played around his lips.

"Think of a man who hasn't tasted food or drink for weeks, and with his hands and feet tied, someone holds a plate of sizzling steak and hash-brown potatoes in

front of him. That's the way it is with me right now. You
see, Kendra, you're the woman I need, the one I have
always needed. Get back here to me safely." He opened
the door and left.

"I'll never get use to that," she said aloud in reference to his leaving without saying goodbye. "And I
doubt I'll ever get used to him, even if I live with him
until I'm ninety."

She had started back up the stairs and at the landing,
she nearly fell backward as shock reverberated through
her. She had just admitted to herself that she wanted to
be with him for the rest of her life. Now, she was a
rational, intelligent person. What was she thinking? She
walked slowly into her bedroom, removed a folded
T-shirt from a drawer and put it in her suitcase.

It's good I'm going to New Bern, she told herself. *I
need to get my feet back on the ground.*

Back in his apartment, Reid looked out of his kitchen
window at the building's moonlight-shrouded garden,
eerily cold and empty. Like his existence. If his life
wasn't on hold, he'd be with her that minute, most likely
buried deep inside her, losing himself in her. He'd never
needed anyone or anything as he needed Kendra, but his
common sense told him that she was right in insisting
that they stay apart until his case was settled.

He worked until after two o'clock in the morning, for
he knew that, still heavy with desire and starved for her,
he would find it useless to try sleeping. At nine that
morning, he walked into Dean Barker's Queenstown
office—Barker's law firm was located in Elizabeth

City—handed the man a folder containing copies of all the information he had relative to his case against Brown and Worley, and took a seat.

"I want you to take the case."

"Since we spoke, I've done some research on this," Dean said, "and I think you have a better than good chance to win. Since they're registered here, we can get a trial in Queenstown. I would advise you to make yourself known here, to the extent that you can, build a good reputation. The jury will be chosen from people around here. I'm going to try and bring this to trial before the end of summer."

"I'm thinking of joining the local theater group. In Baltimore before all this happened, I had an a cappella boys' choir of about twenty voices, but I don't have any place here for them to practice."

"If you join the theater group, I'm sure they'll give you space for that. I'll phone Mike Reinar if you'd like. He's a friend of many years."

"Thanks, and I'll phone him later this afternoon." Dean handed him a contract, which he read twice and signed.

"I'll call you Monday week," Dean said, "and let you know where we stand. Thanks for your confidence."

After shaking hands with Dean Barker, Reid got into the company car and headed for Caution Point. He liked the office at the airport, for he could sit at his desk and look at the space where his building would stand. He worked until three o'clock, packed his briefcase and phoned Mike Reinar.

"I'm Reid Maguire, Mr. Reinar, and I'm interested in joining your theater group."

"I was expecting to hear from you. I've got something I'd like you to try. Would you mind reading for me? Dean told me you want to start a boys' chorus. We have plenty of space, a piano and an organ. You're welcome to use our facilities. What time can you be here today?" ·

"I'm in Caution Point. Say, about five o'clock? That'll give me time to change out of this business suit."

"Right. We're a jeans and Reeboks club. I'll look forward to meeting you."

"Tell me something about the story line," Reid said to Mike Reinar when they met.

Mike dropped himself on the floor and positioned himself lotus-fashion. "It's about a sixteen-year-old girl and her parents' problems in raising her. She's daddy's little girl, but mama wants to discipline her and ward off the problems she sees down the road. You're the permissive father."

Reid leaned against the wall and crossed his ankles. "I can do that." He read for the part and got it.

"Our next rehearsal will take place Monday week. Come with me. You can practice your boys' chorus in here. We have an armed guard downstairs, if you ever have a problem. Here's a master key. It opens the building and any room except a private office. What day will you want to practice?"

"I've found Saturday morning at ten to be best. I'll start rounding up boys. Thanks for your help." He went home, looked through the phone book until he found the local radio station, got a disc jockey on the phone and told him what he wanted. The following Saturday morning, sixteen boys auditioned, and all but three suited his purpose. Before the hour ended, he had taught the thirteen boys to sing the refrain of "Mariah" in four-part harmony and got a beautiful sound from them. He called the disc jockey, thanked him and asked him to repeat the ad.

A few minutes before noon, he arrived in Caution Point. He hoped to buy a car within a couple of months; in the meantime, he would rent one when he needed it. He drove to Marcus Hickson's house at the end of Ocean Avenue, parked and got out. He'd bought a box of chocolates for Marcus's nine-year-old daughter and an assortment of rubber animals for his four-year-old and two-year-old sons.

"Reid, this is my wife," Marcus said with so much pride that Reid had a moment of jealousy. "Amanda, Reid Maguire is a schoolmate and good friend."

"I'm so happy to meet you, Reid, and I'm glad you'll be working with Marcus." Her left arm went around the girl who walked up to them. "Mr. Maguire, this is our daughter, Amy," she said, and he noticed that Amy's arm tightened around her stepmother.

"I'm glad to meet you, Mr. Maguire," she said with a slight curtsey.

"And I'm glad to meet you, Amy," he said.

"I have two little brothers," she said. "Do you want to see them?"

"Yes, I do."

By the end of the day, he decided that life would be complete if he had children like these, and especially if he had a beautiful and intelligent daughter like Amy. He said as much to Amanda.

"Happiness is something that you have to seek, and when you find it your work has just begun. Concentrate on keeping everyone around you happy, and their joy will bring happiness to you."

"I'm divorced, Amanda."

"That's because you were not careful. I know Marcus and I are blessed, because we began in a marriage of convenience, but I did everything I could to make him happy and to give Amy a mother's love. She's so dear to me. Don't look at the outside alone, Reid. The inside is so much more important. Do you have a significant other?"

He got a handful of beans and began helping her string them. "Yes, and I'm…I think I'm falling in love…no." She stopped stringing beans and looked at him. "I'm beginning to love her, or I do already, but I'm not sure."

"So the two of you are not intimate."

"Not yet, but we will be." He explained why they had agreed to see less of each other for a while. ·

"That's tough," Amanda said, "but she's a wise woman. If you lose because of her, you will always resent her, and that's no basis for a marriage or any other kind of relationship."

"I know she's right, but it's driving me up the wall."

"Does she love you?"

"Yes. She does."

"You sound as if you're awed."

"I am. I no longer see myself as the powerhouse I used to be, and I'm no longer so arrogant that I think a woman like Kendra Rutherford, intelligent, accomplished, well-mannered and beautiful to boot, is no more than what I deserve. I had years to learn how to be humble."

Marc, the four-year-old boy, ran into the kitchen. "Mummy, where is Daddy? I think he and Todd are hiding from me."

"Look in the music room. Daddy went there to get something that he wants to show Mr. Maguire."

The boy ran off, and she said, "Biologically, Amy is Marcus's child, Marc is mine, and Todd is ours, but those distinctions don't exist in our hearts. They are our three children."

They finished stringing the beans. "You're a remarkable person, Amanda. Marcus is lucky, and he knows it."

She looked up at him. "We love each other, Reid. Each comes first with the other, and our children come before both of us. That's what makes it tick."

"I'm glad we talked, Amanda. You've given me added confidence in the route I seem destined to take."

Chapter 4

Kendra left work that Monday afternoon, rushed home, changed into jeans, a shirt and loafers and drove to the theater group. She rehearsed the first scene with her stage daughter, and checked the lines of her first scene with the man who would play opposite her as the father.

"What? What's this?" she gasped. "Since when did you… I mean… gosh, this is a surprise."

"It's just as big a surprise for me," Reid said, "but I'm willing to go on with it, if you are."

"Of course," she said, frowning. "It's odd that we both decided to do this. I was keeping myself busy so I wouldn't think about…" She thought it prudent not to finish that sentence.

"My lawyer thought I should get active in the community, and Mike is an old friend of his. You're not going to show up looking like a boy Saturday morning, are you?"

She stared at him. Perplexed. "Like a boy?"

"I'll explain that later. Let's try this scene. I'm Don, and you're Lissa. Right?" She nodded.

"Why can't Tonya have the jeans?" Don asked. "They're just jeans, for heaven's sake."

Lissa rose from the chair, walked over to Don and shook her finger at him. "That's what you said last Saturday when she wanted new ice skates because her friend got new ones. 'It's just a pair of skates,' you said, although she already has three practically brand-new pairs."

"Look, honey, don't blow a gasket now. She wants a little BMW for her birthday, and I told her she could have it."

"Are you crazy? I can't stop you from giving it to her, but she'll get the keys to it over my dead body. Take the money and get her a reading coach. She's sixteen, and can barely read 'Little Bo Peep.' All she wants to do is watch TV and talk to boys on the phone that you put in her room. Damn school. She couldn't care less about it."

He stood and raised both hands, palms out. "Okay. This is getting too hot. We'll solve it later. You mad at me?" He leaned down to turn off the lamp on the table beside the chair in which he'd been sitting, and she turned aside at the sight of his tight jeans hugging his perfectly sculptured behind. Her fingers itched to stroke him.

"No. I'm troubled," she read.

"If you're not angry, kiss me." He walked over to her and stroked her back.

Caressing her was not in the directions that accompanied the script. "I don't—" She hated that her voice trembled.

"Yes, you do," he said in a low, sultry voice. Startled, she forgot that they were playing a role and backed away from him, and as if he, too, forgot, he pulled her into his arms, bent his head and flicked his tongue across the seam of her lips. She opened to him and took him in, but her soft moan brought them back to reality and to the present.

He stepped away from her, but quickly she closed the space between them, furious and embarrassed, and punched his chest with her fist. "I'll remember that."

"Fantastic!" Mike shouted. "We've got a hit. The two of you are born actors. How did I get so lucky?"

"Would you believe it?" Reid said to Kendra later as she drove them down Albemarle Heights to her home. "When we kissed, he actually thought we were acting."

"Of course that's what he thought. As far as he knew, I'd never seen you until you walked into that theater. What do you suppose an audience would think if you did that to me in their presence?"

He shrugged, but she knew he had deep concern for what happened between them in that scene. "I expect I'd get the reputation for being bold as hell," he said. "The play is so much like real life that it's hard to avoid becoming Don."

"You want to become the character. That's the whole

point of acting. I sure hope the script doesn't call for you to sock me."

"Not to worry, sweetheart," he said as they entered her house. "I'd revise that script in a hurry. Wait here, while I look around." He ran up the stairs, then down the basement steps, went into the kitchen and the downstairs bathroom. "You're safe. Give me a kiss."

"You had a kiss."

"That was a mere tease. By the way, I've started a boys' a cappella chorus. That's what I was referring to when I said I hoped you wouldn't show up there Saturday morning looking like a boy."

He held out his arms. "Come here, baby. I've been so lonely for you. You haven't even told me that you missed me while you were down in New Bern."

"I'm not supposed to tell you that. We're not seeing each other. Don't you remember?"

He pretended to sulk, and it was all she could do not to run to him. "I got a taste of you, and I…Kendra, don't you need me?"

She wouldn't have thought she could move that fast, but in less than a second she was in his arms, and his hands were stroking and caressing her. "Kiss me. Love me. I need you," she whispered.

She parted her lips for his kiss, and he grabbed her hips and lifted her to fit him. She felt him then, with his tongue dancing in and out of her mouth and his penis at the apex of her thighs. Jolts of electricity whistled through her body, and she sucked vigorously on his tongue trying to get more of him as he sent the fire of desire spiraling from her head to her toes. She needed all of him.

"Honey, kiss me. Kiss me," she begged. "Oh, Reid."

"Baby, I *am* kissing you."

She grabbed his right hand and put it on her breast, and it was all the invitation he needed. His hand went into her blouse and freed her right breast. He bent his head and sucked her nipple into his warm moist mouth. She let out a keening cry as he began to suckle her, tugging on her nipple, feasting as if he were hungry for it. Reckless now, she clutched his shoulders and wrapped her legs around his hips. She had her back to the wall, and he leaned into her. His erection bulged against her, and he stopped, but she pressed his hips.

"Easy, baby. You don't want our first time to happen right here."

"I don't know what I was thinking," she said when she could collect her thoughts. "It can't happen right now, anyway. Nature must be orchestrating this relationship."

He picked her up, carried her into the living room and sat in an oversized chair with her in his lap. "No apology or explanation is necessary. You and I are in this together, and we start the fires together. I realize it happened in the heat of passion, but you told me to love you. Do you want me to love you? Your answer is important to me."

With her head in the niche between his neck and his shoulder, she put an arm around his shoulder and the other one across his chest. It never paid to lie. "Yes."

"I already love you," he said. "I've never been more certain of anything, and I want you to love me. If you'll let me, I'll teach you to love me."

She raised her head and kissed his lips. "You won't have much work to do."

"Will you go with me to Caution Point Saturday after rehearsal? I want you to meet my friends there."

"Yes, I'd love to meet your friends. Does Marcus like your design for his building?"

"He's already approved it, and I'm working on the plans. I'll rent a car, because I don't want to drive yours. Scratch that. We are not going to drive your car to Caution Point."

Suddenly, she laughed. She couldn't help it. Didn't he know that practically everything he said sounded like a command, that he didn't need to be extra-forceful? She raised her hand in a mock salute. "Yes, sir. I got the message, and I'll be ready when you get here Saturday. What will you have on?"

"Since I'm taking you there for the first time, I'll wear a business suit. I'd better leave while the temperature in here is still at a moderate level. I'll call you."

"Okay. By the way, did you hire Barker?"

"I did, and he's already busy." He stood, set her on her feet and walked with her to the door. "Sleep well." He left.

There is a man who knows his limit, she thought, and wondered what Saturday would be like. With his friends, would he be the Reid she knew or the one he used to be?

Reid locked the front door of his apartment and leaned against it. Exhausted. Maybe he'd better start going to church. His feelings for Kendra were beginning to get the better of him, to control him. During that rehearsal, he'd bent over to turn off the light, and when he looked up, the expression on her face nearly caused him to have an erection. He'd never seen such blatant lust on a woman's face. When she spoke, her voice trembled, and he knew she wasn't acting. He'd wanted her at a gut-searing level. He took a deep breath. He'd better wear a jockstrap when he was acting with her in that play, because there was no telling what kind of scene they'd create. He only hoped they'd stay close to reality and not do anything that would reflect adversely on her as a judge.

He telephoned her. "I have an idea," he said when she answered. "Maybe we can see each other outside the Queenstown area. We can meet some place on Saturday afternoon and come back Sunday night. Kendra, I just can't go on not seeing you."

"We'll be together with your friends in Caution Point Saturday afternoon, and we'll see each other at rehearsals Thursday nights. Let's not move beyond that, Reid. I am not going to allow myself to forget what's at stake."

"I'm not forgetting that."

"No? If you lose that case and can trace the reason to me, that will be the end of our relationship. Even if I didn't believe that, I wouldn't risk causing you to lose something that is so important to you. So let's try to be patient."

"All right, baby, but I'm so damn frustrated. Do you love me?"

"Yes."

"What? What did you say?"

"Reid, honey, this is not the time for this discussion,

with me here and you there, and you're not coming back over here tonight."

He stared at the telephone. "No, I don't think I should. See you Saturday morning."

If he went across Albemarle Heights, unless she called the police, he wouldn't leave there until he buried himself deep inside her.

On Saturday morning, he drove the rental car to the theater group quarters and parked. Once he would have rented a big and impressive Lincoln or Cadillac, but he no longer felt the need for such trappings. "I don't worry about what people think," he said to himself, "and that is a relief."

Kendra stepped out of her door and raced down the walk before he could get out of the car. He walked around it, opened the door for her, hooked her belt and closed the passenger door. When he'd seated himself, and moved away from the curb, he said, "What's the matter? Don't you trust me?"

She leaned over and kissed his cheek. "I trust you, and I trust me, but I don't trust *us* together." She took a thermos from a bag, opened it and poured coffee in the top. "Here. Drink this. If I didn't trust you, would I bring you coffee?"

He took a long sip. "Ah. This is great. When it gets warmer, I want us to spend a long weekend in Maryland at Dickerson Estates. I haven't been back since I left, and I miss my friends there. We can swim or ride. It's a wonderful environment."

After turning onto Route 34, he drove half a mile and pulled into a roadside farmer's market, bought a bunch of yellow lilies and got back into the car.

"These are for Amanda. Marcus is a figure of a man, at least an inch taller than I am, and she isn't big as a minute. When we were in college, he went for those lean, willowy model types. Funny, I went for the little ones. Both of us learned that it's the inside that matters, and we both learned the hard way. Not that your outsides aren't mind-blowing and don't attract me. Lord knows I can get high just looking at you, but it's what I found *in* you that binds me to you. It's a whole lot of things put together."

"Will it be warm at Dickerson Estates around the first of May?"

"It's getting warm there now. I've swum in the Chesapeake numerous times late in April."

"Then we'll go. I love to swim. How far are we now from Caution Point?"

"Three or four minutes."

He parked in front of the white brick house at the end of Ocean Avenue and got out to open the door for Kendra, but when he reached her side of the car, she stood beside the door as if in awe.

"What is it?" he asked her.

"It's so beautiful. The willow saplings swaying so quietly and so sensuously among the blossoming dogwood trees. Pink ones, white ones. It's so lovely. And the breeze. So soft and fragrant. I'd be so happy here."

He felt a rush of blood, a swift tightening of his groin, and ordered his libido under control, for what she stirred most deeply in him at that moment was love. For a moment, he remained transfixed by the powerful elixir of her feminine sweetness. And standing beside the car with the sun warming their bodies and her words caressing his heart, he put his arms around her and kissed her lips.

Her smile told him that she understood all that he didn't say. "I love you, too," she said. "Let's go inside."

As he walked up the stone walkway holding hands, Amy came around the side of the house.

"Hello, Amy," they said in unison.

"Hi, Mr. Reid and Miss Kendra. My mommy is in the shower, and my daddy is changing my baby brother's pants. He spilled milk all over the place and on his pants. Come with me. The front door is too heavy for me to open." She walked up to them, shook their hands and started around to the side of the house. "We're going to have a nice barbecue brunch. You can smell what my daddy's roasting. And it's always good."

Kendra hadn't expected such an adult nine-year-old. "I'm happy to meet you, Amy," she said.

Amy had been walking ahead of them. She stopped, and with a mercurial smile said, "Thank you, Judge Kendra." She opened the screen door. "We're going in here."

They entered an airy room that seemed to be a family room. "My daddy will be down in a minute," she said. "I'm going upstairs and let him know you're here."

At that moment, a four-year-old boy charged into the room. "Be nice, Marc," Amy said, "and keep the guests company while I get Daddy."

Marc walked up to Reid and rested his hands on Reid's knees. "I could show you my airplanes, Mr. Reid, but I'm not supposed to bring them in here." He looked at Kendra. "My daddy said you were bringing your sweetheart. Is she your sweetheart?"

Reid pulled the child between his knees and patted his shoulder. "Yes, she's my sweetheart, and you may call her Miss Kendra."

The boy gazed at Kendra. "Nobody said you were so pretty. Do you have any little boys and girls?"

"Thank you, Marc, for the compliment. No, I don't have any children yet, but I'd be happy if I had a little boy like you."

"I'm sorry," he said, wearing a sad expression, "but I belong to my mommy and my daddy. Maybe they will find a little boy for you."

"Don't worry, son," Marcus said, laughing, as he walked into the room. "They know how it's done." He opened his arms to Reid in a brotherly embrace and then gazed down at Kendra. "You can't imagine how happy I am to meet you. I'm so glad you came." He looked at Reid and winked. "She's lovely. Excuse me for not being down here to greet you, but seconds before you got here, Todd decided to try his strength and knocked a half-gallon bottle of milk all over himself and everything around him. And would you believe the little rascal clapped his hands and laughed?"

And so began one of the most enjoyable afternoons Reid remembered having spent. As he'd expected, Amanda and Kendra found that they had much in common, but what he hadn't anticipated was the joy that Kendra seemed to experience with the children, all three of whom seemed attracted to her.

Two-year-old Todd seemed fascinated with her, and when she opened her arms he crawled into her lap and made himself comfortable. Reid wanted badly to hear what she was saying to the child, but she was sitting too far from him. When it seemed that the boy had gone to sleep, he suspected that she had been singing to him.

"I hope you love barbecued everything," Marcus said to Kendra. "I already know that this brother will eat anything that isn't nailed down. Well, almost anything. Look, I have a boat at the pier down at the end of Bay Street. I haven't been on her since last October, but if you come down at the end of May, she'll be ready to sail. It's good fun. I'll take my brother and his family along, and we'll have a great time."

"I'll look forward to it," Reid said to Marcus. Amanda lifted a pile of dishes and started toward the house. "Let me help you with that, Amanda," Reid said to her when he noticed that Marcus was rescuing Marc from a fence. He took the dishes inside, cleaned them and put them into the dishwater.

"You're handy in the kitchen, Reid," she said. "I consider that a good sign."

"Thanks. I figure that as long as I eat, I should know my way around the kitchen. So I learned to cook and to clean up after myself. I got that from my father."

"Kendra is a lovely woman, a down-to-earth loving and tender person, and you are blessed to have her in your life."

"I know, and I'm going to do all I can to take care of our relationship. She…she's precious to me."

"I can see that, and you're precious to her."

"I'm going back out there and see if I can pry her away from Todd. The kid has taken my woman."

"Which is interesting," Amanda said. "Todd always refused to go near strangers. But she radiates love. Take good care of it."

"I intend to."

"I hope you'll visit us again soon, Kendra," Marcus said when they stood to leave. "We've enjoyed having you and Reid with us."

"Yes," Amanda said. "I want us to be good friends, Kendra." To Reid, she said, "Remember to take care of what's precious."

"Bet on it. Thank you both for a wonderful afternoon."

He let a minute pass after driving off before he said to Kendra, "Do you want children? When I saw Todd curled up in your lap wrinkling this beautiful suit while you coddled him as if he were the most precious thing you possessed, I got a lump in my throat. I hadn't thought about you and children. I guess I thought that didn't seem compatible with being a judge."

"You didn't think about it at all, I suspect," she said. "Yes, I love children, and I want some."

He glanced at her with his peripheral vision. "Hadn't you better get busy?"

She didn't look toward him, but kept her gaze straight ahead. "With whom do you suggest?"

"Hey, I didn't mean to pull your chain, baby. If you want to get started, I'll be the last to complain."

"Back up, Reid. I don't think you meant for that comment to head us in this direction. I've always thought it best to raise children in a marriage, and since

I'm not married, I don't have children. By the way, you don't have any. Don't you want a family?"

"Yeah. I want a family. Myrna didn't want children, but she didn't let me know that until after we married. As I got to know her, I realized that it was a good thing she didn't want them. Children need dependability in their lives, and they need it from both parents."

They talked about their lives growing up, their parents, her sister and the brother with whom he'd lost contact. "What does he do?" she asked him.

"He's a state assemblyman, and it didn't suit him to have a brother accused of designing a shoddy building that collapsed and ruined the lives of possible future constituents, such as when he runs for president." He heard the bitterness in his voice and couldn't stop himself. "He's another reason why I want vindication. Nobody deserves the pain he gave me. He was my only living relative, and he wasn't there for me. I'm over it now."

"It doesn't hurt anymore?"

He shrugged. "I suppose it will always hurt, Kendra, but I feel as if I can love him again, and that's a load off me."

"What about…Myrna? Do you feel as if you can love her again?"

"That's not remotely possible. I need to love my brother. He's my brother, my own blood and our parents would be sad at the way things are between us now. Myrna made God and me a promise that didn't mean one thing to her. She's no longer a part of my life, and she doesn't have the power to make me happy or sad.

My rare thoughts of her elicit nothing but anger at my own stupidity. Does that answer your question?"

"Yes. Sorry I brought it up."

"Here we are." He parked in front of her house. "I'm not sure whether I should go in with you."

He sat there for a minute. "Come on, I want to check things out for you." He did and walked back to the foyer where she waited for him. "I'll see you Thursday night at rehearsal." He opened his arms because he couldn't stand to leave her without holding her and loving her.

"None of the heavy stuff, love," he said. "Just let me feel that you love me."

To his amazement, she eased her arms around his shoulders, stood on tiptoe and kissed his eyes, cheeks, lips, neck and then, with her hands cupping his face, she parted her lips over his, took him in, sucked the tip of his tongue and released him.

He stared down at her, his heart racing like a spooked Thoroughbred. "You make me feel as if I could harness the moon and hand it to you. How did I ever live without you?"

She stroked the side of his face in a loving gesture and contented herself with saying nothing, as if her silence would preserve his words for all time. Suddenly, she rested her head against his shoulder.

"I'll be glad when we don't have to hide the fact that we see each other."

He hugged her to him. "I want that more than anything. Sleep well." He left, because he couldn't risk staying longer. After their first time, he wanted to wake up with her in his arms, and he didn't want to expose her to gossip by creeping out of her house at daybreak. And he didn't want to sign in at a hotel or a motel under a false name in order to protect her. Not that he hadn't thought of it, but what if there was a fire or another catastrophe? He couldn't take the chance.

The next day, he called Philip Dickerson. "Is the bay getting warm enough for a swim?" he asked his friend after their greeting.

"I doubt it. I haven't been down there yet, but it should be pleasant in another three weeks. Why don't you come down for a few days? We're anxious to hear how things are going with you."

"Couldn't be better, at least for now." He brought Philip up to date on developments in his work. "I'm hard at it fourteen hours a day, but I'm glad for it. Getting used to reporting to a boss and getting his approval of what I've done is tough, but I guess it's not the worst that can happen. Jack Marks is a brilliant architect, and he has confidence in me."

"I knew that all you needed was a chance. But remember that man doesn't live by bread alone, friend. Have you found anyone who takes your mind off your problems?"

"Yeah. Off my problems and my work, too."

Philip's laugh reached him through the wire. "She must rival the Venus de Milo. Don't you dare come down here without her."

The following Thursday night at rehearsal, he breezed through his scene with his stage daughter, pampering her as usual. "Now run upstairs to your room and study like a good girl," he said to her in his role as Don.

"Tonya, didn't I tell you not to wear that T-shirt again? It's three sizes too small," Kendra said in her role as Lissa.

"Daddy said he didn't see anything wrong with it."

"Oh, he did, did he? Take it off this second."

Don put his newspaper aside and looked at Lissa. "I don't like your contravening me when I tell Tonya she can do something or she can have something. Lately, you go against me every time. She's young, and this is the only time she'll ever have to find herself, to know who she really is."

"Oh, please," Lissa said. "She'll have the rest of her life to confirm that she's a slut. Whoever heard of a father giving his sixteen-year-old daughter permission to walk around with her nipples showing and half of her breasts hanging out? Tonya, get up those stairs and take off that shirt. This second!"

"Look, baby. Do you want our daughter to be an old maid? She's got it, and she should take advantage of it. That's what you did."

"I did not."

"You did so, and I sucked your nipple into my mouth on our second date."

"That's not true."

He grabbed her arm. "It is, and it's all I've ever had to do to get inside you. Tell me I'm lying."

"She can hear everything you're saying."

"She can't. I heard her close her room door." His hand brushed across her left breast, and he gazed down into her face. "Do you want me to prove it?" She swallowed hard and tried to back away from him. "I'll be inside you in a minute." His hand reached for the V-neckline of her blouse.

An expression of terror settled over her face. "Reid, for goodness' sake!"

He backed away from her, alarmed at what he'd almost done.

"Hey, what happened there?" Mike asked them.

Reid dropped his body into the nearest chair and shook his head. "I got carried away. I'm sorry, Kendra, I'll try to keep it between the lines."

"You do that," Mike said. "We have to remember that Kendra is a judge."

Reid glared at Mike. "I remember that as well as you do, and I have as much concern for her reputation as you do."

"I didn't mean to jerk your chain, man," Mike said, "but neither you nor I want Kendra to back out of this role. The two of you fit like Tracey and Hepburn." He looked at his watch. "It's nine-thirty. Let's wrap it for tonight."

Later, as she drove home, he said, "I wonder why we get these roles confused."

She laughed to let him relax, for she supposed he had worried that she might resent his familiarity with her when he had caressed her breasts in front of Mike and the other players. "You really could cause a problem for yourself when you start playing with my breast. So you'd better tell your hands to control themselves when we're on that stage."

"Hmmm. Does that mean they can play fast and loose when we're not onstage?"

"That question does not deserve an answer. When did Mike say we'll perform for an audience?"

"A couple of weeks from now, and it can't come too soon. I'm tired of tying up my Thursday nights. I love the acting, but…well, you know what I mean."

"I do, but if we didn't have this, would we be able to see each other without raising suspicion?"

"No, and I'm grateful for it. When it gets a little warmer, we can sit out in my garden."

"But won't your neighbors on higher floors be able to look down and see us? We can sit out in my back garden on my deck and no one can see us."

"Damn, Kendra. I'm sick of this secrecy." He got out of the car and, without glancing back, sprinted across the street. Stunned by his odd behavior, she locked her car, went inside her house and locked the door. She didn't need Reid or any other man to check her house.

"I hear you're a terrific actress, ma'am," Carl Running Moon Howard said to her when she got to work the next morning. "The first show's two weeks off, and it looks like the whole town is geared up to see you. The mayor's niece is playing your daughter."

"His niece? I had no idea."

"You should have suspected she was somebody's *something,* ma'am, because she can't act. She once played my little sister, and you should've seen her. I hear the man playing with you is real good, too."

She wanted to ask if he was fishing for something, but

thought better of it. "Yes," she said instead. "He doesn't seem like an amateur," and continued with, "Carl, this coffee is delicious, but I see no reason why we shouldn't make it ourselves. I'm going to buy a coffeemaker."

"Yes, indeed, ma'am, and don't forget the microwave and the mini refrigerator."

"I won't," she said, glad to have deflected his thoughts from her and Reid.

She wasn't getting the results she had hoped for from her acting. One could say that she was doing it for herself rather than for the community, even if she was volunteering.

After hearing two cases that morning that bored her to the extent that she could barely keep her eyes open, one dealing with shoplifting and the other with a man's ruses to avoid paying child support, she decided that if she didn't branch out, she could lose her sanity. At the end of the court's second, third and fourth sessions that day, she announced that she would give free civics classes to high school students at the local school.

"The classes will deal with women's rights and laws affecting them," she said, "and the high-school senior who scores highest on the exam at the end of the class will receive a one-thousand-dollar college scholarship."

Eleven girls signed up for the course, which she would conduct twice weekly from three-thirty to five o'clock.

"How'd you happen to decide to give this course and the scholarship?" Reid asked her when they spoke by phone.

"This town is hard to crack, and I figured I have the time, so why not?"

"Is it limited to girls?"

She enjoyed a good laugh. "Don't be so transparent. No, but it's limited to high-school seniors."

"I hope they learn something. By the way, would you be willing to go with me to the eastern shore of Maryland next weekend? It's warm there. Do you have riding pants or some heavy jeans, and a bathing suit, of course?"

She had been sitting on the edge of the bed when she'd answered the telephone and heard his voice. "What about the boys' chorus?"

"I'll cancel it and give them an extra hour tomorrow morning. Will you go?"

She stretched out on the bed and let herself enjoy hearing his voice while she pretended that she had only to turn over and she could touch him. "You know I will." It sounded like a come-on.

"Are you lying down? Look, sweetheart, life is hard enough without my getting these…uh…pictures of what you must look like right now."

She sat up. "I assure you that I am fully dressed, and I am not lying down."

"Not now, you aren't," he said.

They talked for over an hour about their work, hinting at everything but their loneliness for each other.

"This is a lousy substitute for having my arms around you," he said at last, "but my day will come, and I intend to make good use of it when it gets here."

Laughter bubbled up in her throat and spilled out like a reluctant gurgle. "I can't believe you're talking about me like that. Behave yourself."

"You're joking. Woman, that's all I ever do. I'm

hanging up before I find myself ringing your doorbell. Sleep well." He hung up, and she sat there thinking of ways to turn their relationship around without jeopardizing her status. She knew that when he'd left her in a huff after the Thursday-night rehearsal without seeing her into her house, he'd been frustrated and tired of their hot exchanges, passion that they needed to consummate. She didn't hold it against him.

"Good night, hon," she said to him. "You sleep well, too."

Several days later, when the chairman of the local gas and electric company—a single father with what Carl Running Moon Howard described as an impeccable reputation—invited her to a local fundraiser, she didn't see how she could refuse. She also didn't mention it to Reid.

She had two evening dresses, and she chose the antique gold one, not that she preferred it, but because it seemed more dignified with its wide skirt and modest neckline.

"You're gorgeous," Clayton Anderson said when he called for her. "Absolutely gorgeous."

Alarm streaked through her, for she hadn't thought he'd be a shallow and frivolous man. Her disappointment increased as the evening progressed. The man had a pair of swiveled hips, and insisted on dancing every dance.

What a show-off, she said to herself. *I'm not going to let him make a dunce out of me.*

The band played "Mary Ann," a famous West Indian tune, and he stood, dancing around her chair in his eagerness to begin the dance.

"I don't care to dance this dance," she said.

"You're not serious," he said. "I never sit out a dance."

"And I never allow myself to become a spectacle," she said, her temper rising. "I am not going to dance this dance with you, Mr. Anderson."

He went to the next table and asked a woman to dance with him.

"How did I get myself into this?" she wondered.

"Dance with me?"

At the sound of that familiar and beloved voice, her eyes widened. "Yes, I'd like that very much." He held out his hand, she took it and knew once more the comfort of Reid's arms as he guided her to the sensuous rhythm of the tune "Mary Ann."

She couldn't believe it when Clayton tapped Reid on the shoulder, having left his dance partner. "This is my date, buddy, and I'm claiming this dance."

Reid stepped back. "We'll settle this another time, Anderson. Thank you for the dance, Judge Rutherford."

"I would appreciate it if you would take me home this minute, Mr. Anderson. If you don't, I'll go alone."

"What did I…I was only demanding my rights."

She forced a smile. "*What* rights? Shall we go now?"

She didn't see Reid and didn't look for him, but she knew that whatever he was, he was incensed. *I'll hear about this,* she thought.

"I'm a judge," she told her date when they arrived at her house. "An officer of the law, and I cannot afford the company of a man who would challenge another in a public place. Good night." She didn't wait for his response, nor did she thank him for the evening.

Minutes after she pulled off her evening gown to prepare for bed, the telephone rang. Her first reaction was that she should ignore it, but then she realized that her caller could be Reid.

"How'd you happen to be with that guy?" Reid asked without preliminaries.

"He called me at my chambers, told me the affair was a fundraiser for an important charity, and asked if I would go with him. I had no way of knowing that he was a jerk, and I thank you for not taking up his challenge. I know it galled you not to give him what-for. I'd already told him that I did not want to dance that dance with him, because by that time I wished I'd stayed home."

"I was there with the Marks and Connerly group. The boss bought a table and the less-senior architects on staff had to fill the seats. I was surprised to see you there."

"Not nearly as surprised as I was to see you."

"What did you do with him? I noticed that you left immediately."

"I reminded him that I'm an officer of the law, and that was enough to sober his judgment. What time are we leaving Friday?"

"I get off at four-thirty, and I'm going to work with my suitcase in the car. We should be there by nine-thirty."

"Okay. I'll be ready when you get here. I'm so excited, Reid."

"I certainly hope you are, woman. After all, you're going to spend an entire weekend with your man."

Chapter 5

"I wish somebody would tell me why I'm so nervous," Kendra said to herself when Reid got out of the rented car and pressed the bell at the iron gate that would allow them to enter Dickerson Estates.

"Who is it?" she heard a voice ask.

"Reid. How are you, Max?"

"Couldn't be better. Come on in, man. We're all in the living room waiting for you."

The big letter *D* atop the gate lit up, and the enormous iron barrier against outsiders swung open. *Well,* she thought, *I'll bet I'm in for some surprises. Something tells me I'll remember this visit for as long as I live.*

"In midsummer, this is a beautiful driveway," Reid explained. "The big trees are willows, and the smaller ones lined in front of them are crepe myrtles. The ground cover is a field of phlox, blue bonnets and a maze of other colorful flowers. It's breathtaking."

"I didn't realize that you like flowers."

"I didn't until I came here. This entire environment was so calming, so tranquil. Imagine living among people who wanted nothing more from you than your well-being and comfort. Oh, I had a job to do, but I was so glad for that that I didn't see it as work."

"Wow," she said when the big white Georgian mansion loomed close. "This house is really something."

"Yeah, and shrouded in moonlight this way, it looks mysterious."

"I'd say it looks romantic."

He glanced at her, his white teeth flashing a smile. "That, too."

"Who's this?" she asked Reid when a tall, Texas-size white man stepped out of the front door and ran down the steps.

"That's Philip." He braked, reached over and unhooked her seat belt, got out of the car and went to meet Philip. She watched while they greeted each other with what was clearly a heartfelt warm embrace. They spoke for a minute, and then Reid came back to the car and opened the door for her. Ordinarily, she wouldn't have waited for that courtesy, but she didn't want to interfere with their conversation.

Reid put an arm around her waist in what she didn't doubt was both a signal to Philip and a show of possessiveness and walked with her to meet his friend. "Kendra, this is Philip Dickerson. I've told you a lot about him and what he's meant to me." He tightened his arm around her. "Philip, from eight-thirty to four-thirty, Mondays through Fridays, Kendra is Judge Kendra Rutherford."

She liked Philip Dickerson. His smile covered his entire face—and what a face in the moonlight—and he shook her hands with both of his. "You can't imagine how happy I am to meet you, Kendra. I'm glad you came." He looked around. "You brought a suitcase, didn't you?"

"It's in the trunk," she said. "Reid has told me wonderful things about you, Philip. It's a pleasure to meet you."

"Come on in, I'll send someone for it."

"What's all this?" Reid said when they walked into the living room, a vast chamber with ceilings almost two floors high and wide windows from which hung antique-gold satin drapes. At least a dozen men and a lone woman of about fifty and with the elegance and self-confidence of a fashion model stood when they walked in. They all greeted Reid simultaneously, and rushed to hug him and shake his hand.

Philip walked over to Kendra. "You won't remember anybody's name, except perhaps Doris's—she's my housekeeper and surrogate mother—and Rocket's." He took her to an older man who stood nearby. "This is my dad, Arnold Dickerson. Dad, this is Judge Kendra Rutherford."

She shook hands with the man, thinking that an apple didn't fall far from the tree, for Arnold Dickerson had passed his good looks to his son.

Philip clapped his hands to get the group's attention.

"Look, everybody, as much as I'd enjoy doing it, I'm going to let Reid introduce his lady friend, because I remember that he's a man who stands on protocol."

Reid walked over to them holding Doris's hand. "Kendra, this is Doris. She's the mistress of this place, and that man over there with the blond hair and white T-shirt is Max, her husband and Philip's foreman."

They greeted each other warmly, and then Reid said, "Everybody, this is Kendra Rutherford, and she's one of the reasons why life is good. Officially, Kendra is a criminal court judge."

"Welcome, Kendra" were words that sounded over and over. "Way to go, man," several said to Reid in lowered tones.

Max came over and shook hands with her, and she observed from his carriage that his status was higher than that of anyone in the room other than Philip and his father. "I'm so glad to meet you, Kendra. You're the proof of the pudding, and I couldn't be happier for Reid."

"Come on, let's get it together," Doris said. "Reid and Kendra must be starving. It's kind of late in the evening for barbecued pig, but that's what Reid likes, so that's what you're getting." She looked at Kendra. "Learn to barbecue. Anything. He doesn't care what it is so long as it's barbecued."

The group followed Doris to the dining room where the barbecued pork, buttermilk biscuits, crabmeat salad, roasted corn, fried chicken, green field salad and apple pie covered the center of the table. At one end sat half a dozen bottles of wine, a tub of beer and several bottles of Moët & Chandon champagne, and at the other she saw a large urn of coffee.

When no one moved toward the food, she asked Reid, "Who starts?"

"They're waiting till Doris comes back from the kitchen and says the grace. Not even Philip risks Doris's lecture by eating before she prays over the food. This place operates like a family."

Reid put a generous helping of shredded pork on his plate along with three biscuits.

"Is that all you're eating?" she asked him, enjoying the expression of joy on his face.

"I can get that other stuff most any place, but not this barbecued pig. Marcus did spareribs, but wait till you taste this freshly killed pork."

She did. "I concur that this is exceptional, so you haven't misplaced your passion for—"

"Of course I haven't," he said, making it clear that he was not speaking of roast pig.

"Doris will show you to your rooms, Reid," she heard Philip say. "You're across the hall from each other. I hope that's all right. Your bags are in your rooms."

She pretended not to hear Reid say, "Somebody guessed which was which?"

Philip grinned at him. "What does it matter? Both of you can damned well walk." He opened three bottles of champagne, rapped one bottle with à knife. "Welcome home, Reid, and welcome to our home, Kendra." He poured a small amount in a glass, waited until the others filled their glasses and then drank it.

Kendra clicked glasses with Reid, drank half of the champagne and said, "I'm ready to turn in." She thanked her host and followed Doris up the stairs and down a long hall toward what was clearly an addition to the house's original structure.

"Here you are," Doris said. "Sleep well. And, Kendra, when I saw Reid walk in here with you, I knew he'd made it, that he was back on his feet. If you don't already know it, you'll discover that he's as solid as they come—a hardworking, capable and decent man."

She thanked Doris, and opened her room door as Reid walked toward them. She waved at him and went into her room, but she didn't expect him to ignore the fact that she'd be asleep across the hall from him. *If he does ignore it,* she said to herself, *I'll be in that rented car and gone before he wakes up. If I could have only one more thing in this life, I'd ask for one night with Reid.*

Philip Dickerson had class, and the pink rosebuds on her night table, the champagne service, grapes, cheese and crackers were further evidence of that fact. She kicked off her shoes, sat on the chaise longue and stretched out her arms. She'd had faith in Reid, but this trip strengthened it. She reached over to answer the telephone, aware that Reid was the caller.

"I understand you've got a cold bottle of Veuve Clicquot over there. Are you planning to drink all of it?"

"If I thought that was a serious question, I might try. I'll share it, but I need half an hour."

"Works for me. See you later, sweetheart."

She opened her suitcase, unpacked, took a quick shower, brushed her teeth and had just managed to slip into a green silk jumpsuit at about the time the phone rang.

"I'll be over in a minute. Thought I'd alert you so I wouldn't have to knock too hard."

She lowered the light a notch and opened the door as Reid was closing his. "I haven't had a kiss in ages," he said, closing the door.

"It's early yet," she said. Her kiss on his cheek was intended to take care of his complaint. She stared at him in an open-collared shirt, his belly as flat as the back of his hand and his trousers tight enough to emphasize his muscular legs. She swallowed hard and told herself not to rush him. "Mmm. You smell so good that I feel like sniffing," she said, and she could see that the comment pleased him.

"You always say things that make me feel great," he told her. "It's interesting that they put the goodies in your room and not in mine. Somebody figured out that you're a woman who doesn't have to go to a man. Shall I open the champagne? Neither of us has to drive."

"Let's not kill the whole bottle," she said. "You, at least, should stay sober."

Both of his eyebrows shot up as he caught the bubbles with the towel. "I can take that a lot of ways."

"Sure you can," she said, making herself comfortable on the gold-colored chaise longue, "but you're a clever man."

"Really?" He poured champagne into each of the long-stemmed crystal glasses. "I hope I'm clever enough not to make any mistakes with you."

"I don't imagine you will."

He clicked her glass with his own. "I don't aspire to be as wealthy again as I was before, but I do want to be able to treat the people I love with as much grace as Philip has shown us tonight."

She wondered what had brought on that thought. "You will be." She patted the place beside her. "Sit here with me. Are you sleepy?"

He looked hard at her. "Sleepy? Me? Has something happened to your sense of humor? Sweetheart, if I could have only one thing, I'd ask for one night with you. This night!" He put his glass on the table to the left of the chaise longue, reached down and flipped on the radio. "Let's finish that dance we started at the fundraiser." The orchestra was halfway through a famous waltz, but she didn't care what tune they danced to; she only wanted to be in his arms. Nonetheless she remained seated, mesmerized as he stood before her with his legs apart and a lover's smile on his face. His masculine aura overwhelmed her, destroying her will to do anything but let him love her. She rubbed her hands up and down her thighs and bathed her lips with the tip of her tongue as her imagination went rampant.

"Are you nervous?" he asked. "I've been talking to myself. Come here to me."

She sprang into his arms and laid her head against his shoulder, eager to let him lead her wherever he would.

"I'm not nervous," she said, but she didn't believe her own words.

He stopped dancing. "This is the first time you've ever been totally submissive to me. Baby, why are you trembling?"

"It's been a long time since I… Please, don't ask me any questions." She moved closer to him and kissed his neck.

Reid stopped dancing. "Sweetheart, if you're planning to send me back to that room across the hall before daybreak, I'd better leave here right now."

She looked at him from beneath lowered lashes. "You haven't given me a single reason to invite you to stay."

"I haven't …" She could feel tremors racing through his body, his breaths came faster and shorter, and his nostrils flared, signaling his rising passion. He bent his head, tightened his arm across her shoulders and traced the seams of her lips with his tongue. "Open up to me. I want my place inside you." She parted her lips for what he'd give her, and he thrust into her. His tongue sent the fire of desire shooting through her, and she sucked him deeper into her mouth.

She needed more, much more. If she could only get him all the way into her. She'd waited so long for this. Years of wanting, longing to love and to be loved, and when he began to stroke her and to move against her with the rhythm of his stroking, a wild and wanton feeling possessed her, and she undulated against him, moving to his beat. She heard her moans of frustration and didn't care.

She wanted him worse than she wanted to breathe, and when he stepped away from her, she moved into him—mindless of what she did—grasped his buttocks and held him while she danced against him.

"Kiss me," she said.

"What? Tell me what you want." She unbuttoned the jumpsuit, exposing to him her firm, round breasts.

"Oh, sweetheart!" He lowered his head, covered her left nipple with his warm mouth and began to suck as if his life depended on it. Hot darts danced in her belly and slithered down her thighs until she felt an unearthly heat boiling in her vagina. Groaning from the sweet torture of his biting and sucking, she reached down and stroked him.

With his head thrown back and his teeth bared, he let her have him, and she stroked and squeezed him until he cried out, "Stop it, baby, or it'll be over in a second."

"I thought you would like it," she whispered.

"I loved it, and I love you. I want to take this thing off you."

Why did he ask her? Couldn't he just hurry up and do it? "There's a zipper in the back."

He had her out of it within a second, turned back the cover on her bed, stopped and looked around at her as if he'd forgotten something. "Good Lord, you're beautiful."

Her breasts nearly spilled out of the tiny yellow bra that was meant to shield only her nipples, and when his hands went to the back of the bra to unhook it, she covered them with her hands. He stopped. He picked her up and put her in bed, and she struggled to keep her hips from swaying as her body hungered for him.

"Don't be shy," he said. "I've longed for this moment."

She held out her arms to him, and within a minute, he'd slipped out of his clothes and stood beside the bed. Realizing that he was waiting for an invitation, she grasped his thigh, pulled him closer to the bed, peeled off his bikini shorts and ran her tongue around the tip of his penis.

"Ah, sweetheart, no more of that right now." He removed her bra, wrapped his arms around her and sucked her left nipple into his mouth, but when she began to thrash in passion, he left it and kissed her forehead. When he'd satisfied himself with that part of her, his lips skimmed her eyes, worshipped her ears, her nose and her throat. She swung her body up to his, but he restrained her.

"I want to feel you," she said. "I want you inside me. Let me hold you."

"In a little while." His hot breath on her nipple sent rivulets of heat cascading along her limbs, and she began to moan when he sucked the nipple into his mouth and stroked the other one in a double assault.

"Please, honey. Get in me," she begged.

"I will, sweetheart, as soon as you're ready."

"I'm ready. I'm on fire."

His tongue trailed down to her belly and then skimmed the inside of her thighs. Nearly out of her mind with desire, she tried to take his penis into her hand and force him, but he moved down until his feet hung over the bed, hooked his forearms beneath her knees, rested her knees on his shoulders and licked the inside of her thighs until, frustrated beyond caring what she did, she raised her body to meet him. He plunged his tongue into her, sucked, nipped, kissed and thrust until screams poured out of her.

"I'm so full. I need to burst. Get in me, Reid. I want to feel you in me."

"I will. It's what I want, baby." He sheathed himself, crawled up her body, placed an arm around her shoulder and the other beneath her hip. "Take me."

She took his penis, thick, hard and throbbing, into her hands, stroked it lovingly and led him to her vagina. He thrust gently, but couldn't enter.

"How long has it been?" he asked her.

"Years. Push a little harder. I don't care if it hurts, I want you in me."

He put his hand between them and let his talented fingers dance at her portal until a gush of liquid covered his fingers. Holding his penis in her hands, she swung her body up to his, and he slowly eased into her.

She had him at last, completely inside her, and he gazed down into her face and kissed her lips. "Look at me. You're mine now. Mine, Kendra, and you'll always be mine." He moved slowly at first, and she began to feel his power as he stroked in and out, moving faster and faster.

"Do you feel me? Am I in the right place?" he asked her. "Talk to me, sweetheart."

"Yes, I feel you, but I have this awful ache, like if I don't burst, I'll die." Her feet seemed on fire, and a surge began beneath them, crawled up her legs and her thighs, and… "Honey, do something. I can't stand this. I'm hanging out here… Oh Lord, I think I'm going to die." Her thighs began to tremble. "What are you doing to me?"

"I'm loving you, and you aren't going to die."

She thought her vagina began to swell, and when a pumping and squeezing gripped it, she tried to steady herself by locking her ankles at his back and tightening her arms around him. All of a sudden, she could feel the walls of her vagina gripping his penis, squeezing, caressing and then she couldn't stand it. She was drowning.

"Reid. Honey. Oh, Reid!" She flung her arms wide and gave herself to him, and he rode her furiously, showering her with stars, giving her the sunrise, the sunset and all the colors of the heavens until she burst wide open. "Oh, Reid. I love you so."

Shouting his release, he gave her his essence and collapsed in her arms.

He didn't have the strength or the will to move. Locked in her arms and legs, he would willingly remain as he was forever. For the first time in years—long before Myrna had walked out—that sense of loneliness did not plague him. He belonged to a woman who belonged to him deep in her heart, and he'd felt it in every sinew of his body the minute she gave herself to him. He didn't ask himself whether the power of his release came from his years of celibacy, because he knew better. It came from knowing that he was wanted and loved for himself and not for the jewels, perfumes and furs that he could buy.

He raised himself up, his elbows taking his weight, and stared down at his beloved. "I love you," he whispered, and when she opened her eyes, smiled and tightened her arms around him, his heart seemed to slide down into his belly.

"How do you feel?" he asked her.

"If I didn't know better, I'd think I'd died and gone to heaven."

Her hand at his nape brought his lips down to hers, but instead of the hot kiss he expected, she gave him a little peck. "It was wonderful," she said. "After the way I felt with you, I know I can't ever be as I was before."

"What do you mean? How were you before?" he asked her. "I'd like to know."

"I guess it's… I feel like a woman, a woman with a man who can make her soul sing. It's… I can't explain it, but I'm different. It's like I'm whole for the first time."

"I feel something similar," he told her. "I've been celibate since my marriage broke up, and not because women weren't available. They're always available. But after Myrna's treachery, I didn't want anything to do with women. I saw them and looked through them. I spent six years on the estate here and never once left it. It was my respite from the world."

He separated them and lay on his back holding her hand. "That's one reason why I was able to save almost all the money I made while I worked here. I didn't have any expenses, didn't smoke or drink. Philip stocked the men's quarters with daily newspapers, magazines and books, and we all had library cards. Drinking and gambling weren't allowed, and we had a house master who valued his job, so nobody broke the rules.

"I'm lucky or blessed, however you see it, and when Doris told me tonight that she'd never seen me look as I do now, I realized how far I've come. She said you're the proof that I'm on the right track."

Kendra sat up and leaned over him. "I'm glad she's happy for you, but you don't need me as evidence of what you've accomplished. You're as much man as

Philip Dickerson or the president of this country. Which of them was ever flat on his back, down and out? Yes, you had help, but many men have passed through my court several times, because they wouldn't or couldn't use the help given them. You are not an ordinary man."

She patted his chest. "Why don't we drink the rest of that champagne? And you used up my energy. I'm hungry."

He pulled her into his arms. "Don't change the subject. You were saying nice things about me. I'm listening."

Her lips brushed his. "Don't get carried away."

If she only knew how great she made him feel! "All right. Let's see what's in this basket." He rolled off the bed, got their glasses, filled them with champagne and handed her one. "Do I still have to stay sober?"

She lowered her lashes, pulled the sheet up to her neck and glanced at him. "It's up to you, but what'll you do if I decide I want to… That I want some more?"

Play with him, would she? He felt a grin teasing his lips. "More of what? There won't be any champagne left?"

"You know what I mean," she said, pretending to pout.

"No, I don't. You have to give it to me straight, baby." He took a long sip of the champagne. "And you'd better do it soon, because this champagne works fast."

"Maybe I'll just lie here right beside you and suffer."

Laughter streamed out of him. He couldn't help it. "Sweetheart, don't even think it. That's the least of my worries. When your engine heats up, you ignite. So what do you think you might want more of?"

"Does it matter? You've just finished off the champagne."

That was enough of a challenge, and the champagne had warmed him just enough, like a tantalizing whiff of perfume fanning his libido. "Do you want any more cheese and crackers?"

"Later, I might."

He took her glass from her hand, put it on the table, joined her in the bed and pulled the sheet down to her waist. All he had to do was get one of her nipples into his mouth, and he lowered his head and began to suckle her vigorously the way he knew she liked.

"Reid! Oh, honey!" He let his hand drift down to the apex of her legs and linger still there until she crossed her knees in frustration.

"Open your legs. I want to get in there." He eased his hand down until it cupped her. "Am I sober enough, or do you want me to stop right here?"

"Honey, please don't tease. I was joking."

"Good." With his forefinger, he rubbed the nub at the entrance to her vagina until she began to squirm and wiggle. Then he let his fingers have sway, playing her as a lyrist plays his lyre, strumming and picking until he could feel her give in to him. At that moment, he knew he had to have it all, so he lifted her, kissed her and, excited by her moans and cries, he sucked on her.

"Please," she begged. "Let me come. I can't stand it."

He lay on his back and pulled her on top of him. "You want it. Take it," he said. "Do anything to me that you want to." He began to rub her nipples. "Go ahead, sweetheart. I'm yours."

To his amazement, she bent to his chest and circled an aureole with her tongue. He flinched slightly, and she sucked it into her mouth. Her hand trailed down to his belly, and she let her fingers stroke and tease him. If she was going any further, he wished the hell she'd do it. Then she was kissing his belly, the insides of his thighs, ignoring his fully erect penis. He struggled to remain still and let her have her way, but with her slow tease, he felt as if he would erupt any second.

Her tongue replaced her lips on the inside of his thighs, and he wanted to shout his frustration. Then he felt nothing, and he realized that she was looking at him. After that long pause, her fingers clasped his penis the way one grasps an object that may be hot.

"Take it in your hand, baby." But instead, she left it and ran her fingers gently over his testicles, exploring them. He'd scream any minute.

His whole body tensed when he felt her warm breath on him, and he nearly jumped out of bed when her tongue rimmed his penis.

"You didn't like that?" she asked him.

"Oh, baby. I've been lying here dying to feel you take me into your mouth. When I tell you to stop, you stop."

She said nothing, and he wondered if he'd ruined it. Then she kissed the tip, and he told himself to relax. But a second later, she took him in and began to suck on him, gingerly at first and then greedily, as if she loved it. He struggled to remain still, but his body began the classic undulations, and she locked her arms around his hips and tortured him.

"Kendra. Honey, stop. *Stop!* I don't want to make a

mistake." He reached down and pushed her away from him. She stared at him until he pulled her up. "You were about to make me explode." He fell back.

"Crawl up here," he said, "and straddle me." She did, and he eased into her.

"Lean forward, sweetheart." He suckled her while she took them on a fast ride to oblivion. When at last he shouted his release, he felt as if she'd drained him of his energy and of his will to do anything but what she desired.

Cradling her atop him, he pulled the sheet up and told himself to sleep, but he didn't want anyone to discover that they had spent the night together. He wanted to protect her reputation. He reached over, got the clock and, without awakening her, managed to set it to five o'clock. That would give him half an hour to get into his room before Philip awakened. But was that the real reason why he couldn't sleep? How would he manage when they returned to Queenstown? So close to her, but unable to have her.

"I've traveled rockier roads," he said to himself and drifted off to sleep.

"Why do I have to get up, and why are you talking to me on the phone?" Kendra mumbled the next morning. "Reid?" She sat up in bed, gazed at her surroundings and remembered where she was and why. "Why didn't you…? Oh. I don't remember when you left."

"I left around four thirty because this house begins to stir at about five. How do you feel this morning?"

"Lonely. I wanted to wake up in your arms."

"So did I, but I guess that will have to wait. Get up, sweetheart. It's the best time for riding. The horses are happiest when all is quiet around them. Wait a minute, I have to answer the door." After a minute, he said, "Hi. I'm back. That was Philip. He always made lousy coffee, but he brought a pot of it, two mugs, milk, sugar and two spoons. I'll be right over."

"Wait a second. How'd he know you were over there and not in here with me?"

"Simple. He didn't dare knock on your door, and if I wasn't in my room, he'd have taken the coffee back to the kitchen, and we would never have known that he brought it. Philip is the epitome of discretion."

"Give me ten minutes."

She brushed her teeth, took a fast sponge bath, straightened the bed, put on her robe and opened the door. "Sorry. I didn't have time to get dressed. I know you would have waited, but I wanted the coffee."

He put the tray on the table beside the chaise longue, put his arms around her and adored her with his lips. "No heavy stuff this morning, sweetheart, my willpower is practically nonexistent." He poured two cups of coffee.

She sipped with great care, fearing that she might burn her lips. "It's not bad at all."

"Doris must have taken Philip in hand. It always tasted like instant before."

"Maybe it *was* instant. Want some cheese and crackers?" He accepted the food that she placed on a napkin. "Is there any reason why we can't spend a weekend at a resort, or some place private where we can swim or just be together?" she asked him. "If there is, you don't have to explain it. Just tell me it would be best if we did it later…or never, if that's how you feel."

He sat on the edge of the bed, topped off his coffee and put the pot back on the table. "Thank you for being so understanding. It's something I won't forget. My priority right now is my case against Brown and Worley, but my salary is good, and I have a private contract with Marcus Hickson, so I'm not pinched for money. Figure out which weekend is good for you. What do you think of Cape May?"

"I haven't been there, but I'll be happy with whatever you choose. It doesn't have to be luxurious like…like this." She waved her hand to indicate all around them. "I just want us to be together."

He put his cup down, bent over and kissed her. "I trust that you mean what you say, sweetheart, but I've been taught by a master. Please start with me the way you know you can continue. Do you understand what I'm saying?"

"I do understand, and that's what I'm trying to get across to you. I don't want you to overstretch yourself to do what you think will please me or make me comfortable. I want you to present yourself as you are, because that's the only way you'll know who I really am."

He looked at her for a long time, as if he wanted to see inside her. Then he said, "I'd better go. You wouldn't believe how tantalizing you are in that yellow robe. Put on something suitable for horseback riding. I'll be in the kitchen with Doris." He kissed her on the mouth, put the coffee service on the tray and left.

She showered quickly and dressed in gray riding breeches, a red-and-gray paisley shirt, a gray tie and black boots. She didn't have a riding hat and didn't want one. She got on a horse twice a year, and she wouldn't have had the boots and breeches if her sister hadn't given them to her. Besides, they were out in the country, and she'd bet that only jeans-clad behinds had warmed the backs of those horses.

She walked into the kitchen to find Doris making biscuits while Reid laid strips of bacon and what looked like two pounds of rope sausage on the grill. "Good morning," she said, not calling the name of either.

"Good morning," the two of them said in unison.

"How may I help, Doris?"

"Here's a knife. You can hull those strawberries, if you don't mind. I already washed them." '

"I don't mind one bit. By the way, how many people are going to eat breakfast?"

"You, Reid, Philip, Max, Arnold and me. Six."

"They why are we cooking all this sausage?"

"Well, Max, Arnold, Reid and Philip will eat most of it plus a few strips of bacon. That, scrambled eggs, grits, these biscuits, juice and strawberries isn't a really big breakfast."

Kendra rolled her eyes to the ceiling. "If you say so. I guess working men eat a lot."

"Yes," Doris said, "and I just remembered that Reid is sitting down these days. Reid, you have to go light on this stuff now. You don't want to ruin your fabulous physique. A big bay window will turn a woman off in a minute." She released a throaty laugh. "Am I right, Kendra?"

Kendra sampled a strawberry. "Probably. It'll take a lot more than a bay window to turn me off Reid."

"Well, hallelujah!" Doris said. "Looks like you hit the jackpot, Reid."

He walked over to her and, with his hands clasped behind him, kissed her mouth. She flicked her tongue across his lips, winked at him and returned to the business of hulling berries.

"I'll get you for that," he told her.

"Naah. Self-discipline is good for a man." She whirled around to see Philip straddle a chair and put a coffee cup to his mouth. "Good morning, Kendra. I hope you enjoyed the coffee. I don't make the best brew, but as Reid will confirm, I'm improving. You two are going riding?"

"Yeah," Reid said. "I thought I'd saddle Bessie Rae for Kendra. I always rode Casey Jones. How's he these days?"

"He'll probably jump all over you. I never knew a horse to sulk the way he did right after you left. He wouldn't cooperate with a soul."

After breakfast, as Kendra walked with Reid to the stables, the men with whom he had worked stopped them, greeting them warmly. Reid kept a firm grip on her hand, and she didn't have to be told that he enjoyed showing his friends what he and she meant to each other. At the barn, Max caught up with them.

"I expect you remember how you used to do it, Reid," he said. "They've been fed. It's a great morning for riding, so you two have a good time. Here's a walkie-talkie in case you need me."

Reid thanked him, brought Bessie Rae to her and

waited until she mounted the mare. "That was as smooth as it gets," he said. "Wait here while I get my mount."

The stallion neighed and swished his tail when he saw Reid. "Casey, boy. You remember me," Reid said, patting the big bay stallion. He saddled the horse, mounted him and reached down and hugged his neck.

"Don't tighten the reins, sweetheart," he said to Kendra. "Keep 'em slack. These horses love to gallop, and if Bessie Rae takes off, there's no holding Casey Jones back. He's as competitive as some men."

They walked the horses toward a brook. She'd never seen such a beautiful brook winding among sleepy willows and pines and with wildflowers of many colors decorating its banks. The sun filtered through the pine trees, and hundreds of birds chirped like a great choir.

"Reid, this is so idyllic. I could stay here forever."

He brought his horse to a halt. "With me?"

"Ask me that question again a week from now. I'm still drunk on you."

His gaze sliced through her. "You pick the damnedest times to say things like that. I'm so full of you right now that I can hardly think straight."

"Consider yourself kissed," she said, and patted Bessie Rae on the rump and broke the tension of the moment. She was becoming besotted with him, and because she'd just decided that she wanted him for all time, she knew she'd better keep her head. She remembered her father's words to her sister and her. "If you give a man all he wants, pretty soon he won't want anything."

* * *

There'd been a miscue somewhere, Reid decided as they headed back to the house. He wouldn't say she'd closed up, but she seemed less—he couldn't think of any other words—open to him.

"Want to see the dormitory I designed for the men who work on the estates?" he asked her when they approached it. She said she did, and a few minutes later he brought Casey Jones to a halt in front of the redbrick building.

"This is it? It looks like a two-story private house, albeit a very big one," she said.

"Each room has a bathroom and a balcony," he explained, "and the downstairs consists of a kitchen, dining room, lounge and recreation room with a bathroom on each end. I was pretty proud that I could do this for Philip. It made me happy to be able to do something for him.

"Want to see the lounge?" It seemed like years since he'd called that place home. He hadn't spent much time in the public rooms, for as soon as Philip had put three laptop computers at their disposal, he'd spent his spare time searching for information on Brown and Worley, and in the three months before he left the estates he'd been looking for a job whenever he wasn't working, eating or sleeping.

"This resembles a very nice hotel lobby," she said of the lounge.

"Philip spent a lot of money furnishing this place, and the men appreciate it. There's nothing they wouldn't do for him.

"We'd better go. Lunch is promptly at twelve, and nobody here goes to a meal late." He took her hand, and to his surprise he voiced a thought that had sprinted through his mind. "I hope this isn't the last time I'm as happy as I am today."

"What brought that on?" she asked him.

"I don't know. It isn't a thought that's spent much time on my mind."

"If you aren't tired," Philip told them at lunch, "we can drive over to Oxford and take a spin on my boat. Dad and I went over last weekend and got her seaworthy. Maybe Dad will come with us. Max can't stand that much water, and Doris wouldn't think of going off and leaving Max on a Saturday afternoon."

"I love living near the water," Kendra said later as Philip headed the cruiser out on the bay. She glanced at Reid, read his sultry eyes and quickly lowered her gaze.

"So do I," he said, "and when I build my own house again, I hope it will overlook a lake, a big river or even the ocean. Water gives such peace."

"Yes," Arnold said. "In the early spring, I go down by the brook right after sunrise. The water rushes along, but everything else is still and quiet, except the birds. It is so peaceful." He turned to Kendra. "Did Reid take you there this morning?"

"Yes, he did. It was heavenly."

"This is Reid's home," Philip said to Kendra, "and no matter where he lives, this will be home for him, so please encourage him to come home often."

"I will, Philip." She glanced at Reid and caught him

gazing intently at her, so she smiled. "But I can only encourage him. The first thing I learned about Reid was that he's a loner—an independent, self-willed creature."

"Don't think I didn't learn it, too," Philip said. "But I also learned that he's got a big heart."

She walked over to Reid and locked her fingers through his. "What is it?" he asked her.

"Nothing. I was too far away from you." She couldn't bring herself to tell him that she needed to touch him.

He didn't know whether he did it because he wanted Philip and Arnold to know that she was truly his or whether it was because of his need of her. He only knew that when he looked down at her inviting mouth, nothing could have stopped him from kissing her. He was in deep, headed down a one-way street. Did he want to go all the way with her? Had being with her, getting to know her and loving her restored his faith in marriage? He didn't believe that was possible, yet all the signs were there before him. And he loved her.

Chapter 6

On Sunday night, Kendra crawled into her own bed nursing her aching limbs and trying to come to terms with the feeling that she'd been separated from Reid for years. A total of four hours on the back of a horse—albeit a gentle one—had left her barely able to walk. She didn't mind that nearly as much as she hated having Reid so far from her. He'd telephoned her twice since they got back to Queenstown around eight that night, but his calls had not abated her loneliness.

"I will not telephone him," she told herself. "I will not be a slave to my emotions." But, man, the way he moved inside her like a borer tunneling for air. And the way he wiggled his hips! At the memory of it, she stretched out in the bed and threw her arms wide. If only she could close them around him!

After a night of fitful sleep, she got up early and was leaving home on the way to work when she heard the drums, horns, bugles and tom-toms coming toward her. She didn't want to be there when the pickets arrived, but she didn't want to run away, either. She saw Reid sprinting across the street. As he got closer to her, he beckoned. She ran to him.

"Hurry!" he yelled. "The radio announcer said they're planning some rough stuff this morning." He grabbed her briefcase with one hand, took her left hand and dashed with her into the building in which he lived.

He closed the door and locked her in his arms. "I'm so glad I caught you," he said. "I just heard a radio announcer say that the pickets planned to damage Brown and Worley's developments, but he didn't say which one. It could be the one they're developing over near the park."

"This is frightening," she said just as he dragged her from the window so roughly, horrifying her, that she felt a pain in her right shoulder. He slapped his hands over her ears, but she heard the explosion.

"What was that?" she asked him.

"A hand grenade. I heard it singing just before it exploded. I hadn't heard that sound since I left Afghanistan, and I'd hoped never to hear it again."

"I didn't know you were in Afghanistan. Do you think it blew up something? What about my house?"

"Two years. A busted collarbone got me out of the army and into university. I think that explosion was a bit farther down the street. I hope I didn't hurt you a minute ago, but I had to get you away from the window. How do you feel?"

"A little displaced. This isn't the way I expected my day to start."

"Stay here a minute," he said and left the building.

She didn't frighten easily, but she felt as if her heart was in her mouth as she waited for him to come back. Relief, such as she had rarely felt, spread through her when he opened the door.

"There's one policeman out there for every picket, or at least it looks that way. I know what you're going to say, so don't bother to say it. I'm walking with you to the courthouse this morning, and that's that. Kiss me now, unless you want me to kiss you when I leave you at the courthouse."

"You're too bossy, but I don't have time right now to put you in your place."

She didn't sound convincing, not even to herself, and the smile of happiness on his face let her know that he didn't take her words seriously. He locked her in his arms and kissed her nose. "Something tells me that I'll never get enough of you," he said, and then his demeanor changed from sweet and playful to serious and, she thought, to a little sad. "Don't let what's happening across the street and my problems with Brown and Worley come between us."

He lowered his head, and his mouth came down on hers hard and possessively. "Let's go."

"One of the most comforting things about my relationship with you, Reid, is that my being a judge doesn't bother you. You're not threatened by it."

"Why should I be? You're beautiful, sweet and feminine, and I like the fact that you're so intelligent, and that we can discuss all kinds of things, enjoy all kinds of things together. I'm proud of you, and knowing that you want me is a helluva shot to my ego."

"Thanks for the nice compliment. I'm proud of you, too. You're not beautiful, but—"

He interrupted her. "I'm not? You wound me."

"Stop right there," she said. "We're not getting into the way you look, because I'm sure that at least a thousand women have told you."

"Have not."

"Have so."

They walked along the side of Albemarle Heights on which Reid lived, so they didn't encounter any of the pickets. "I'll call you tonight. Consider yourself kissed," he said. Reid didn't cross the street with her but watched until she entered the courthouse door.

She had to find a way to get out of that house. She didn't have enough equity in it to avoid losing money if she sold it, so she could do nothing at the moment. She walked into her chambers, saw that the appliances she'd purchased had arrived and that Carl had already installed them.

"Coffee's ready, ma'am, and it sure does taste better than what we've been getting."

"Thanks, Carl. Did you know that the pickets are out this morning? Somebody threw a hand grenade."

"I expect that was one of those rabble rousers that sometimes follow the pickets. Did it damage anything?"

"I only know it didn't damage my house. I got out of the area as fast as possible."

"The pickets aren't going to hurt you in any way,

Judge Rutherford. I've told the tribe how you feel about the whole mess, and they're aware of what you're trying to do for our young people. By the way, how's the civics class?"

"I'm pleased with it, Carl. I'm thinking of having a civics teacher from Edenton grade the exams and the papers, and I'm going to give a second prize of five hundred dollars."

"It was a good move, ma'am."

She wasn't sure that she should ask the question, but she wanted the answer. "Are any of your ancestors buried on that hill, Carl?"

He looked into the distance and then bowed his head. "Yes, ma'am. Both of my parents, my grandparents and my whole family."

Her lower lip dropped, and her eyes widened. "I'm so terribly sorry."

"It's all right, ma'am," he said, and seemed to stand taller than his six feet two inches with his shoulders square and straight and his chin defiant. "Those builders will get what they deserve, so you needn't worry."

She pushed aside the notes she had intended to study before hearing her first case. "Why do you say that?"

"My people don't bother the innocent, but we always see the score settled with our enemy one way or the other. We know that you are not our enemy. May I get something else for you, ma'am?"

"No. Thank you, Carl. You've given me a feeling of security, and I appreciate it."

He turned and left.

She donned her robe and took her seat in the courtroom. *I hope I don't have to slap this attorney's wrist again,* she said to herself when the defense attorney arrived with his client. *Doesn't he know that his behavior sets the jury against his client?* The trial ended with a verdict of guilty, and she couldn't help wondering how many prisoners were incarcerated only because they'd had an incompetent lawyer.

Concentration didn't come easily, because, in spite of the assurance Carl gave her, she couldn't help being concerned about her house. "Happiness is seeing your house still standing," she said to herself when she got home that afternoon.

"So where was that explosion we heard this morning?" she asked Reid when he called her.

"An uprooted tree about four doors south of you," he said. "The guy's in jail. He doesn't even live in Queenstown, just went along to foment trouble.

"I've done some research. The possibilities are Cape May, Miami Beach, Bermuda, Ocean City and Fort Lauderdale. Think about all possible ramifications, and let me know which you prefer. If we waited until July Fourth, we'd have an extra day, but that would require early planning."

"Let's go to Cape May. That's what you suggested at first, and I think it's what you'd prefer. I mean it when I say I only want us to be someplace where we can behave naturally with each other."

"All right. Cape May on the July Fourth weekend. Check carefully, and let me know if that suits you."

"I will. I've already begun to anticipate it."

"Wait a minute. That's the weather guy on my radio.

He said we're in for a terrible storm, and that a storm watch will be in effect from six this evening until three o'clock tomorrow morning. Close and lock your windows, roll up your awnings and put your car in your garage. Maybe I'd better come over there and roll up those awnings."

"Thanks, but they go up and down with the push of a button. I'll run out right now and put the car in the garage. Oh, dear. What about my civics class?"

"Not to worry. It's getting dark outside. They'll check the weather forecast. I wish I could be over there with you. Nothing's more exciting than a rousing storm."

"Maybe it'll storm while we're in Cape May," she said, feeling a bit wicked. "I'd better put my car away. I'll talk with you later."

She wasn't fond of any level of storm, especially not if lightning was a part of it. She put her car away, closed and locked her windows and doors and secured the awnings. The problem was that the dark clouds were so eerie as to be breathtakingly beautiful, and she wanted to sit out on her deck and enjoy the scenery. However, a loud clap of thunder quickly disabused her of that notion.

What a pity she couldn't be with Reid at a time when she felt the need to be close to him. Rain pelted her windows until she thought the panes would shatter, and then the winds began. She curled up in a chair thinking that she would read in order to take her mind off the storm, but the lights flickered and died away. Why hadn't she thought to gather some candles and matches?

She fumbled her way toward the closet in the foyer in search of a flashlight, stumbled and skinned her knee.

At the sound of the doorbell, she pulled herself up, certain that only Reid would be at her door in such weather. "I didn't know whether you had any candles," he said when she opened the door.

"Oh, Reid, you're soaking wet. Come in the kitchen and let me see if I can get you dry."

"I don't mind being wet," he said. "I want to be sure you have some light." He turned on a flashlight and walked with her to the kitchen.

She found her flashlight, ran down to the cellar, opened a trunk and got a blanket. "Let me wrap this around you. What a chance you took," she said as the thunder cracked. "You could have been hit by lightning. Take off your shirt. It'll dry in front of the gas oven."

He looked at her with a devil-may-care expression, daring her. "What about my pants?"

She winked at him and started out of the kitchen. "Behave yourself. You can take those off, too, but you'll have to stay in here until they dry."

"You're a very mean woman. I want to be with you," he said.

"I'm not looking at you," she said over her shoulder, "so get that little-boy look off your face."

"Maybe I'd better change tactics. I'm exhausted. Do you mind if I lie down?"

Laughter spilled out of her in spite of her effort to contain it. "Honey, I didn't dream you could be such a baby," she said. "Hmmm. That oven is heating up this kitchen."

He gazed at her. "You think it's the oven, do you? Well, come here."

Ignoring his remark, she took two of the candles he'd brought, put them in bud vases and lit them. "Let's see, I have some frozen quiches, frozen spinach and the makings of a salad. Will that fill you up?"

"Depends on the size of the quiche."

She put three individual quiches in the oven, sautéed the spinach and put dressing on the mesclun salad. "I forgot I have some good German ham. Want some?"

"I'll take anything you give me."

"Here," she said, handing him a bottle of pinot grigio wine. "Open this, please."

"My pleasure. I can't think of anything you're likely to ask me to do that I wouldn't do for you. And you're supposed to believe that."

"I do, so I'm going to be careful about what I ask you to do." Suddenly, she laughed.

"What's funny?"

"Suppose you were mad as the devil at me—and it can happen—and I told you I wanted you to make love with me? What would you do?"

He looked at her and grinned. "You think that's far-fetched? Well, it's not. What would I do? I'd do my damnedest to make you climb the wall."

She regarded him with a withering look, but thanks to her experience with him, she wasn't sure of her ground, so she didn't voice the quip that came to mind. Clap after clap of thunder roared above them, and a flash of lightning revealed the storm in his eyes.

"It's good, Kendra, when the storm on the inside of

you is just as fierce as the one that's roaring above you and all around you." He let the blanket fall to the floor. "Come here and let me love you."

"I…uh…I have to take this stuff out of the oven."

"Damn that stuff, baby. Don't you need me?" he asked her in a voice gruff with tenderness.

She turned off the oven and rubbed her thighs with her hands, up and down. Up and down.

"Don't you want me to do that?" he whispered.

She stared at him, transfixed by the impassioned turbulence in his eyes. He stood before her wearing only his shorts, his fists balled and his legs wide apart, and her heart began to hammer out a wild rhythm as the man in him jumped out to her. Oh, she could smell the male in him breaking loose. He wanted her. And she wanted him. Zombielike, she opened her arms to him. He picked her up, carried her to the living room and sat down with her in his lap.

"I want to be inside you so badly," he told her.

"Then stop talking and do something about it," she said.

A second later, her T-shirt landed on the floor at his feet, his hand went into her bra, released her left breast and his warm, moist mouth began sucking on her nipple. Caring for nothing now but the feel of his marauding lips on her, she unhooked her bra and began to tug at her pants. He removed the remainder of their clothing, sat her facing him in his lap, entered her and suckled her while he drained her of her will and strength.

"Put me on the floor," she begged. "I want to feel your power the way I did before."

He did as she asked, and within minutes he was storming within her. The lightning flashed and the thunder roared, but she was conscious only of the man inside her, under her, around her, everywhere. She tightened around him, screaming his name, and he splintered in her arms. *Hers.* He belonged to her as she belonged to him, and she knew she would love him forever.

"I didn't come over here to seduce you," he said. "I hope you believe me. I wanted to be sure you had light and that you could handle the storm." He rolled over, got up and looked around for her clothes and then down at her. Completely vulnerable in her nudity. "I could make love to you all night long," he said, barely recognizing his own voice, hoarse with desire. He got the flashlight and went to the closet in her foyer for a raincoat to cover her. "I liked what I was looking at, but I don't want to wear out my welcome."

She slipped on the coat, grateful for his thoughtfulness. "Thanks. I'll be back in a minute."

She tripped up the stairs, and he collected his clothes, washed up in the powder room, dressed and set the table. He didn't see anything for dessert, but he found some gingersnaps and sherry and a container of Reddi Whip.

"Let's see what this tastes like," he said, soaking a gingersnap in sherry. "Hmmm. Not bad." He got a small mixing bowl, soaked some gingersnaps and placed them between layers of whipped cream, topped the concoction with cream and put the container in the freezer.

"It can't be too bad," he said to himself. "Ginger-snaps are good, cream is good and sherry sure is good."

"What's holding you up there?" he yelled to her.

"I'll be down in a minute."

"What was keeping you?" he asked when she came down.

"Try moving around in the bathroom in the dark. I forgot to take a light up there."

He rubbed her nose. "Supper's ready. Have a seat."

She looked at the table and then at him. "You're growing on me. You know that?"

"I'm doing my best. What was that?"

He got up and went to the window. "The water's standing over a foot deep out there, and the wind just tossed somebody's deck chair into your garden. If this continues until three in the morning, Queenstown may be a wreck."

They finished the meal of ham, quiche lorraine, spinach and salad, and he said, "Want some dessert?"

"I'd love it, but I don't have any."

"Really? Trust your man to perform miracles." He served the trifle in two glass bowls that he suspected were intended for salads and brought them to the table.

"What's this? When did you do this?"

"You stayed up there long enough for me to make it. Taste it."

She did, and licked her lips. "It's delicious. What's in it?"

"My secret. Would you mind cleaning the kitchen tonight? I have to adjust the design of the building I'm doing for Marcus, and I told him I'd e-mail the changes tomorrow. I need to get home."

Her smile seemed to illumine the darkness that had encompassed them. She had so many ways to let him know that she was there for him. He knew she didn't want him to get soaked again, but he also knew that the alternative—remaining all night with her—was not an option.

"Considering this storm," she said, "Marcus won't expect you to send him anything tomorrow."

He let his shrug express what he thought of that idea. "No dice. I don't believe in excuses."

"Would you like to wrap my raincoat around you?"

"Thanks, but I'm probably twice as big as you are. Walk me to the door, sweetheart. I need to get moving."

"Here's your flashlight."

He grasped her hand and walked toward the door. "Thanks." At the door, he wrapped her in his arms and seared her with a kiss. "Good night, precious."

She took the blanket down to the cellar, and when she got to the bottom step she stared at six or more inches of water. What on earth? Maybe a drain was clogged. Tomorrow, she'd see what Reid thought of it.

The rain continued to pour throughout the next morning. Half of her jurors failed to report for duty, and when at one o'clock the rain had not slackened she recessed the court until Monday morning and went home.

Concerned about possible damage from the storm, she put on a pair of boots and walked around her house to determine the extent of the damage, but she saw only a large amount of debris that had blown onto her property. However, when she checked in her basement she discovered that the water had risen another inch or two.

She telephoned Reid and after their warm greetings worked up slowly to the condition of her basement. "Did you finish revising your design?" she asked him.

"I did, and he's satisfied with the changes. Have you checked the back of your house, your garden and fences?"

"Nothing serious out there, but I need an architect or somebody else familiar with building structures to check out my basement."

"What? Is this serious, or are you lonely?"

"Both. I have six or eight inches of water in my basement."

"*Don't step in that water!* There may be a loose wire somewhere down there. I'll be over in half an hour."

They had agreed not to see each other—at least not in Queenstown—but they *were* seeing each other, and she'd told herself not to have an affair with him and prejudice his case against Brown and Worley, but she *was* having an affair with him. Furthermore, she no longer called the shots, because he knew that if he could get her alone in a private place, he only had to get his mouth on her nipple and she'd melt. She let out a hearty laugh. If he got that far, she was already a goner.

She gathered a couple of bottles of water from the pantry and unwrapped the cranberry scones that she'd bought on the way home. A few minutes later, she heard his knock, and as if she hadn't seen him in years, she raced to the door. He stepped into the house, took her into his arms, and her world spun off its axis. He kissed her on the lips, hugged her and attempted to step back, but the quivers that he'd sent racing through her continued their path through her body, and she had to hold on to him.

"What is it?" he asked her, cradling her in his arms.

"You take some getting used to," she said. "I bought scones. Want some?"

How much more of a man-in-charge he seemed than when he'd picked her up off the ice a lifetime ago. His smile, so sweetly seductive, and his grayish-brown eyes with their long and curly lashes sometimes seemed incompatible with his rough masculinity, but she loved the tough man as much as the sweet and sexy one.

He sat down at her kitchen table and bit into one of the scones. "You're not used to me yet?" he asked her.

"I'm comfortable with you, but I'm definitely not used to you. I don't want to get used to you, either," she heard herself say. "Scratch that last part. It wasn't meant for your ears."

"I see you take care of your middle, but you don't worry about mine," he said as he savored the treat. "This is delightful."

"Thanks. Your middle is perfect, but mine bears watching."

"Believe it, sweetheart, and I intend to watch it every chance I get."

"Oh, you!"

"I'll take a look downstairs. I sure hope it isn't what I think it is. By the way, let's duck out of here tonight and go somewhere for dinner. If you don't want us to go together, we'll both drive, and I'll meet you at the restaurant. There's more than one way to crack a nut."

"You'd rent a car for that?"

"Why not? I want to eat dinner with you, and I don't want either you or me to cook it. I'll be back after a while."

She heard his cell phone ring as he reached the living room, and she could tell from his voice that he had taken a seat and was involved in a conversation about something important to him. But she didn't listen and she didn't plan to ask what it was about. In any relationship, trust was essential. If he wanted her to know, he'd tell her. After about ten minutes, she heard his booted steps and knew he'd gone to the basement.

What a rotten job! A roof-to-basement leak in a brand-new house. In a couple of years, that side of the house would have to be refurbished. He didn't rejoice in it, but if he wanted to use it, the evidence would be added ammunition for his own case against Brown and Worley. He needed tools that he didn't have, and with rain forecast for the entire weekend, he didn't want her to stay here. One live wire could cause a fire or even take her life.

"I have to go to a builders' supply store for something," he told her when he went back upstairs.

"Then take my car." She handed him the keys. "It's parked out front. Is the problem serious?"

He didn't want to alarm her, but he couldn't lie. "Serious enough. Thanks for the car. I'll be back shortly." He found what he needed and went back to her house.

"Is there anything I can do to help?" she asked him.

"Thanks, sweetheart, but I don't want you to come down here unless you're wearing rubber boots. Plastic won't protect you." By the time he assured himself that the water had not seeped in from the ground outside but from the roof, he'd found four major flaws in the building's foundation.

Halfway up the steps from the basement, he removed his rubber boots, carried them and placed them on the mat at her front door. He had a decision to make and not much time in which to make it.

"Where are you, Kendra?" he called as he walked toward the kitchen.

"I'm in here. Are you ready for your coffee?"

He sat in a chair at the kitchen table and reached for her hand. "You have a leaking roof, and the water is running down beside a couple of pipes. Some walls upstairs are probably wet. There are some other problems. I'd like another builder to check out this house inch by inch first thing next week."

"Are you serious?"

"Oh, yes. Definitely. With the rain continuing to come down like this, I can't leave you here, and Philip needs me. We got a part of the hurricane, but he got the brunt of it. When I left the estates, I told him that if he ever needed me, he had only to call."

"And that was who called you before you went to the supply company?"

He nodded. "The only way I can handle this is to take you with me down to the eastern shore. If you don't want to go, I won't leave you here, I'll stay. You come first with me, but I need to help my friend."

She handed him the coffee and sat down. "What happened down there?"

"The barns and stables need a major repair, tree limbs need support and there's damage to the men's quarters. I can help a lot with those repairs. His strawberries and lettuce are ready for market, and the men have to see to that. Three days of overgrowth, and they won't be salable."

"I see. I think we should leave now."

He stared at her. "But we have to move your things out of those closets and maybe clean up a bathroom."

"Come on. We can put everything on the bed in the guest room."

He followed her up the stairs, hardly able to take in his surroundings, for his thoughts were on her readiness to help him. It was not an experience he'd had with any woman other than his mother.

After they cleared out two closets and the guest bathroom, she said to him, "Go home, pack whatever you need and phone Philip. We can take my car. I'll be ready to go in half an hour."

"No, sweetheart. I'll get a rental car and be back here for you in forty-five minutes. The fact that you offered is good enough for me, and I won't forget it, but I'm not going to take advantage of your generosity."

After phoning for the rental car, Reid took a shower and packed what he needed. Philip would have tools, but he wanted to be sure that he had the essentials. He stood at the door of the building in which he lived, and when the rental car arrived he dashed to it and got in. "I'll return it Monday morning," he told the driver. Normally, he would have driven the man back to the rental-car office, but doing that would mean leaving Kendra open to gossip. Seeing her leave town with him when they both carried suitcases would be too tempting a subject for most of the local citizens to pass up.

Reid couldn't drive as fast as he liked because the rain made that hazardous. Nonetheless, they reached the estate around seven that evening. As he'd done on their previous visit, Philip came out to greet them.

"You don't know how glad I am to see you, friend," he said to Reid. "You can show these fellows how to repair these buildings." He greeted Kendra. "Thank you for coming. I know Reid wanted to stay and take care of your house. You're a very big person to do this."

"It's important to him," she said simply.

"You're in time for supper," he told them, "and since I know approximately what time you left Queenstown, I know you didn't stop to eat. I'll take you up to your rooms." He picked up Kendra's suitcase. "Neither of you will ever know what your coming here this evening means to me."

He put her bag in the same room she'd had previously. "You're over there, Reid. Doris is waiting supper, so come on down."

"I'm going to turn in early tonight, sweetheart," Reid told Kendra after supper, "because I want to be up at four-thirty, but you may sleep as long as you like." He brushed her lips with his own, hugged her and headed for his room. The less time he spent in her company, the better, for he faced some back-breaking work in the morning, and making love all night was not a way to prepare for it.

* * *

"I've never harvested lettuce," Kendra said to Doris, Max, Philip and Philip's father after Reid went to his room, "but I know when strawberries are ripe, and I can pick them. I can also tie up the limbs of saplings, and I can hand shingles and boards to the men."

The three of them stared at her. "I didn't know you intended to help," Philip said. "I think it's best that you walk around, see what you want to do, and if you feel inclined, do that."

"All right. Thanks for that great meal, Doris. See you in the morning."

She slept well, and found that getting up at four-thirty posed no problem. She walked into the kitchen a few minutes after five, stunning Philip, Reid, Doris and Max.

"What's the matter?" she said with a laugh. "Did the four of you think I had the backbone of a piece of twine? Bring on the grits, scrambled eggs, sausage, biscuits and strong coffee. I'm ready for a man-sized workday."

Her words brought a round of laughter, and as Doris rose from the table, Kendra placed a hand on her shoulder. "I know where the stove is, Doris." She helped herself to a plateful of food, poured a cup of coffee and went back to the table.

"I could get used to eating good food that I don't have to cook. I suppose Doris said grace."

"Oh, she did," Max said, "or none of us would be eating. You can bet on that."

She quickly found a job sorting shingles that had become detached from the roof of the barn. Half of them were useful only for burning.

"These are perfect," she told Max shortly before lunch, "but this pile is good for nothing but starting a fire. I counted seven hundred good ones and about as many useless ones."

"It's good you counted them," Max replied. "Reid will know about how many Philip has to buy. It's a quarter past eleven, and we eat at noon. Do you want to rest now?"

"Not really. I'm tired, but I'm not exhausted. Give me something to put them in, and I'll pick some strawberries if you show me how."

He got a crate of empty cups and walked with her down to the strawberry patch. "Take them by the stem and break the stem with your fingernails. Like this. Run your hands over and through the leaves and especially along the sides where the sunshine strikes them. You ought to get about a quart every two feet of row, sometimes more. We usually hire berry pickers, but there's no help anywhere around today. People are cleaning up after the storm. Put this marker on the row where you stop."

She filled the crate in no time, picked it up and started toward the house with it.

Reid came toward her, shaking his head as if perplexed. "What the hell are you doing carrying that thing? What *is* that?" He got close enough for a good look. "You picked strawberries? Max told me you sorted those shingles. That's back-breaking work." He took the crate of berries from her and kissed her cheek. "Looks as if Philip finally got a modern crate for these berries."

"I picked them, and it was fun," she told him.

"You must be exhausted."

"I wouldn't be able to run in a marathon right now, but I'm not ready to keel over, either."

After lunch, he suggested that they swim, but she knew that if she hadn't been there, he wouldn't have considered it, not with the work facing them. "Maybe after dinner—'scuse me, I mean supper—if you don't mind swimming at night," she told him. "I didn't pick more than twenty feet of that row of berries, and there must be a hundred more rows."

"You want to pick berries?" Reid asked her.

"I want to help, Reid. I didn't come here to pose while everyone else works. At least I'm being useful if I pick strawberries."

"You were useful this morning when you sorted all those shingles. Philip ordered what he needs for a replacement, and tomorrow morning I'll show Jack and Max how to repair the roof of the barn and the stables."

"Have we accomplished much so far?" she asked him.

"Yes, indeed. We'll finish the men's quarters today. A couple of the men have put supports on the biggest trees with sagging limbs and cut away the limbs that couldn't be saved."

"Then I think I'll pick strawberries. When you see Max, please ask him to get me some more empty cups. I have only about a dozen out there." Reid didn't know what to make of her, she realized, but it was time he accepted that she wasn't a fragile doll, but a flesh-and-blood woman who didn't mind rolling up her sleeves and doing what had to be done.

She said as much to Doris later that day when they

sat in the living room, along with the three men, relaxing with drinks before supper.

"Max had to learn that," Doris said. "I work all day here looking as if I'm almost ready to go dancing, but when we're alone in our apartment, I let my hair down and allow him to feast his eyes and body on the woman he married. I'm always there for him when he needs me, and, honey, I know he needs me. It's a great feeling."

"I imagine it is," Kendra said.

"Honey, don't you know Reid needs you? Funny thing is you've had him completely flabbergasted all day. Maybe he thought that since you're a judge, you won't soil your hands. He came in here this morning, sat down and asked me if I thought you'd get angry if he told you to come down off that stable. I told him to give you a sturdy ladder and leave you alone."

Kendra couldn't help laughing at that, because she didn't think that was the advice Reid wanted to hear. "He's very protective," she told Doris.

"Yeah, and bossy, too. I've been working here since Philip was seven. I raised him. Of all the men Philip has helped find a new life—and there've been at least thirty—Reid is the only one who's come back after getting on his feet and leaving. They write and call, but they don't come back. Reid is an exceptional man. Loyal as they come."

Kendra hadn't thought a great deal about Doris, but she realized that if she got to know the woman, she would probably like her. "Thank you for telling me this," she said.

After supper, Philip turned on the lights around the

pool area. "I'd wait at least an hour before going in," he said.

She looked at Reid, whose gaze, she discovered, had been locked on her. "You want to swim for a little while?" he asked her.

"Why not? My muscles could use it."

"Philip said we should give our food an hour to digest, so I'll be back down in about an hour."

Once in her room, she showered, applied lotion to her body and put on her red bathing suit. "This must be the skimpiest bathing suit ever made," she said aloud, wishing she'd brought the more generously cut yellow one instead. She wrapped the floor-length transparent red and tan beach skirt around her hips, but, still dissatisfied with what she regarded as her near-nudity, she put on the white terry-cloth robe that she found in the closet.

She told herself that she'd experienced a sudden case of modesty because she didn't want to shock Philip's father, but in truth, she feared that Reid might be embarrassed, though she didn't know why she felt that way. She put on the flip-flops she found in the closet and went downstairs. Reid met her at the bottom of the stairs.

"I was beginning to think you'd fallen asleep. You look pretty. It's hard to believe you worked in that sun all day." He wrapped his arms around her and bent to kiss her.

"Please," she said, stunning him. "Do you want me to drown?"

"Do I want you to... What's come over you?"

"Kissing you makes me drunk, and if I swim while I'm drunk, I'll drown."

She could almost see the words sinking in, along with the slow exposure of his pearl-white teeth and the grin that gradually changed the contours of his face until at last, he doubled up with laughter.

"I wouldn't take anything for you," he said and brought her into his arms. Though his kiss was brief, through the thin fabric of her swim top, her nipples felt the naked skin of his chest, and desire sent her hot blood racing to her loins.

He looked down at her. "You were right. That wasn't such a good idea."

"For Christmas, I'm giving you a pair of red bathing trunks," she said. "Boy, what a sight that is."

They left the house by a side door off the dining room and found Philip sitting on the deck beside the pool drinking a margarita. "You're getting fresh," Reid whispered to her.

"Just because I said you look cute in that nothing you're wearing? Be glad that's all I said," she whispered.

"You seem as fresh as if it were morning, Kendra," Philip said. "I know you don't drink much, Reid," he said, "but I have lemonade and soft drinks or wine." He pointed to the bar. "You two help yourselves to whatever you want."

"Thanks," she said, smothering a laugh, because he'd used the same word to describe her that Reid had used, though in a different sense. "I think I'll swim first." She dropped the robe on a chair, untied the skirt, threw it across the robe, strolled out to the pool and dived in. What a luxury, she thought. There was much to be said for wealth, and Philip Dickerson had a good share of it. She didn't envy him; he was too nice a person, a man whose hard work and common decency had made him a blessed individual.

She heard a splash and knew that Reid had joined her. They swam together for three laps until she began to tire. "I think I've had enough," she told him. "A few more minutes, and you'll have to carry me into the house."

"Want me to get your robe?" he asked her after they climbed out of the pool.

Taken aback, she stared at him. "Why?"

"Because…because…your… You haven't got anything on."

She looked down at her bikini, saw that it was still there and relaxed. "If I get it myself, you'll be mad, won't you?"

"He can see the same thing I can see, and his attitude toward what he sees will be the same as mine."

"What if we compromise, and I go in the house through the kitchen, on up to my room and change into a shirt and a pair of shorts?"

"Uh…all right. I didn't know you were so stubborn."

"Well," she said. "If I'm stubborn and you're bossy, are we going to make a go of it?"

"We'll probably learn to compromise. At least I hope so."

When she got back downstairs, Reid and Philip were laughing about something and Arnold, Philip's father, had joined them. "I think I'll have a glass of white wine," she said. Arnold got up immediately, poured a glass of wine and brought it to her.

"You and I haven't had a chance to talk, Kendra," he said, "but I want you to know that you had my admiration when you first visited us, but today you won my deep affection and gratitude. I wish my son had met you first."

"Thank you," she said. "That's the nicest compliment you could have paid me." They talked for an hour, about her work as a judge and his before he retired as an automotive engineer.

"We didn't make the money those guys make nowadays, but we designed far better cars. Philip wanted no part of it. He had a desire to make things grow, so he's a professor of agricultural science, and he loves what he does. I think that's how he and Reid became so close. They're both dedicated to doing their very best. Reid designed the men's quarters as if he had a commission from the White House and acted as the engineer for the project. You see how it withstood that storm. Didn't lose a thing but some roofing. Those two men love their work, and they're both good at it."

"I'm enjoying talking with you, Arnold, but I'm sleepy. Getting up at four-thirty is a new experience for me. What time do we rise tomorrow?"

"Early," Reid said. "We'll leave around three, but I'd like to get some work done on the stable roofs before we go." He looked at Kendra. "Will that suit you?"

"Yes, of course." She told them good-night, picked up the robe and skirt and went to her room. When she heard Reid open his door, she peeped out of hers.

He walked over to her. "Thanks for all you did today. We'll talk about this another time. Right now I'm bushed. I haven't done this kind of work since I left here, and I didn't have to work that hard when I was here. Open up for me a little bit." He slipped his tongue into her mouth, and immediately her tiredness vanished, but she didn't advertise it.

"I'll make up for it," he said, letting her know that he understood her emotions.

She enjoyed a sound and peaceful sleep, rose early and went out to pick strawberries. To her chagrin, the part of the row that she had finished the previous day now glistened with red berries. "Well," she said, refusing to start the row over, "I'm not retracing my steps."

After lunch, as they prepared to leave, Reid had a sense of accomplishment, but he knew that Philip still needed his help. "I'll try to get back next weekend, Philip, but I'm not sure I can bring Kendra. She bought a new house, and a couple of hours before we left to come here, I discovered that it has serious flaws. I haven't told her yet, but she may have to indict the builder. And that's a sticky wicket, because he's the same builder who cost me my reputation."

"If you need me, just call. I have to ask you something personal, but first I want to remind you that you are my brother, that I love you as if we had the same parents. Whatever you tell me will be gospel to me. I've observed that Kendra is attached to you, but a man can want a woman and not be serious about her. Are you serious about Kendra?"

Reid was accustomed to Philip's straight-shooting,

so he was hardly surprised. "I'm in love with her. If you're interested, I'm sorry, because I'm in deep."

"Your answer doesn't surprise me. She's beautiful and a credit to herself and to any man. Please don't mention this to her, because I wouldn't want her to be self-conscious around me. There's nothing lost, because I haven't spent time thinking about it, so not to worry."

Reid threw up his hand for a high five. "It won't bother you if I bring her back with me?"

"Not for a second."

Chapter 7

"I didn't expect you to break your back working like a laborer," Reid told Kendra during their drive back to Queenstown. "I brought you with me so I'd know you were safe, that you wouldn't be fooling around in that basement."

"I was glad I could help."

"And I appreciate it. I learned a lot about you these past two days. Believe me, I hope I never see you pulling shingles off the top of another barn again, or that one, either. Woman, you almost gave me a heart attack."

"I thought it was my bathing suit that rang your bell."

He wished she hadn't brought that up. "Why can't you wear a one-piece bathing suit? That thing is skimpier than your underwear."

He glanced at her to see her reaction, but she seemed

unconcerned, a signal that she didn't plan to change her style. "One-piece bathing suits for women my age are almost as hard to find as those modest swim trunks that men wore back in the 1950s," she replied. "Trust me, your bathing trunks are definitely an advertisement for your equipment, so why can't I show off *my* assets? Did I make a stink about Doris seeing you like that?"

He pressed his lips together, because he didn't want to laugh. "Doris wasn't out there, and you didn't even notice. You're making it up."

"Who says I didn't notice? You bet I did. I could hardly take my gaze off… I could hardly stop looking."

"You didn't act like it."

"I was too tired. Are we having an argument?"

"If so, I hope it's an example of the amount of heat we can expect in all of our disagreements. By the way," he said, choosing his words carefully so as not to alarm her, "you've got a real problem with your house. I think you should charge Brown and Worley with criminal negligence. It will cost you between thirty and fifty thousand to correct the defects in your house."

She jerked forward. "You're not serious."

He slowed down for the exit onto Route 17. "Oh, yes, I am. If I were you, I'd get a registered, certified examiner to check the house from roof to basement and provide a notarized report. If you like, I'll ask my boss which one he uses. It will stand up in court."

"My goodness! You *are* serious! I'll check with the bank and see what I can do about this."

"The bank doesn't care, baby. It gets its money no

matter what. But Brown and Worley do care, because they're already in trouble with the community."

She leaned back and clapped her hands. "True. What am I thinking? Get the name and phone number of that examiner for me, please."

He supposed that humming a gay tone meant he'd pleased her.

"Reid!" She said his name as if she had just discovered a treasure, and maybe she had.

"What is it?"

"It's just occurred to me that whatever that examiner documents will support your case, as well."

"You're right." He parked in front of her house. "It's only seven o'clock. Let's go to a decent restaurant, but first I have to go home and change."

"Good idea. I was going to eat a peanut butter and jelly sandwich and call it a day. I'm not up to cooking."

He went inside to look around for problems that might have cropped up during her absence. He did not rejoice in her discomfort; far from it. But what he saw gave him a peculiar kind of pleasure, for it validated his claim that the partial collapse of Worley Towers in Baltimore was the fault of the builders and not of Reid Maguire, the architect.

"You've got a flood in your guest bathroom," he told her, "but since it's stopped raining, I don't think it will get worse. It would be a good thing to leave it so that the examiner can document it. Do you want him here tomorrow?"

"If possible, yes. Reid, what would I do without you?"

He guarded his facial expression, because he didn't

want her to know what he felt right then. "I'm trying to make myself indispensable, so please don't raise that question. I'll be back shortly."

Kendra did not intend to allow Brown and Worley to cheat her and get away with it. Two days after returning from Dickerson Estates, she looked at Helligman's notarized report on the condition of her brand-new house and decided that it represented her opportunity to get out of the controversial property. A lawyer would counsel repair and damages, and she didn't want that.

Deciding to be her own lawyer, she telephoned the builders' office and spoke with Aaron Brown. "Mr. Brown, I'm Judge Kendra Rutherford, presiding judge at Queenstown Court. This is about the condition of the house I purchased from you at Albemarle Gates." She told him about the examiner's report. "We can go to court, but you'll lose in a jury trial, and you know it."

"What are you asking for?" Brown wanted to know.

Best to be bold, she knew, so she said, "Buy back the house. If you don't, I'm going to court and sue you for the price of the house plus what it cost me to move in and out of it and the pain and suffering this mess caused me. Think of the fun the local media will have at your expense. In fact, I'd prefer that." Taking advantage of her status, she added, "I want your answer by noon Friday. You may reach me at my chambers in the courthouse."

"I'll…uh…have to speak with my partner."

"What happened?" Reid asked her when she phoned him a few minutes later. She repeated her conversation with Brown. "They wouldn't dare go to court here in Queenstown."

"Anyway, Reid, I'd rather your case was the first opportunity the people in this town have to take a crack at Brown and Worley. There's a house around the corner from you that I'd like to have if I get what I want from Brown and Worley. Will you check it out for me?"

"Of course. You don't have to ask. By the way, next time I see you I'll have my own car. I'm picking it up this afternoon."

And what you bought will tell me a lot about you, she said to herself. To him, she said, "What kind is it?" She'd never cared for a man whose pride was not in himself but in his automobile and snakeskin or alligator shoes and who, consequently, wore the most costly handmade shoes and drove the flashiest and most expensive car for which he could obtain credit.

"It's a Buick Century."

Hmmm. Modest. "What kind did you drive before?"

"You mean kinds. The day I lost that court case, my three-car garage held a Town Car, a Caddy and a Jaguar. It's hard for me to believe that I was ever that frivolous."

She relaxed and let out a long breath. "I definitely prefer the Buick, Reid."

His laughter reached her through the wire, warming her heart. "I like this one better, too, and I'm sure glad you do."

She received Aaron Brown's phone call minutes before court convened Friday morning. "I think we can settle this out of court, Judge Rutherford. Can you meet me at the bank this afternoon at two-thirty?"

She could and did. Three weeks and two days later, she moved into her new home at 103A Pepper Pot Lane, around the corner from the apartment building in which Reid lived.

Tired and dusty from cleaning and dragging furniture around, she sat down for a brief respite and phoned her sister, Claudine, to tell her that she had moved and why. She hadn't told Claudine about the problems with her house, because her sister wouldn't have bought a house without having had it inspected several times by different experts. Claudine wasn't poor, but she treated what she had with respect.

"I wish you'd come see me," Kendra said. "I can look out of my bedroom window at the Sound. Last night, we had a clear, full moon and the sight of that over the water was spectacular."

"My show went so well that I was asked for copies of some of my sculptures. That wouldn't be ethical, so I'm making some similar models. I should finish them in four or five weeks. Maybe I can visit you then."

"I'll probably be in Cape May a month from now, so that—"

Claudine interrupted her. "Wonderful, I've always wanted to see Cape May."

"That won't work, Claudine. You don't think I'd go up there by myself, do you?"

"Well, *excuse* me. Now I know I'm going to find time to visit Queenstown."

"Really? If I thought man-hunting was on your list of things to do… Say, next time I go down to the eastern shore of Maryland, maybe you can go, too. There's a genuine hunk down there, hardworking, accomplished and unattached."

"Does he like women?"

"I didn't ask him, but from my observations I'd say he definitely does."

She hung up and thought about it. Claudine might be just Philip's type. He liked black women, and Claudine's gentle ways had always been more attractive to men than her own disposition.

"Now, who could be banging on my back door?" She raced down the stairs, through the hallway and into the kitchen and… "Reid!" She opened the door. "How'd you get around here?"

He kissed her lips and handed her a pot that contained a four-foot ficus plant. "Where do you want me to put it? I decided I'd better not show up at your front door with this, because I've already seen some of your neighbors looking out their windows at this house. So I came through the alley, but I don't suppose I should do that too often, because I met two people as I walked through it. Give me Baltimore. Nobody cares what you do."

"No," she told him, "and that, too, can be a problem."

He ran his finger down her nose, and she liked it when he took little liberties with her, playing with her nose or her ears, stroking her back. "You look cute with that dirt on your face," he said. "While I'm here, let me help you. Anything to be moved?"

They had waffles with syrup and sausages along with coffee and strawberries for dinner, as neither had the energy to cook anything more elaborate, and by the time eleven o'clock arrived and they had all the furniture in place, she was ready to fall from fatigue. She turned out the lights in the front part of the house and walked with him to the front door.

With her sandwiched between his body and the wall, he imprisoned her. "Kiss me. Put your arms around me and let me know that I'm your man."

She parted her lips and took him in, and she could feel the exhaustion flowing out of her body as he claimed her. She sucked his tongue deeper into her mouth and felt the solid print of his penis as it jumped against her belly. He stepped back then. "I've got a lot to make up for, and I don't want to start on it this time of night when you're ready to drop. Just remember that when I start collecting, you'd better be prepared." He kissed her eyes and the side of her mouth. "Tell me you love me. I need to hear it, baby."

"I love you," she whispered, "and I need to hear it, too."

"I love you, woman," he said and stared down into her face. "You're my life." He turned and left before she could respond, and maybe that was a good thing. She didn't switch on the hall light until she was sure he'd turned the corner.

"I wish I'd seen my current house before I saw the other one in Albemarle Gates," she told Carl Running Moon Howard on her first day at work after moving. "If I had, I'd have a lot more friends."

"They'll come now, ma'am. People here are neighborly."

That afternoon around five o'clock while she stored

items in her pantry—a convenience that she hadn't had at Albemarle Heights—her doorbell rang. She put the chain on the door, cracked it open sufficiently to see who rang, and looked into the faces of three women. Strangers.

"We just thought we'd welcome you to our neighborhood, Judge Rutherford," one said.

Kendra blinked rapidly, as if to confirm with her eyes what her ears heard. After recovering her aplomb, she opened the door. "This is a wonderful surprise. I've been on the town's black list, and I haven't had any visitors."

"We know, Your Honor," one woman said, presenting Kendra with an apple pie, "and we're glad you moved. We appreciate the support."

"I'm still settling in," she told them, "and the place isn't quite presentable, but I hope you don't mind. Come on in. I make great coffee."

They introduced themselves, and to her surprise they talked without further reference to Albemarle Gates. She didn't think she had ever discussed with a group of women topics that she considered frivolous, such as where to shop, the best hairdressers, weight gain and the kind of cosmetics to wear. And she discovered that she not only enjoyed the camaraderie, but learned some important things.

"I'm going to join your civics class in the fall," the woman called Reba said. "I don't know a friggin' thing about my rights as a woman. Judge Judy told a man that half of what he earns belongs to his wife. The man didn't believe it, and his wife didn't know it. My husband wouldn't believe it, either."

"Neither would mine," Bell, a younger woman, said, "but he thinks what I earn is community property. Which is why he doesn't know how much I make."

Kendra didn't mention the law to them, for she didn't wear that role unless she was in court. She merely allowed herself to enjoy the fun.

The following Thursday evening when the curtain rose on the first performance of their play, she received a standing ovation when she walked out on the stage, and her three new friends sat front-row center. She glanced at Reid, who stood in the wings awaiting his cue to join her onstage, and he, too, applauded her.

After the applause died down, Reid sauntered out, picked up a newspaper from a magazine rack, sat down on the sofa and opened it.

"Tonya walked out of the room right while I was talking to her and slammed the door so hard that that copy of Matisse's blue nude fell off the wall," she said, speaking as Lissa to her husband, Don. "I won't stand for such behavior from my own daughter."

He opened the paper to the sports section. "So you won't stand for it. What did you do about it?"

She walked over to the man, whose face was hidden behind the newspaper, and stuck her hands on her hips. "What *could* I do? She's a princess spoiled by you." She pointed a finger at him as he turned the page. "She left the house and hasn't come back. I want you to do something."

"If you're smart, woman, you'll let me read. I worked my ass off all day. I'm tired, and I'm entitled to a little relaxation." Suddenly, he rested the paper on his right knee, and she jumped back. "What did *you* do today?"

Angry now and puffing to show it, she poked out her chin. "I worked mine off, too, but I can't come home, sit on my behind and read the newspaper. Right now I have to cook your freakin' supper. So don't get me started."

"You've already started," he said, picking up the paper, "and if I can't read in peace, I can go to the bar and read. If you force me to do that, I'll be back when I get back."

She tossed her head and rolled her eyes. "Like I care. While you're out there, see if you can find your daughter. I wash my hands."

He threw the paper on the coffee table, knocking over the bud vase that contained one half-dead yellow rose. "My daughter?" he exclaimed. "You're the one who... Oh, what the hell! What are we fighting about? I'll give Tonya a good talking-to when she gets home."

"Don." She lowered her voice. "Suppose she doesn't come home. She's been gone every bit of two hours."

"Oh, for Pete's sake. Don't be so melodramatic, Lissa. I can take just so much of it."

"That last part was not in the script," she hissed at him under her breath.

"No, but you're enjoying browbeating me," he hissed right back.

"Suppose our Tonya becomes a missing child," she said, her voice syrupy sweet for the benefit of the audience.

He took out his cell phone and dialed a number. "Where are you?"

"I'm with my friend Denise in the ice cream parlor," Tonya said.

"If your behind isn't in this house in fifteen minutes,

it'll be a year before you get another penny in allowance. I am not buying you another thing for six months. School's out at three-thirty, and you're grounded after four-fifteen. When you learn how to treat your mother, I'll treat you differently, and not before. Two of your fifteen minutes are up, and I'm not joking." He closed his cell phone to the audience's thunderous applause.

Lissa stared at him, her mouth agape. "What's come over you?" she managed to say.

"I'm damned tired of... I didn't get married in order to live as a celibate. Whenever I do something to annoy you, you either have a migraine at bedtime or you turn over and say no, and you're never annoyed at me unless Tonya acts out or I pamper her. Well, the pampering is making her foolish, and from now on, if she acts out with you, I'll punish her. I'm through giving up the good stuff."

She looked at him from beneath lowered lashes, patted the back of her hair and said, "Oh yeah? Well, honey, you just say what's what."

The curtain fell on the first act, and they walked backstage together. "You overdid that flirtation at the end there," he said. "Remember I've been celibate for weeks now."

"Right, and you just told the whole town. That part about your being celibate is not in the script. Watch out! I can come up with some cute ones, too."

"You have to take a curtain call," Mike Reinar told them. "Go ahead. They're yelling for you."

They took a bow separately and then together. Mike greeted them with his hands spread out, shaking his head. Perplexed. "I don't understand it. You guys perform perfectly as we rehearse, then you start making it up and it brings down the house. Well, go for it."

"I never know when it's going to happen," Reid said to Mike. "She comes on so strong sometimes that I feel I have to defend myself. The problem with the script is that the writer has never met Kendra Rutherford. Man, she's standing there wagging her finger in my face, and—"

Mike released a soft whistle. "Give him a break, Kendra. You got the man frustrated."

"Hang it up, you two," she said, using slang she'd heard that morning. "It's time for the second act."

"You don't know how close I came to shaking you during that first act," he said when they met at a restaurant north of Queenstown later on. "You were like a ball of fire on that stage. All I could think of was getting you in bed and wearing myself out with you. Try to keep it between the lines, baby."

"I was acting, and you weren't, Reid Maguire. You were Donald I-forget-his-last-name."

"Woodson. Well, you sure as hell were Kendra Rutherford when you stuck your hand on your hips and swung your butt for emphasis."

She couldn't help laughing at him. "I think I would have enjoyed acting as a career," she said.

"You would have been a first-class actor. You make me forget that you're acting."

"What a nice compliment! I hope I have the same effect on the audience."

"From that ovation you received when you walked out onstage, I'd say you do."

"Oh, I think that was because I left Albemarle Gates. Did I forget to tell you that I had visitors for the first time the day I moved in?"

He put his fork aside and gazed at her. "Yes, you forgot to tell me. What happened?" She told him about her visitors and the pleasant hour that she had spent with them.

"That's wonderful, sweetheart. Good news, indeed." A grin formed around his lips. "Hereafter, I'll have to call before I go to your house." The smile faded. "I'm glad you're going to have friends. I've always enjoyed friends, but I discovered that, as Billie Holiday sang, '...when the spending ends, they don't come back no more.'"

"I'm your friend," she said, wanting to erase the sadness in his eyes.

"I know that, and it means more to me than anything."

Reid wondered if Kendra knew how much he'd just told her. "I think we ought to celebrate," he said. "Tomorrow evening after the play, let's have dinner at a first-class restaurant and then dance until the music stops." He reached across the table and caressed her hand. "What do you say? You're starving me to death for good loving, so you can at least keep me happy otherwise."

"A celebration would be wonderful. As for the rest of that verbalized daydreaming, I'm not going there," she told him.

"What time shall we get together?"

"Seven. I'll go to you, since no gossipers will be watching your place."

"I certainly hope not. I'll expect you at seven."

"My nose itches," she said, and began to laugh almost uncontrollably. "My granddaddy always said that means good news."

He wondered if she was about to become hysterical, but that didn't suit her personality, so he asked her, "Is your grandfather living?"

As he guessed, she sobered at once. "He died when I was little, and I still miss him."

"Do you think he would have approved of me?"

To his amazement, she didn't hesitate. "He would have loved you. My granddaddy thought highly of your type of man, and don't ask me what type that is. Let's go. I'm still pooped from all that work you and I did tonight."

He gazed at her, expecting a reaction, and when there was none he quipped, "Please don't say that around anyone else. Much as I'd enjoy a strong manly reputation, I don't think that suits a judge."

The implication of what she'd said seemed gradually to dawn on her. "Right," she said, with what had to be a greatly restrained facial expression. "Let's go." But since she refused to laugh, he figured he'd better not do it, either. As they strolled through the restaurant's parking lot to his car, he took her hand, enjoying the precious anonymity. At the moment, life was good.

He had tried to maintain a low profile among his co-workers, for he didn't want any of them to think that he expected or deserved special favors. Jack Marks gave him permission to design the building for Marcus Hickson, but he knew that Marks and Connerly would not have taken the job.

"I know you're not an engineer, Reid," Jack said to him after he arrived at work the following morning, "but I'd like you to have a look at our terminal in Caution Point. I understand that it's attracting photographers, so I'd like to know that it's going precisely according to your plans."

"I thought Kennedy was the engineer for the project. Won't he get his back up if I'm snooping around?"

"Point taken. What do you suggest?"

"We could have a weekly or bi-weekly conference on it, give him a chance to say whether he sees any problems. If so, I could check it out. I'll go there if you think it's necessary, but I'm fairly certain it would cause hard feelings, Jack." Reid shrugged. "But it's up to you."

"I'll have an informal meeting with the three of us tomorrow."

His next assignment would tax his abilities. It occurred to him that Jack intended to use him for the most difficult jobs, and he didn't mind the experience, but he was no longer dejected, no longer in a pit trying to see daylight, and he was not going to permit Jack or anyone else to take advantage of him. Little did he know that opportunity would knock soon, bringing with it both discord and dilemma.

"Would you come to my office?" Jack said to him over the intercom after lunch that day. He wondered that the man didn't greet him, and that he spoke like a boss, just short of ordering him to come to his office.

"Yes," he replied with equal detachment and wondering if his cordial relationship with Jack Marks had come to an end.

He walked into the office where Marks and Connerly sat at the conference table. Jack did not ask him to sit down. With his guard up, Reid said, "You want to see me, Jack?"

Jack leaned back, his demeanor that of a boss certain of his status and power.

"You've been soliciting work for yourself again, and that is not permissible."

"I've done no such thing," Reid answered, "and I want you to withdraw that accusation. If anyone says that I've solicited an architectural design job since Reid Maguire and Associates folded over seven years ago, that person is lying."

Jack leaned forward. "You're telling me that—"

Reid narrowed his eyes, not bothering to hide his annoyance. "Who told you that I solicited work? I want to see that liar."

"Now, Reid, maybe I shouldn't have said it the way I did, but it comes from someone I've trusted for years."

"You've misplaced your trust. You'll have my resignation in twenty minutes." He turned to leave. Talk about a downer!

"Wait a minute. Not so fast. I don't want your resignation."

"And I won't work for a man who doesn't respect me."

"You're the best architect I've got. I don't—"

Reid interrupted Jack for the second time and didn't care if he did. "I know I'm the best architect you have, and I also know that you take advantage of me, but I'd do the same if I were in your place, so I don't mind. For now. When I get tired of it, I'll leave."

"Mr. Marks," a voice said over the intercom, "a Mr. English is here to see you. He says it's urgent."

"You deal with your guest," Reid said to Jack. "I'll be in my office."

"All right, but I don't want you to resign. I'll make you a junior partner."

"Yeah," Reid said, "but you've exploited me for the last time. I'd like to know who the hell told you that lie."

Twenty minutes later, his phone rang. "Maguire speaking."

"Reid, this is Jack. Would you mind coming to my office? I apologize for that scene earlier. I was totally misled."

Reid took his time. He didn't want to be buttered up, and he was in no mood to be gracious. He walked into Jack's office and saw, with Jack, a man he hadn't seen before.

"Reid Maguire, this is Reginald English, and he tells me he's come a long way to see you."

Reid walked over to shake hands with the man, skipped the preliminaries and asked, "Why do you want to see me?"

Reginald English stood, tall, gray-haired, chalk-white and blue-eyed. He extended his hand. "I've been trying to find you for a good eighteen months. I was about to give up when I mentioned it to Marcus

Hickson, who's rebuilding my son's grand piano, and he told me where to find you. I want to build an office building and a vacation house on the Outer Banks. I want them stormproof, and that means money. You can do it."

Reid sat down. If he did that job, he could call his shots. "You didn't tell anyone that I solicited this job, did you?"

"Me? Hell, no. I've never spoken to you before. Is there a problem?"

He decided to let it all hang out. Telling the truth never hurt. "Do you know why my architectural firm folded?"

English crossed his knees and leaned back. "Of course I know. When I enter into a business deal, I know all there is to know about the other party. You're back on your feet now, and I assume you're going to contest that judgment. I can recommend a crackerjack lawyer."

"Thanks. I'll get to that," Reid said, careful not to show his hand.

"Well? My only reason for coming to Queenstown is to get your signature on a contract, Mr. Maguire. I've had a man examine over half of the buildings you designed, and I'm satisfied that you'll bring me something solid and exquisite."

"Thanks for the compliment. How may I reach you? You're asking for a decision that I can't make at this time." Moreover, he wanted to talk with Jack Marks, now that Jack had evidence of his innocence in respect to that accusation. Once you're down, people find it easy to step on you. He was grateful to Marks for giving

him a job as an architect in spite of his blemished reputation, but not so grateful as to accept an unwarranted
rebuke. He wanted an apology or he was out of there.

Reginald English stood, and in Jack Marks's presence, he said to Reid, "You don't have to work for
anybody but yourself. All right, so you got the short end
of the stick and you didn't deserve it, but what about
the thirty-some other buildings that bear your name?
Not to speak of private houses. They're a testament to
your competence. I waited eighteen months, and I'm
willing to wait another twelve." He handed Reid his
card. "I'll be expecting to hear from you." He turned to
Jack. "Thanks for your help, Mr. Marks. Good day,
gentlemen."

Reid watched the man leave the office, then turned
to Jack. "It's your call, Jack."

"Look. It was unfair of me to accuse you without first
hearing you out, and I'm sorry about it. I saw myself
losing you, just when I'm ready to accept a job that,
frankly, I don't think any of my other architects can do.
And it's been so long since I designed a building more
than fifteen stories high that I'm probably not up to it,
either. But you can do it."

"That's a tempting offer, Jack, and he'll pay
whatever I ask. I won't mislead you. I'm going to give
it serious consideration. I appreciate your confidence in
hiring me, all things considered, but I have to be honest
with you." He looked Jack in the eye, saw that the man
regarded him with heightened esteem and asked him—
not because he was seeking advice, but because he

wanted Jack Marks to show his integrity or lack of it. "If you were in my place, would you take that job?"

"You don't pull punches, do you? I expect I would, if for no other reason than it would allow me to form my own company again. That's what you're after, isn't it? And of course, it's bound to be a lot of money."

"I know. The name *English* is synonymous with wealth and has been for generations."

Jack made a pyramid with his hands and propped his elbows on his desk. "It hurts me not to be able to take on the job of designing the tallest building in Chowan County. But if you leave, I'll have to pass it up."

"This town won't support two architectural firms, Jack, so I have to think this thing through."

"Well, let me know your decision as soon as you can. I won't hold you to your contract. That would be un-conscionable."

"I didn't think you would. Besides, it has a release clause that I could probably meet. See you tomorrow." He couldn't wait for four-thirty; he had to get out in the fresh, clean air, spread his arms and pay homage to life. He didn't remember ever having felt so free, so strong, so capable of changing the world. For two cents, he'd reach up and fly. He got into his car, his very own car, and headed home, wrapping his deep baritone around the words of his favorite song "Shenandoah." Shock re-verberated through his system; he hadn't heard himself sing in years. What a day!

Already, as he drove, he sensed that mental stress—something he hadn't felt since he went to Dickerson Estates—had begun to creep up on him as his mind dangled his options by the weight of their positive aspects. A building's design and its plans represented a hefty percentage of the cost of any building, and Reginald English would erect a building that was a credit to his name. As for the summer house, that would surely be a mansion. But could he risk leaving a sure position with a promise of a junior partnership—Marks, Connerly and Maguire, Architects—for a job that, although it would carry fame and prestige, was unlikely to last more than two and a half years, if that long. He didn't need that dilemma.

At home, he parked in the underground garage of his apartment building, rode the elevator up to the first floor, walked slowly into his apartment and closed the door behind him. Everything looked the same, but he didn't feel the same. As if he were tied to a bag of helium, he could hardly prevent himself from floating up to the ceiling. If only his father were alive to rejoice with him. He was, at that moment, experiencing his psychological ascent from that deep, dark pit, and he needed to shout it to someone who would appreciate how far down he'd been. He telephoned Philip.

"I just had to share this, man," he said to Philip after they'd greeted each other. "You're the only person who knows how far down I was, so I want you to be the first to hear this." He told Philip about Reginald English's offer and Jack's counteroffer of a junior partnership less than an hour after having accused him, in effect, of lacking integrity. "I've never been easily overwhelmed, but, man, this is a plateful."

"Surely you're not wondering what to do?"

"In fact, I am. Mad as I was at Jack, I still have some allegiance to him because he gave me a chance when others didn't."

"How many places did you apply to before you got a contract with Marks and Connerly?"

"Five. Four firms turned me down, and I received an offer from a fifth one after I signed on with Marks and Connerly."

"As far as I'm concerned, Marks hired you because he knew you'd be gunning to prove yourself, and he'd get a bargain. He knew your history as an architect. Look, it's up to you, of course, but I'd go for it. What does Kendra say?"

He scratched his head. Why hadn't he called her before he phoned Philip? Then he remembered: Kendra didn't get home until around five o'clock. "She's still in court, so I haven't told her, but I pretty much know what she'll say. I asked Jack what he'd do, mostly because I wanted to test his integrity, and would you believe he said he'd take English up on that offer?"

"If he's an honest man, he couldn't have said otherwise. I can see that a partnership at this stage of your life, the past considered, sounds tempting, but don't forget that your status as an architect has been higher than that. When do you think you can get back down? I bought a summer place right on the bay. If the weather's good, we can fish and swim for a whole weekend."

At the moment, a weekend on the Chesapeake Bay held about as much interest as the art of catching butterflies. He had to decide what to do with his life. "As soon as I get my head straightened out, man, I'll let you know. Thanks. Somehow, the estate is the place that means home to me, so I'll get down there whenever I can."

"Make it as often as you can, brother. Your room will always be empty."

Reid went outside and sat in his garden, which had been his reason for taking the terrace apartment. He kicked off his shoes, pulled off his socks, stepped on the lawn and let the blades of grass tickle his toes. He had a sense of being completely alive. The Dutch irises, planted by some previous occupant of his apartment, bowed in reverence to the brisk wind, and he turned to face the breeze and receive its exhilarating magic. Ah, what a day!

"I think I'll go down to the Sound," he said to himself, but when he looked at his watch, he saw that in a few minutes Kendra would be home. He put on his shoes, locked the door of his apartment, got into his car and headed for the market. He wanted to do something special for her, something different. He walked through the supermarket, but could find nothing that interested him, so he went to the fishmonger and bought four large lobster tails, then went back to the supermarket and got what he needed to complement the lobster. Finally, "I'll take that nice red one," he said to the woman who sold roses beside the newsstand.

"This is Reid," he said when Kendra answered the phone. "Did you eat yet? No? That's good. May I come over in about forty minutes for a while?" He listened more to her voice than to her words of welcome. At times, the sweetness of her voice captivated him. He hoped that he would never get used to it. He showered and dressed, steamed the lobster tails and put them in the picnic basket along with the remainder of the meal, got the rose and two bottles of white wine and walked through the alley to her house.

"I was watching for you at the front door," she said, and took the rose from him and kissed his cheek. "Oh, Reid, sometimes, you touch me right where I'm most vulnerable. Thank you." She saw the picnic basket. "What's that?"

"Allow me the pleasure, ma'am, of serving your dinner."

He shifted his gaze, for he was sure that her eyes glistened with unshed tears, and if one teardrop left her eyes, he knew that—considering how he was feeling—that lobster would be ice-cold by the time they ate it.

Chapter 8

This man had more ways of locking himself into her heart. She was in trouble, big trouble, and she knew it. She had looked at him standing there with a rose in one hand and a picnic basket in the other one and told herself that she had better not cry, that crying because a man showed that he cared was juvenile behavior. But she couldn't help expressing her feelings, so she kissed his cheek, took his hand and pulled him into her house.

She kissed the rose and asked him, "Are we having a picnic?"

"No, madam, I have prepared your supper, and if you will lead the way to the dining room, I will set the table and feed you."

A funny, drunken sensation settled in her stomach, and she leaned against the wall in the hallway that led to the kitchen and looked straight into his eyes. "I'm a strong woman, Reid, and I've proved it to myself many times, but when I got a broken heart wasn't one of those times. You shower me with affection and caring, but if it's…if it's because there's nobody else available, I want to know right now."

He put the basket on the floor and stared at her. "I came to you because I'm bursting with happiness, because my ship came in today, and I want to celebrate it with you. Why do you think I would hurt you? Do you doubt me?"

She shook her head. "I'm feeling so much in here, Reid." She pointed to her heart. "It just scared me all of a sudden."

"Let me hold you." His lips brushed her forehead, but she could tell from the tension in his body that he was using an inordinate amount of self-restraint. "You will hurt me long before I hurt you."

Regretting her moment of weakness, she said to him, "Come on in here. When you called, I had been wondering what to cook for my supper." She put the rose in a bud vase and watched, marveling, as he set the table with utensils from the picnic basket, and placed the warm lobster, a bowl of butter sauce, steamed tiny waxy potatoes rolled in butter and minced parsley, asparagus tips and a green salad. He poured two glasses of Château de Rodet, a rich white burgundy, bowed and held a chair for her.

"Madame, dinner is served." She sat down and dabbed at her eyes with a napkin. "What's wrong, Kendra? If you cry, I won't be able to eat."

"I'm not crying. My eyes do this sometimes. This is

wonderful, and I love lobster. I wish something good would happen for you."

"Something good has happened." He told her about his day and added, "Sweetheart, I feel as if I could fly with my own wings. If you knew…

"Ten months ago when I left Dickerson Estates, I saw a rough road ahead. I'd been so far down. When I stopped Philip on the street in Baltimore, I was ready to commit suicide. I hadn't eaten in almost three days, but I wouldn't stoop to stealing. I asked him for a dollar, and he asked if I wanted a chance to rebuild my life. I had nothing to lose, so I went with him. And now this.

"Loyalty is deeply ingrained in me, Kendra. My father poured it into my head. Jack needs me, but I need to work at my full potential. If I take a junior partnership, I'll be fixed for a long time, because Marks and Connerly are the top firm in this entire region. But I'll be selling myself short."

"I can't believe you'd even consider turning Reginald English down. Tell Jack you'll design that building for him as a consultant, if he likes, and reestablish your own firm. If I were in your shoes, I wouldn't sweat over that."

"You're serious, aren't you? Even knowing that after a minimum of four years I could be without work, you think I should do it?"

"If Jack Marks has a dozen of the best architects around, and he thinks none of them is as capable as you, why would you worry? You can do anything you set out to do. Anything. Only such a man as you would be able to pull himself up—even with help—and come out of pure hell unscathed."

* * *

He lifted his glass of wine with fingers that he could barely control. Finally, he had to steady the glass with his left hand. "I brought us some dessert," he said, and couldn't let himself lock gazes with her, an indication that his composure had slipped, "but if you continue to say these things to me, I...doubt we'll eat it tonight."

"Please, Reid," she said, and he knew that his eyes mirrored the desire that threatened to strangle him. "I can't afford to slide into an affair with you."

"We're having an affair whether you can afford it or not," he heard himself say in a voice that seemed to him unnatural, more like a growl. "I want you this minute so badly that I think I'll explode. You can't know what it does to me when you—a woman of your accomplishments—let me know that you believe so strongly in me. No other woman ever made me feel as if there's nothing I can't do. Kendra. I need to give myself to you."

"Honey, we're headed for heartbreak. Both of us."

He stood and walked around the table to her chair. "Why? We're both unattached. Why can't we love each other? I'm tired of sneaking around to spend time with you. A judge is human, and a female judge needs male company as much as any other woman."

"Yes, but suppose your case comes before me? I could be fired as a judge and disbarred as a lawyer. I want to do all I can to ensure that you get a fair trial."

"I hear you, but you're overstating it. I'll get a fair trial, because I've done my homework." He pulled her chair back from the table and lifted her into his arms.

"You gave me heaven, and now you tell me I can't have it? Until that night in your arms, buried inside your body, I didn't know who I was."

Tremors raced through him when he recalled the minute he had exploded inside her. "For the first time in my life, I held back nothing, and I didn't want to, because you gave yourself to me without reservation. I'll never forget it, and I want it. I need it. I need *you*." He could feel her relax as the tips of her nipples hardened against his chest.

"You said we'd go to Cape May. Even if we went public, so to speak, you shouldn't be seen leaving my house late at night."

"I'll never knowingly expose you to censure or ridicule. You mean too much to me. And I'll do what I can to avoid it."

"You didn't eat all of your potatoes," she whispered, grabbing at anything that would reduce the tension between them.

"Potatoes are not what I want in my mouth right now." He let his eyes mirror his feelings, wrapped his right arm around her shoulder and let his left fingers stroke and pinch her erect left nipple. She grabbed his wrist, and though he knew what she wanted, he didn't accommodate her, but waited until, frustrated, she guided his hand into her scooped-neck blouse. He freed her breast, lifted her to fit him, sucked her nipple into his mouth and suckled her until she undulated against him.

"Reid. Honey. Get into me." She locked her legs around his hips and pressed herself to his erection.

"Not here, sweetheart. I need more than this."

"I can walk," she said when he picked her up, but he ignored her and carried her up the stairs to her bedroom. He hardly glimpsed the lavender taffeta in a sea of white, including carpet and window treatments, as he unzipped her dress and let it slide to the floor. When she stepped out of it, he rose to full readiness, threw aside the covers and put her on the bed. "You said you love me, Kendra, and I'm holding you to it, because I need you to love me." He leaned over and pressed a kiss to her lips. "You're everything to me."

Her arms opened, reached out to him and happiness suffused him. In a flash, he shed his clothing and lowered his body into her waiting arms. How had he been so fortunate as to find a woman like her? Her fingers stroked his back, his buttocks, every place that she could reach, and then she let him know that she wanted him to lie on his back. With her tongue, she fired his libido as she teased and sucked first one aureole and then the other. Warm, feminine fingers danced on his belly, promising him heaven if she would only move lower. She skimmed his inner thighs, barely touching him, until his body rose to meet her hand, but she ignored his rising frenzy and explored his testicles.

He heard his moans as she toyed with him. Finally, when he thought he'd go insane, she grasped his penis in her hand and stroked him. Nearly mad for the feel of her moist lips, he cried out, "Take me. One way or the other, but stop tormenting me."

His body nearly sprang upward when her breath, warm and sweet, fell on him. She wrapped her arms around his hips, imprisoning him, and took him into her mouth.

"Oh, my sweet, sweetheart."

He steeled himself, concentrating on self-control. She had no technique, but she made love to him as if he were the most precious… "Kendra. Easy, honey. Stop. Listen to me, baby. St—" He pulled away from her, using force to separate them.

"Come up here, love. Did I hurt you?"

"No. Why? Can I…?" She didn't finish the question, but evidently realizing her advantage, she mounted him and took him with her to a shattering climax. She fell over onto him, clearly exhausted.

"Why did you decide to do that?" he asked her later when he was able to get his breath back.

"You needed me."

He turned over, putting her on her back and looked down into her face. "I'm having trouble believing that any woman could be as selfless as you were a few minutes ago. You didn't want anything for yourself. You only wanted to make me feel good. If you're serious about not wanting an affair with me, you just killed the possibility. I'd have to have a Herculean will to stay out of your arms."

She had given him everything a man could want, and he meant to repay her in full and then some.

"Are you tired?" he asked her.

She shook her head. "Who, me? No, indeed."

To his mind, her reply gave him license to love her until she screamed for relief. After leaving nothing to her imagination, stimulating every nerve ending in her body, he tested her for readiness.

"Do you want me?"

"What do you think I am, a piece of wood? You can ask me that when you know I'm going out of my mind?"

He wanted to shout for joy because he had her where he wanted her, irritated and frustrated. "Take me in, baby," he whispered.

She swung her body up to him, grabbed his penis and he sank into her. Within minutes, she began thrashing wildly beneath him, begging for completion, and he took her on a wild ride to that place reserved for them alone. She flung her arms wide and gave herself to him.

"Are you all right?" he asked her when he could get his breath.

"I guess so. Oh, Reid. That was… Is this going to get better each time?"

"The more we learn about each other, the more skilled we should become in pleasing each other."

"I don't want you to get any more skilled than you are now. Believe me, that's skill enough for me. You had me feeling as if I was going to die sure enough."

"Yeah? What do you think you did to me?"

She wrapped her legs around him and purred like sated feline. "You got what you asked for."

He stared down at her, a warm bundle of sweet mush. Compliant and yielding. His lover. "I love you," he said, and for some reason his willingness to say that without provocation seemed strange, even worrisome.

Kendra didn't doubt that her heart belonged to Reid Maguire. Her problem was the unknown. She believed that Reid would protect her from any semblance of harm, to the extent that he could, but if she behaved indiscreetly, he could not protect her from the law. And "the law" would respond to anyone who decided to complain that, for a judge, her behavior was unseemly.

Deciding that she needed a focus other than Reid, she telephoned her sister, Claudine, and invited her to spend a week, now that school had closed for the summer. "It's very nice here, and you can swim in the Albemarle as often as you like. It's only four short blocks from my house. We can go boating, too, but not very often, because the winds tend to come up suddenly. How about it?"

"Okay, but don't let me cramp your style."

Wasn't that precisely why she'd called her? "When are you coming?"

"I signed up to teach summer school because I didn't have anything else to do, but I don't start till Monday week, so I could come this weekend. Sure I won't be in the way?"

"Listen, Claudine. You're talking to Kendra. Am I in the habit of deliberately making problems for myself?"

"Well, no. What's the nearest airport?"

"Caution Point."

"Okay, I'll let you know what time I'll get in Friday afternoon."

On Friday, with the county clerk sitting in her court, Kendra was reluctant to adjourn an hour early in the afternoon in order to drive to Caution Point to meet her sister. She recessed for ten minutes, went to her chambers and called Reid.

"Are you going to Caution Point today?"

"Why?" She told him of her difficulty in meeting her

sister. "All you have to do is ask, sweetheart. I have an office right in the airport terminal building, and I can work there as well as here. What's her name?"

"Claudine Rutherford. She's half an inch shorter than I, two years younger and we resemble each other."

"Just in case, I'll wait for her at four o'clock with her name printed on a piece of paper. Not to worry."

"Thank you. I hope I'm not inconveniencing you."

"It gives me pleasure to do things for you. Kiss me?"

She made the sound of a kiss. "I won't be home until five or a little later."

"If I don't see your car in front of your house, I'll show her the town. Okay?"

She went back to court, ended the recess and the prosecutor continued her cross-examination of a man charged with child neglect and abuse, a man who, Kendra was reasonably certain, was being unfairly accused. The prosecutor rested her case early, so Kendra was able to adjourn and be home just before five o'clock.

When she opened the door to her sister and Reid, his move caught her off guard. He stood by while she greeted her sister, then closed the door, pulled her into his arms and, with his tongue dancing in her mouth, drugged her until she collapsed against him.

"I like your sister," he said.

"Right now I don't care whether you like her or not. Why did you do that?"

"So it won't be necessary for you to fudge the truth. You're my girl, and your sister should know that." He turned to Claudine. "I'm happy to have met you, Claudine, and I expect I'll be seeing more of you. Good night." He walked over to Kendra and kissed the side of her mouth. "I'll call you later."

Claudine's eyes seemed permanently arched. "Well, how do you like that?" she said.

At the supermarket that Saturday morning with Kendra, Claudine felt a hand on her arm and turned to see Reba, one of her sister's neighbors. "You must be Judge Kendra's sister, 'cause you look just like her. I'm Reba. How long you staying?"

"At least until midweek, I'm not sure. How are you, Reba?"

"Me? I'm fine, thank the good Lord." She looked at Kendra. "Maybe I'll drop by and bring Claudine some of my pecan Noels I made yesterday. She'll love 'em. See you later."

"I thought you said people here give you a cold shoulder," Claudine said to Kendra.

"That was before I moved out of Albemarle Gates. Now I'm practically a hero. They think I moved because of that controversy, but I moved because the house was shoddily built and the company that built it was too vulnerable to put up a fight.

"I'm also in the local theater, and that doesn't hurt my popularity. You haven't told me what you think of Reid," Kendra said later as she drove them home.

Claudine let out a long breath. "He's a hideous-looking man, a runt of minimum intelligence and totally lacking in charm and personality." Kendra nearly slammed on the brakes. "If he was mine, I wouldn't let him out of my sight," Claudine continued.

Kendra had forgotten about her sister's oddball sense of humor. "I'm glad you like him," Kendra said dryly.

She had just finished putting away her groceries when the telephone rang. "Hi, sweetheart. I just spoke with Philip, and he wants us to come down there Friday. The whole place is in bloom, and this time we won't have to work. His cruiser's ready to sail—plums, blueberries and apricots are getting ripe." He paused. "Please?"

"Just a minute." She asked Claudine if she'd like to go.

"Any decent-looking men down there?"

"He's as good-looking as they come, well-educated and independent."

"Does he have all of his teeth?"

Kendra couldn't help laughing. "Absolutely, and they glisten. You may not think he's eligible, though."

"Why? Does he have one leg? So what? They still make crutches."

"Nothing so simple. He's a green-eyed blond."

"How tall is he?"

"I'd guess about six-four."

Claudine slid off the kitchen counter. "The man's six feet four inches tall and you're telling me some garbage about the color of his eyes? Girl, I haven't had on a pair of three-inch heels in years. Tell Reid we can leave tomorrow."

"We can't, because I have to work Monday, and so does Reid. Claudine is anxious to go," Kendra told Reid.

"Yeah. I heard most of that conversation. Your sister has a wicked sense of humor. I detected that when I was bringing her here. We'll have a good time down there."

* * *

Reid rang the bell at the wrought-iron gate leading to Dickerson Estates at precisely five minutes after seven that Friday evening, and gave thanks that he had not been given a ticket for speeding.

"This is Reid with two stunning females," he said to Philip, who answered his ring. The gate swung open and in the still-bright summer evening, they drove up the sleepy land to the white Georgian mansion.

"This place is breathtaking," Claudine said of the long lane that wound between moss-filled willow trees, crepe myrtles and fields of colorful flowers. "Who owns it?"

"Blond and green-eyed Philip," Reid said with a laugh, "and trust me, he's got both legs."

"If you tell him I said that, I'll…I'll poison my sister against you," Claudine said to Reid. He parked, and Philip ran down the steps to greet them.

"How's it going, brother? Hello, Kendra. Welcome back. This must be…" He stopped as if shocked. "Hello," he said, and Reid took Kendra's arm and went to the back of his car to get their bags. "Come on, baby. Let them deal with it." He removed their bags and closed the trunk of the car. "I'll put these in the foyer. Philip will tell me where we're sleeping."

"But Reid," Kendra said, seemingly distressed, "shouldn't you introduce Philip to Claudine? It's improper to bring a guest to his house and not—"

He couldn't believe she'd said that. "You couldn't be serious, sweetheart. Their hormones have given them all the introduction they need. Can't you see that? What they need from us is privacy."

"But they…" She looked up and saw that, with his arm around Claudine's shoulder, Philip guided her toward the side of the house where he'd installed the swimming pool, barbecue pit and basketball court. "Oh! Good Lord! He's a fast mover."

"That's just it," Reid said. "He is not a player. He isn't even a ladies' man. Philip is a loner, and apart from the people who live on the estate, he stays to himself. Doris said he was once engaged, but he wasn't rich enough in those days, and his fiancée dropped him for a rich man who she later sued for neglect and wife abuse. Philip's richer now than that guy ever was. Talk about justice!"

He rang the bell, and Max opened the door. "Come on in. Glad to see you again, Kendra. Philip tells me you're flying, Reid. You can't know how happy I am to hear it. Doris barbecued a young pig, Reid, because she knows how you love her barbecue, and we're eating out by the pool tonight. Where's Philip?"

"I was wondering the same thing. He disappeared with my sister," Kendra said.

Max's eyebrows shot up. "Yeah? Well, she couldn't be in better hands." He looked at Kendra. "Maybe you want to freshen up before dinner? I'll take you up to your room now. If Philip's got your sister occupied, I sure hope it means something. Reid, nobody sleeps in your room except you." Max put the bags belonging to Kendra and Claudine in their rooms and went back downstairs.

"He just met her," Kendra said to Reid. "What's with him?"

"She poleaxed him. That's what's with him. And if

you'd been looking, you'd have seen that he did the same to her. Your fast-talking sister couldn't open her mouth."

"I must be losing it. That ran right past me. I hope you're right, and I hope he realizes that Claudine runs her mouth because she's self-conscious."

"Self-conscious or not, she's obviously Philip Dickerson's type. Meet you down at the bottom of the stairs in fifteen minutes."

The first time he'd looked at Kendra, he'd thought something exploded inside him, shaking him so that he wanted both to run away from her and never to leave her. He unpacked, washed his hands, scrubbed his fingernails, brushed his teeth and changed into a yellow, collared T-shirt and a pair of white pants. When she drifted down the stairs, he laughed aloud, for she wore a yellow, collared T-shirt, white slacks and white sneakers.

"This is proof positive," he said, swinging her into his arms, "that we're soul mates."

"They'll think we planned this. Don't tell them it was accidental," she whispered, "because they won't believe us anyway."

"I don't give two hoots what they think. Next time, let's plan it. I want everybody to know I'm your guy and you're my woman."

She raised an eyebrow, and he wondered at that. Staring down at her with his feelings bare, he said, "I *am* your man, am I not?"

"If you asking me whether you have privileges that no other man has, the answer is yes."

Whether to gain strength from a coming blow, he

couldn't say, but he widened his stance and looked her in the eye. "That's not the answer to my question, Kendra. Am I your man?"

Her countenance darkened, and he thought she appeared sad. "I'm old-fashioned, Reid. You're as important to me as the air I breathe, and no one, not even Claudine, who is my only living relative can boast that. To say that—"

He grabbed her shoulders. "If you had my ring on your finger, would you object to my saying that I'm your man?"

She sucked in her breath and something in the vicinity of her feet engaged her attention. "I guess not, but fiancé would be more appropriate."

"Ah, sweetheart!" He pulled her into his arms, and she snuggled against him, holding him tight. How had he ever lived without her? He took her hand and headed for the recreation area.

"I wondered if you two had decided to fill up on love," Max said.

Kendra greeted Doris with a hug. "That comment seemed out of character for Max. Was he telling me something?"

Doris's smile showed her pride in her husband. "He sure was. Max is so fond of Reid, and he won't be satisfied till he sees a minister pronounce the two of you man and wife. Girl, my husband is so romantic." She patted the back of her hair, which looked as if she'd just left the hairdresser, and looked toward the ceiling. "After twenty-four years, he's still the best, most eager lover a woman could want."

"That's because you probably look and behave exactly as you did twenty-four years ago, a perfect size ten with everything where it should be. How do you do that and eat this great food you cook?"

"I don't overeat, and I swim every day in the year." She took a deep breath. "Philip is really taken with Claudine. I never saw the like of it, and that sort of thing always happens to both people. I tell you, this is something! Take this cornbread out to the table, will you? Wait a minute? You think Claudine would agree to live here? We're so isolated. Lord, I hope she's flexible."

"Doris, they haven't known each other an hour."

"I know, but, honey, I've known Philip since he was seven, and what he's going through right now isn't going to leave him during this lifetime."

Kendra didn't know what to make of Doris's words, but she had a hunch that the woman knew whereof she spoke. She hastened outside to observe for herself the interplay between Philip and her sister.

"Excuse us for a couple of minutes," Philip said to the group. "Claudine wants to change before dinner, and if we don't hurry we'll be on Doris's black list." He extended his hand and Claudine took it, rose from her chair with the grace of Aphrodite rising from the Aegean Sea, and didn't even glance at her sister as she left the group, holding Philip Dickerson's hand.

"Well, if that doesn't beat all," Kendra said to herself. To Max, she said, "Something's happening here. Does this place have magic? Reid certainly cast a spell over me when I was here before. What is it about the place?"

"No magic here," Max said, and stretched out his legs and fastened his gaze on his wife, who sat across the room from him. "The people here care about each other, down to the last man. No one here has anything to fear. We treat each other with respect and care for each other when there's a need. Nothing here to get stressed out about."

When Philip and Claudine returned a few minutes later, Claudine wore white pants and a pink T-shirt, and Kendra thought that Philip's color had heightened considerably. Doris said grace, and the three couples, along with Arnold, Philip's father, who joined them for the meal, enjoyed barbecued fresh pork, stuffed baked onions, stewed collards and baked spicy cornbread and lemon tarts for dessert.

Reid leaned back in his chair and said for all to hear, "Kendra, baby, you're going to have to learn how to do this barbecue. I've tried to make it at least half a dozen times and screwed it up on every occasion."

"Just let me know when you're coming, and I'll show you," Doris said, "but you have to promise not to give away my recipe."

"I'll promise you just about anything," he said.

Arnold walked around to Claudine and extended his hand to her. "I see that my son is so taken with you that he's forgotten to introduce us. I'm Arnold Dickerson, Philip's father, and I am delighted to meet you."

Claudine stood and shook the man's hand. "Thank you, Mr. Dickerson. I'm very happy to meet you, too."

At least she's still got presence of mind, Kendra said to herself.

"I suggest we all go over to St. Michael early

tomorrow morning and take the cruiser out," Philip said to the group. "What do you all say?" He turned to Claudine. "I hope you brought along a sweater. Early mornings are cool on the bay."

"Yes, I did. Thanks."

Arnold returned to his seat beside Kendra. "Your sister is also a lovely woman. I'm tempted to ask if there are any more Rutherford women."

"Thank you," Kendra said. "We're all that's left. Our mother passed a couple of years ago."

"I'm sorry about that. You know, it saddened me that Philip didn't meet you before Reid did, but well, that was that. Philip and Reid are brothers. They've been through a lot together, and as stubborn as Reid is, he wasn't so intractable as to ruin their relationship, because Philip stands his ground. You can't imagine how happy I am to know that Reid's ship is upright again. He's a terrific man."

"Thanks for telling me this," she said. "How do you feel about this obvious attraction between Philip and my sister?"

"She's a beautiful, elegant woman. I've never seen him this way. Reminds me of myself when I fell in love with his mother. I hope she'll love him as deeply as Ellen loved me."

These people take some getting used to, Kendra thought as she sat around the pool with them later, sipping a mint julep and staring at the fire in the barbecue pit. She knew from the sound of the bird's song that the singer was a mockingbird, although she had never heard it before. The smell of gardenia blossoms wafted among them and night creatures seemed to greet each other and to respond to the many different noises. Crickets chirped, frogs croaked and somewhere an owl hooted. *What a heavenly oasis!*

"That was an owl, wasn't it?" she asked Arnold.

"Absolutely. They can sound eerie, too, on a dark night when the wind is ominous. If you're not accustomed to 'em, they'll scare the living beejeepers out of you."

Kendra turned to Reid. "I could get used to country living. Nobody can find this much peace in the city."

He reached for her hand and held it. "This place gave me a second life. It's so tranquil. Here, a man can think, explore himself, appraise his life and find his salvation."

"Oh, honey," she said and put her arms around him because she couldn't help it.

The poignancy of the moment was broken when Arnold said, "Reid, I hear you got a great offer of a contract from Reginald English. I hope you're going to accept it. That's an old and solidly placed family. I remember that my father had some dealings with Reginald English Senior, a lot of years ago, before the man got into the oil and gas business. I think he bought lumber from one of his mills, couldn't meet his payments and offered to work it off. Old man English erased the debt. It wasn't huge, but it sure meant a lot to my father. Anyway, you deserve your own company, and that deal will cement your status."

"If I have to get up at five," Kendra said, "I'd better crawl in. Thanks, Doris, for this wonderful meal, and, Philip, thanks for the best—and first—mint julep I ever tasted. Its reputation for putting people in a stupor is well earned," she added, drawing a round of laughter from the group. She patted Arnold's hand. "I'm always glad to see you."

Reid rose and reached for Kendra's hand. "Kendra's turning in, and I'm going to walk with her to her room. I'll be back, Philip, to finish this dynamite drink you mixed. By the way, everyone, I've decided to leave Marks and Connerly and strike out on my own."

"Right on, man," Philip said. "I knew you'd do it."

"Yeah. Now that I've made up my mind, I can't wait to get started. Thank all of you for the support you've given me. Be back shortly."

"Are you surprised?" he asked her as they walked up the stairs.

"Not a bit. You're loyal, but you're also logical, and because you want to regain your status, this is the proper road. I'm proud of you, and when I get some privacy I'm going to give you a proper kiss."

"Not tonight, please, sweetheart. If I don't go back there, they'll know why."

"I can still kiss you. A little self-control is good for a man."

"When I repay you, be sure you remember how I incurred the debt."

At her door she stroked the side of his face. "I'm so proud of you. I would have accepted your decision if you had decided to stay with Jack, but I'm glad you chose to leave. Not because of the money, but for the man you are. You're the best, and you don't need to bow to any man. See you in the morning."

"Aren't you gonna kiss me?"

She knew that her grin had all the elements of deviltry. "If you want me to."

When he released her, she stumbled into the room, closed the door and fell across the bed.

"That was a real party Philip put on yesterday," Reid said to Kendra as they pointed their horses toward Bachelor Bay on Dickerson Estates, on Sunday morning. "I never cared much for those big boats. He was always trying to get me to go out with him, but I wouldn't. That's one sweet cruiser."

"Yes, and that weekend house is nothing to sneeze at. The entire day was memorable. Imagine, the man who owns Dickerson Estates actually sitting down and scaling fish! Max said Doris wouldn't think of cleaning fish."

"Half the time, Doris is more like his mother than his housekeeper. She raised him from the time he was seven."

"Without the moonlight to put scales over their eyes, Philip and Claudine seemed even more mesmerized by each other," Kendra said. "What do you think about it, Reid?"

"I think they're both almost as lucky as I am. Don't worry about your sister. Philip Dickerson is not going to hurt her."

"She's pie-eyed, and not in the thirty-seven years I've known her—except when our parents died—have I seen her this serious for periods longer than thirty minutes."

"Have you talked with her?"

"When could I? He hasn't let her out of his sight."

He had thought that Philip and Claudine would be

attracted to each other, especially because of Philip's deep appreciation for intellectual wit, and on the short ride from Caution Point to Queenstown, he had discovered that Claudine was a very witty person. But it pleased him immensely to know that Claudine had destroyed whatever interest Philip might have had in Kendra.

"If I was smart, I wouldn't let you out of my sight, either. Are you comfortable on that horse? She seems a bit agitated."

"I'm okay," Kendra said. "I don't ride often enough to be good at it, but I'm comfortable."

He hadn't often ridden to this part of the estate; during his stay here, he'd spent most of his spare time planning for the day that he hoped was at hand, the day he would face Brown and Worley in court once more. The day of vindication. The acres through which the bridle path roamed were resplendent in wild flowers that grew among the peach trees and pecan groves. He wanted to stop his horse and pick a bouquet for Kendra. At last, they reached Bachelor Bay. He dismounted, and then helped Kendra dismount.

As soon as the others arrived, Arnold, Philip and Max built a fire, put up a table and set it for a meal. "I'll cook," Reid said, "that is if you don't mind eating gourmet food."

"Since when can you cook?" Doris asked him.

"Since before you met me, and after eating your cooking, my standard went up, and I got better at it. I had to because I couldn't stand lousy meals."

"Then, let's the four of us cook," Philip said. "Here's

the bacon, the sausage and a frying pan, Reid." What a difference having a woman he cared for and who cared for him could make in a man, Reid thought as he watched Philip use every opportunity to touch Claudine. And how her eyes adored him! He walked over to Kendra.

"I'm damned proud of myself. I thought up this trip just to get those two together. I'm a helluva smart man."

Her eyes sparkled, and the low, sexy laughter that he loved trickled out of her. "It isn't the first solid evidence I've had of your cleverness, sir."

"You mean that I stayed after you till I got you in bed? That sure was clever of me."

The group passed jokes among themselves, ate a breakfast of blueberries, grits, eggs, waffles, bacon, sausage and coffee, and after the men cleaned up, they all lay down on straw pallets and dozed in the morning sun.

Glancing around, Reid saw that Claudine lay in the curve of Philip's arm, while his friend gazed down at her, then bent over and kissed her lips. A smile altered the contours of his face. Reid didn't do it often, but he couldn't help thanking the Lord. Life was good.

The sun climbed and the temperature rose. "It's time we packed up and started back," Philip said at about nine-thirty. "By the time we get home, it'll be hot."

Reid rolled up Kendra's mat and his own, singing "Shenandoah" in his deep baritone as he did so. Then he packed them on Casey Jones, his favorite horse, and he and Kendra joined the others for the trip back to the mansion.

Sitting on his horse, Monument, a big chestnut stallion, Philip called to Reid, "In all the time I've known you, I had no idea that you could sing. You never sang here."

"No. I don't suppose I did."

"You never smiled as much, either," Doris said. "Next, you'll tell me you can dance."

"I love to dance, Doris, and I think I'm pretty good at it." He couldn't help looking at Kendra. "Things are so different now. I feel like singing."

As they neared the house, a rabbit dashed out of the lettuce field in front of Kendra's horse, spooking her, and the horse rose on her hind legs, throwing Kendra to the ground. She landed on her back and writhed in pain.

"Philip!" Reid yelled as he jumped down from his horse and ran to Kendra. "Are you hurt? How do you feel? Oh, my God, baby. I'm so sorry."

"My back and my shoulder."

"I'll get the doctor and a stretcher," Philip said. "It's best not to move her, because we don't know where or how badly she's hurt. Do you have any pain in your neck, Kendra?"

"No. Don't worry. I feel all my toes and my fingers. It's my shoulder and my back."

Reid let out a deep breath. If she had feeling in her fingers and toes, she wouldn't be paralyzed. Claudine and Doris hovered around her, but he refused to give way.

"I'll cancel my classes and stay with you," Claudine told Kendra.

"You don't need to do that," Reid said. "I'm going to take care of her. She won't want for a thing."

"Are you sure?" Claudine asked him. "I don't feel right going off and leaving her."

"You may stay if you like, Claudine. You're her sister, but she's my woman and my responsibility, and *I* am going to take care of her."

Chapter 9

"She has a dislocated shoulder and three broken ribs," the doctor said, "and she's a very lucky woman. I've taped her up, and she should be able to travel tomorrow if she can lie down in the backseat."

"She can," Reid said. "We can make her comfortable with pillows. Can you give her a painkiller, doctor?"

"Yes. I gave Philip a prescription."

"I'll take that to the drugstore, Philip." Reid sat on the side of the bed in which Kendra lay, her face registering her surprise at the sudden change in her circumstances. "I'll be back shortly, sweetheart. We'll stay here tonight and leave sometime tomorrow. I'll call my office. Do you want me to call your clerk?"

"I don't have his home phone number, but perhaps we can get it through Information."

"You're going to take her back to Queenstown tomorrow?" Philip asked him with a note of incredulity in his voice.

"That'll be fine," the doctor said, "so long as he makes her comfortable."

"Tell you what," Philip said to Reid. "You take the town car and leave your car with me. The backseat in my car is roomier, and it's a heavier car, so she won't feel the bumps."

"Thanks, brother. I'd do the same for you, and I'll get it back to you as soon as Kendra's well."

Philip's offer surprised her until she remembered Arnold's words to her the evening of their arrival. The two men were indeed brothers in their hearts, and they shared some admirable traits, too. She prayed that Claudine and Philip would love each other and build a life together. Thinking that she couldn't wish more for her sister, she fought the drowsiness.

"What did you give me?" she asked the doctor.

"Something for the pain. If I hadn't given it to you, you'd be in agony."

"Thank you. I'm sorry to be so much trouble."

"You're no trouble," Doris said. "I was just thinking how much fun it would be to throw a wild party right here in your room and out there in the hall."

"Don't believe her," Max said. "Doris hates loud parties."

"I thought you'd never wake up," she heard Reid say. "Claudine and I are going to help you sit up, so we can get you out of those clothes and put on whatever it is that you sleep in."

She helped them ease her into a sitting position. "Reid, you can't undress me."

"Really? Thank God, this thing buttons in the front."

"Claudine, get him out of here."

"Honey, don't mind me. I don't think he'll get any surprises."

"What do you mean?"

"Don't push me, Kendra, because you know I'll tell it like it is. Tell you what, I'll go out and let Reid do it."

Claudine left the room and Reid eased off her blouse, turned back the bed cover and removed her slacks and socks. "You are one sexy woman," he said when he took off her bra. "Lord! Can I have just a little taste of this?" He flicked his tongue over her erect nipple and then pulled it into his mouth.

"You're asking for trouble," she said as the glow of desire began to warm her.

"I know, but it was worth it. What did you bring to sleep in?" She told him. He looked at the yellow-and-black lace teddy. "Why bother? You might as well sleep nude."

"Lots of times I do. I'm really impressed with Philip. He's very generous, and it's clear that he loves you a lot. I hope his interest in Claudine is genuine."

"Trust me, it is. He told me he'd give anything if she'd stay here with him."

"He doesn't know anything about her."

"They fell in love with each other. What do you expect them to do? Drop it? They want to be together, just as you and I want to be together." He sat on the side of her bed and took her hand. "She isn't your little sister anymore, Kendra. She's twice-grown. Let them love each other."

"Oh, I'm happy about this relationship. I see how they feel and I'm praying it will last forever."

"Good. Philip's going to bring you a television, and I'll bring you some food."

She didn't relish the thought of a four-hour ride lying in the backseat of a car, but she didn't see an acceptable alternative. *He'll make it as pleasant as he can,* she told herself, *so grin and bear it.*

What surprised her was Philip's obvious reluctance to let Claudine leave him. He stood beside the car looking down at Claudine, and finally, as if he had exhausted his willpower, he took her into his arms and kissed her as if he would never again get the chance. She hadn't seen Claudine cry since they were in their early teens, but her sister put her head on Philip's shoulder and wept.

"Are you in love with him?" she asked Claudine when they finally headed off the estate.

"Love him? I'm crazy about him. I never dreamed I could feel this way about a man. He said, 'Hello.' That's all. I looked up and saw him staring down at me, and I...I just lost myself to him. That minute. And I knew it was mutual."

"Did you two make plans to see each other soon?" Reid asked her.

"He's coming to Alexandria next Saturday. I don't know how I can wait that long."

"You will," Reid said. "He's a prince of a guy, but don't make it too easy for him, and be sure you don't get out of character. Always show him the real you. If he can live with that now, he can live with it forever."

* * *

"Why can't I go to work?" Kendra asked Reid the following Thursday morning. "I can walk, and I can get my robe on."

"I can't force you to stay home, sweetheart, but please, at least let's have a doctor examine you before you go back to work. Or wait until Monday." She agreed, and later that day, a doctor told her to wait until Monday before returning to work, and gave her a doctor's certificate. "You'll need to be very careful for a while," he told her. "You can easily reinjure this shoulder."

"Have you forgotten that the performance of our play in the park is two weeks from now?" Reid asked her. "As much as you like to move around on the stage, you need to be healthy for that."

"You've done everything for me except bathe me, Reid, and I won't ever forget your tenderness and patience, but I want to sit out in my garden and feel the sun on me."

"Okay. Tomorrow after I come from work? Speaking of work, I have something to tell you. My lawyer said the date's been set for a retrial of my case. He's negotiating for the venue."

She didn't ask him the date. She didn't want to know the day on which he would probably walk away from her.

"I couldn't turn down this opportunity," Reid told Jack Marks after signing the contract to design a twenty-five-storey office condominium building and a summer mansion for Reginald English on the Outer

Banks. "But you can take that other deal anyway. I'll design the building for you as a consultant, if you want me to."

"You're a straight guy, Reid," Jack said, working his mouth in the manner of one clearly touched. "I won't forget it. If you ever need me, you know where I am. I'll let you know what I envisage for this building, and you draw up a contract as a consultant. Is this your last week with us?"

Reid nodded. "Yeah."

Jack stood and extended his hand. "Could we have lunch together Friday? Oh, yes, and will you let me know if you get a retrial in that Brown and Worley case? I just got a new customer who wants me to renovate a house they built less than two years ago. I may be of some help to you."

"Thank you. I'm probably going to need it." He went back to his office, phoned Marcus Hickson and gave him the news. "The signature on your factory will be Reid Maguire, Architect, Incorporated. I'm back in my own business."

"Knock one back for me, man. This is the best news I've had in ages. Get ready to sweat, because I've had at least eight calls about this building. People like your work. It looks nothing like a factory. Amanda said that from the outside, it looks more like a private club. I'm going to give a big party when I open, and I want you and Kendra to come."

"I'll look forward to it."

He hung up and looked at his watch. Four o'clock. *I'm a free man. I can do as I like, and what I want to*

*do right now is find something real nice and take it to
Kendra.* He drove to a gourmet caterer midway between
Caution Point and Queenstown and bought a quart and
a half of lobster bisque, an assortment of imported
cheeses—Stilton, Chaumes, Saint Andre, Pipo Crème
and Cheshire—pumpernickel bread, mesclun salad and
several bottles of Châteauneuf du Pape, his favorite red
wine. Kendra had to be tired of his cooking; he certainly
was. She didn't want him to do her housework, but she
hadn't hired anyone to clean, and he knew how to do it.
So he did it. She wouldn't allow him to help her bathe,
so he imagined she took a sponge bath with her left hand
while he stood outside the bathroom in case she needed
him. He'd seen every inch of her flesh, front and back,
and he didn't see why the devil she risked falling in the
bathroom because of a foolish modesty.

As he'd done at least three times every day since he
brought her back from Dickerson Estates, he walked
down the alley beside the house in which she lived and,
using a key that she had given him, entered her house
through the back door.

"Hi," he said to alert her to his presence, "it's me,
Reid." He knocked on her bedroom door.

"Come in."

"Did you do this?" he asked her, handing her a red
rose and frowning as he observed the tidy room.

"My friends, Reba and Letty, heard that I was sick
and dropped in. They just left."

"How nice! And they straightened up your room.
We're having something different tonight. I hope you
like what I got." He told her that he'd resigned from

Marks and Connerly, signed a contract with English and that he would plan Jack Marks's building in the capacity of consultant as she had suggested.

"That idea pleased Jack, and you know what? He may have evidence that will support me in my case against Brown and Worley."

"I'm glad, Reid. You're rebuilding your company, and you don't feel that you're being disloyal to Jack. Does Mike want us to rehearse before our performance in the park?"

"I imagine he does, but if you're not up to it, we'll have to skip it. I'll call him."

He used his cell phone to call their producer/director. "Mike, this is Reid. Are you planning another practice session before our performance in the park?"

"Tuesday night. The show is Thursday evening."

"I suppose you know that Kendra is recovering from three busted ribs and a dislocated shoulder? She thinks she can make the Thursday date, but she's not sure about an earlier practice date."

"I heard she wasn't in court. How's she doing?"

"Sorry, man. I have no idea what kind of progress she's making. I'll ask her to call you." He hated lying, but he wasn't going to be tricked into exposing Kendra. He busied himself setting the table and laying out the food. After heating the lobster bisque, he went to Kendra's room to help her out of bed, but saw that she was up and had managed to put on her robe.

"When are you going to return Philip's car?" she asked him.

"I told him I'd bring it back when you're well."

"In that case, you should return it to him this weekend."

"Philip will be in Alexandria with Claudine this weekend. I'll call him and see if he'd like me to meet him there. It would certainly save me more than half the distance between here and Denton." He telephoned Philip, who agreed that they should exchange cars in Alexandria that Sunday morning.

After helping Kendra with exercises that the doctor had prescribed to ease her into the free use of her right arm and hand, Reid took her left hand, walked with her into the living room and sat with her on the velvet sofa. He preferred leather furniture coverings, but he liked Kendra's taste. Indeed, he liked everything about her.

He draped an arm around her shoulder and tugged her closer to him. "We love each other, we like each other and we're friends," he said. "We also suit each other as lovers. I'm ready to commit to you for the long haul, but I don't feel free to ask you to marry me until I get that last stumbling block out of the way."

She'd been relaxed against him, and now she sat up and turned so that she could face him. "I don't expect you to lose that case against Brown and Worley, but if you do, does that mean it's over between us?"

"I...I haven't thought in terms of losing."

"Well, think about it," she said. "Don't you believe my faith in you will survive any loss you sustain, whether it's a court case, your architectural firm or every penny you own? Huh? Don't ask me to pay for Myrna's crimes, Reid. I refuse to accept a maybe-if relationship with you."

"And I don't think I suggested that, either. I want so

much for you, for us, and I can't see myself offering you the shame of a man disgraced in his profession. Until I clear my name, that's the tag I carry."

She leaned away from him. "My good sense told me that we shouldn't become involved in an affair."

He suppressed a laugh, because he knew she was not in a mood for jokes. "Good sense doesn't have a lot to do with what goes on between a man and a woman who are attracted to each other. From the moment I first saw you, I knew I had a choice of yielding or leaving town. Leaving town never occurred to me. Look," he said, settling for what he could get, "let's at least remain the closest of friends. These next two weeks are going to be hard on both of us."

"I know. Probably harder than you realize."

Two days later, Reid cleaned out his desk at Marks and Connerly, packed his personal belongings and went to each office to tell his colleagues goodbye. He believed in courtesy, even though, in this case, he thought that some of his fellow architects there would be glad to see him leave.

"I read in the *Maryland Journal* this morning about that plum of a contract you got," Gene, one of the senior architects, said when they shook hands. "You've got your work cut out, but I don't expect it will stretch you. It must be a great feeling to have your hat in the ring again."

"It is. But it's been so long since I was stressed out that I probably won't recognize myself after a month or so."

"Anytime you feel like swearing at the top of your voice, give me a call and we can share a beer instead."

"Thanks, man. I appreciate that, and I'll be in touch." Among his associates at Marks and Connerly, Gene Faison was the only man, other than Jack Marks, who had welcomed him as a colleague. He was also the most competent. *When you know your stuff,* Reid thought, *you don't envy your competition.* So he'd gotten some press coverage. He hoped that news didn't encourage Brown and Worley to strengthen their hand. When he got home, he phoned his lawyer.

"Dean, this is Reid. Any rumblings from Brown and Worley?"

"They wanted the trial moved back to Baltimore, but you're legally a resident of North Carolina, and they're registered here, so you're entitled to sue here if you want to. Other than that, they've been quiet. I suspect their lawyer won't accept any Native Americans on the jury because of the furor over Albemarle Gates, so we'll probably have a one-sided jury. But if Judge Rutherford will permit me to enter into evidence the architectural examiner's report on her house, that along with the mountain of information you and I collected gives us a very strong case."

"I think we have a good one, too," he said, "although if Rutherford is the judge, we can't use Helligman's affidavit."

"I'm not so sure, Reid."

Early Sunday morning, he left Queenstown for Alexandria, Virginia, arriving there shortly after nine o'clock. "How's it going, Philip?" he asked his friend.

"Great. How'd you know Claudine and I would get on so well?"

"She's so witty, and she has such a fast mind."

"Fine, so far as it goes, but by the time I discovered that, I was already a goner. Anyhow, I'm grateful to you. How's Kendra?"

"She's improving, and she plans to be back on the bench Monday. As soon as the trial is over, I hope to get a permanent commitment from her. Man, she's changed my life. I'd better start back. I don't want her fooling around in the kitchen yet. She doesn't move her right arm to suit me." They embraced each other. "Thanks for the car, Philip. I'll be in touch."

He drove back to Queenstown without stopping. Kendra thought she was well, and he didn't doubt that, in his absence, she would overextend herself. It surprised him that, as he turned his key in her back door, she opened it, her face blooming in a big smile. She had dressed in pants and a T-shirt that didn't button down the front, but he didn't question her about that. The doctor had cautioned her about raising her arm. He shrugged off his concern, bent and kissed her.

"Mind if I get something cold to drink?" he asked her. "I'm practically dehydrated. I spent exactly thirty minutes in Alexandria. I was in such a rush to get back here and fix your lunch that I didn't even see Claudine." He headed for the kitchen to get whatever thirst-quenching drink he could find and stopped at the kitchen door. Dumbfounded.

"Woman, what on earth have you done?" He stared at the mess that covered the stove and a part of the floor in front of it. "What were you doing and why couldn't you wait until I got back? It's only a quarter of one. Why does it bother you to be dependent on me? I know this is the twenty-first century and that women are as competent and as efficient at most things as men are, but while you're recovering, you are not.

"I'm not playing at being the superior male, Kendra. I love you. I thought you needed me, and I wanted to take care of you, but—hell! Just look at this mess in the kitchen. Did you scald yourself?"

"No, I didn't," she said in the voice of one vacillating between regret and anger. "And I'd appreciate it if you wouldn't chew me out. I don't like it."

"I stand corrected," he said, but he was damned if he'd apologize.

"You didn't see Claudine? Are she and Philip all right?"

"According to Philip, they are. I forgot where you keep your towels." She told him. "I want you to get comfortable somewhere while I do this." He tied the towel around his waist for an apron, cleaned the stove and mopped the floor.

"I suppose you're hungry. Since you're dressed, would you like to go out for lunch? I guess you're tired of the house."

"I am, and I'd like us to go somewhere for lunch, but not if you're mad at me."

He grasped her arms and looked into her eyes. "Angry at you? My temper is not so subdued as this. Trust me. I'm disappointed, not angry. I am concerned that you may have retarded your progress. Sweetheart, can't you see that I want to help you and to…to protect you? Oh, hell. If you can't see it, there's no point in telling you. Let's go eat."

* * *

It didn't surprise Kendra that Reid knocked on her back door Monday morning—he had returned her key because she had declared herself well—with a thermos of coffee and a toasted bagel unwrapped in a saucer. "Here," he said. "I'm not coming in. I just wanted to be sure you got something to eat before you left home."

She grasped his right forearm, pulled him into the house and kissed his mouth. He put the thermos and the saucer on the floor, wrapped her in his arms and ran his tongue across the seam of her lips.

"Let me in, sweetheart. It's been so long." She sucked his tongue into her mouth and, at once the fire of desire shot through her. She wanted to drag him to her bed and have her way with him. He stepped back and looked down at her. "Can we be together this evening? I'll be practically a cripple all day."

"If I'm not too tired for company," she said, for she refused to make that kind of date with him. He stared down at her for a long minute. "Right. After all, it's your first day back at work. I'll call you at five."

"All right. What will you do today? I mean, where will you be?"

"I have to find office space, and I'm thinking of locating in Edenton. It's only a thirty-minute drive from here, and there's no architect located there. It's also a much bigger city than Queenstown."

"How far is it from the location of your projects on the Outer Banks?"

"Same distance as from here, and the driving is easier."
She traced a finger down the front of his shirt. "I

hope you find something suitable. Thanks for the food. See you this evening." She kissed him again and watched him lope down the lane while she devoured the bagel.

She would have welcomed a better supply of energy when she walked into court. On her first day in that court, she'd had to reprimand the lawyer who was there representing another client. The man liked to pull tricks, and she knew she'd better remain alert. By the end of the last session, tiredness hung over her like an iron yoke.

"You've had it pretty tough your first day back, ma'am," Carl Running Moon Howard said when he handed her the following day's schedule. "Can I get you anything?"

"Thanks, Carl, but I'm fine. I'm going home and get some rest. See you in the morning."

She'd barely had time to pull off her shoes when the phone rang. "This is Reid. How'd it go?"

"I had Emerson all day again," she said. "He's a very incompetent defense attorney, and he has a problem with me. I had to put him in his place the first day I was in that court. So I didn't dare let my attention drift today, and it was a struggle. I'd love to kiss you, but I'd have to keep it light."

"I'll bring you some supper and get my kiss, but I won't stay very long. Be over in about an hour."

"Thanks. Call before you leave home, because I'm going to lie down, and if I fall asleep, I might not hear you knock."

She wondered at his long silence. Then he said, "I

wouldn't want to awaken you. If you have food in the house, I'll see you tomorrow."

"I've got several cans of soup, bread and eggs. I can make a meal of that, but I'd love to kiss you."

"And I'd love to get a kiss, but I don't think I'd enjoy its aftereffect. Get some rest. See you tomorrow."

She arrived at the theater in the park an hour early that Thursday night because she hadn't attended the Tuesday night rehearsal and she wanted to familiarize herself with the stage and with Mike's stage directions. What a night, she thought, as the warm breeze brushed her face and stars blanketed the sky. It seemed to her that the moon's brilliance made electric light redundant. She went backstage and spoke with Mike.

"You only have to worry about the second act," he said. "It's very emotional, real drama and it may exhaust you, because you're not up to snuff. So don't use up too much energy there. You have another act facing you."

"All right. Thanks for alerting me."

However, she failed to heed his warning. At the beginning of the second act, Lissa said to Don, "Betty's got a job at the casino, making fistfuls of money. I think I'll try it. She said she can get me in."

Don got up from his favorite chair, walked over to her and, with his face an inch from hers, said, "No, you are not. There's adequate money for Tonya's education in the trust fund I set up for her the day she was born. I make enough to support my family and save adequately for our retirement. We don't even need the money from your job as an administrative assistant, so why the devil do you need to work at a gambling casino? You don't need fistfuls of money."

"You're telling me what I can't do? I didn't marry you to get a boss," Lissa said. "I married you for a husband and a lover, and if I want to be a croupier I'll take the course and apply for the job."

"Dammit, letting me take care of you is like eating ground glass, isn't it? You had to have your own car, and why? I drive right past the building you work in every morning on my way to work, and pass back by there every evening. You also had to have your own bank account, even though I put your name on mine."

Lissa jerked away from Don and pranced across the room. "I need my own identity. Left to you, you'll take over my life. A woman needs her own life, her own name and her own authority."

"Yeah? What the hell does that mean?"

"It means she won't allow herself to be smothered by a man. That's what it means, and if I want to deal blackjack at a casino, you are not going to stop me."

"We'll see about that. You know I can make you do anything I want you to do."

Lissa started backing away from Don. "That's what you think. You get nothing here tonight, buddy."

"Who said so? And don't you call me buddy." His hand went to her right breast. "If I get my mouth on you, I can be inside you in a minute."

"It's not true," she said, and suddenly she forgot that it was Lissa and not Kendra speaking. "You're out of line."

"Really?" Don said. "It'll give me great pleasure to prove it." His right hand caressed her other breast. The curtain fell, and the audience rose as one, applauding and yelling, "Bravo!"

"You weren't supposed to do that, man," Mike said when he rushed to them. "Kendra, I told you not to get carried away in this act." He threw up his hands. "Go take a bow."

"You rewrote the script, not to speak of the stage directions," Mike said after they took a bow. "True, the audience loved it, but this is not a reality show." He threw up his hands again. "It's a howling success, so what the hell?"

Suddenly, Mike seemed to sober up. "Reid," he said, "in the next act, please try to remember that Kendra is Judge Kendra Rutherford, and keep your hands off her pretty breasts. I'd hate to see her slap your face and ruin the play."

"Do you really think that you only have to touch me, and you can do anything to me that you like?" Kendra asked Reid when he took her key to open her back door. "I wouldn't be much of a woman if I was that weak."

"And I wouldn't be much of a man if, at this age, I didn't know how to get a woman, so let's not fight about it."

"You were still mad because I tried to cook Sunday and made a mess."

"You also pulled that T-shirt on against the doctor's orders. Were you trying to show me that you didn't need me, and doing it at the risk of injuring yourself permanently?"

So that was it. She realized then that she had hurt him

and that he had a deeply ingrained desire to know that she needed him. "Oh, Reid. I needed your help when I couldn't look after myself, but that's not the important way that I need you. I need you to hold me when I hurt, to laugh with me when I'm happy, to share good news and bad news. I need you to love me. When I see a beautiful sunset or an exquisite painting, I want you to see it with me, or if I hear beautiful music or a funny joke, I have a need to share it with you. I need *you*, Reid!"

"When you say things like that to me, I'm almost happy." The tremors in his voice told her more than his words, and she opened her arms to him.

"Someday soon, I hope this secretiveness won't be necessary," she said and tightened her arms around him. "You're such a sweet man, and I…I don't like to remember what my life was like before you made it so beautiful."

He gazed down at her, saying nothing, seemingly content to look at her. She couldn't divine his mood or what he might be thinking. "Say something," she said to him.

"I don't trust myself to talk right now. Hold me for a minute, and then I'll leave."

"Why?"

"I don't want to spoil one of the truly wonderful moments of my life." After a minute, he kissed her cheek and left. She didn't understand his behavior, but it didn't matter, for she had seen in his eyes, his countenance, his whole demeanor, pure love for her, and it was what she felt when she held him.

Her phone rang, and she answered it, knowing that

Reid was the caller. "Are you going to tell me why you left so suddenly?"

"Words of love, I mean genuine love, such as you expressed to me are… I don't know. What you said to me was like a healing potion, something sacred, and I didn't want to diminish it by following it with anything else, not even something that I valued. What I'm saying, Kendra, is that it wasn't a time for lovemaking, although I wanted that, needed it like I needed air to breathe. I left because your sweetness and gentleness only made me want you more. All things in their season."

Reid left home Saturday morning around nine for a drive to Edenton. He wanted to see that office space in daylight on a weekend, and he also wanted to inspect the neighborhood at night. He wanted Kendra's appraisal of it, too. When it came to real estate, he didn't take the owner's word. As he approached a traffic light one block from the building in which he lived, he slammed on the brakes with such suddenness that, had anyone been following him, he would have caused an accident. It couldn't possibly be, he assured himself, collected his wits and drove on. But who else looked like that? God forbid he should have problems with Myrna just as he'd begun to enjoy living once more.

Chapter 10

"I was in Edenton this morning," Reid told Kendra after he returned to Queenstown, "and I liked the office space I found. It suits my current needs. It's in a decent-looking building and the neighborhood's presentable. But I need to see the area at night, and I'd like you to look at it. You may see something that I missed."

"Sure. When do you want to go?"

"Now, if you have time." They drove to Edenton, and he watched her carefully for her gut reaction to the building and office space.

"After you renovate the bathroom, you'll have excellent accommodations," she said. He liked that way she had of making her criticisms sound almost like compliments.

"My thoughts exactly," he said. "Let's hang out someplace until dark. I want to see how this area looks at night."

He parked across from the city park, went to a convenience story and bought two large cups of pecan-praline ice cream and a bag of roasted peanuts. He took her hand. "Let's walk over by the river and feed the squirrels." They sat on a bench at the edge of the Chowan River, ate ice cream and shelled nuts for the squirrels.

Kendra gazed down at his bare feet, and though she didn't frown, she seemed skeptical. "Do you always pull off your shoes when you sit down?" she asked him.

"Let's put it this way. I only wear shoes when I have no alternative. Why? Couldn't you live with a man who goes around barefooted all the time?"

She cast him a sidelong glance and leaned back. When she did, her T-shirt tightened across her breasts causing them to jut out, and he nearly swallowed his tongue. "I could if he always washed his feet before he went to bed."

He didn't know why, but he'd almost guessed she'd say that. "If I tell you I don't have a single bad habit, can we live together?" He hadn't planned to ask her that, but he had, and he'd go with it. "I can move here to Edenton, and you'd only have a half-hour commute."

She stopped eating ice cream and placed the lid on the container and appeared thoughtful, for she realized that he wasn't smiling. "Is that a serious suggestion, and how am I supposed to take it?"

"I need to be with you, Kendra. We love each other, so why can't we live together?"

"The answer to that shouldn't cost you any sweat, Reid. We're not married. I'm a judge, and your case may come before me. To me, shacking up is a way to avoid commitment, and if a man won't commit to me, I'm not going to live with him."

"I am committed to you, and you know it. Oh, hell, if you don't want it, I'm not going to nag."

Her shrug told him that she had dug in, and that she wouldn't be moved. "You mean you're not going to beg. I didn't say I don't want to live with you, I'm saying that I am not going to shack up with you."

"It would only be temporary," he said.

"And that could be a problem, couldn't it?" she said. She ate the remainder of her ice cream, and he took the empty cup from her and threw it into the refuse basket. When he returned to the bench, she looked down at his bare feet.

"The grass under my feet is a great feeling," he said. "Pull off your shoes and try it. It's like getting back to nature."

She pulled off her shoes and as he stared into her eyes, he rubbed her toes with his own. "I'd give anything, yes, anything, to kiss you senseless right here, right now."

"And that would be the minute in which the county clerk would stroll by," she said. "We're safer watching the sunset."

But, somehow, when the big round disc slipped behind the distant hills, he'd never felt lonelier in his life. Lonely, although his arm was tight around her.

When twilight settled, he drove back to the street where he would open his office, and circled the area block by block. "This doesn't seem real," he said to her.

"It's Saturday night, the streets are empty, and it's so quiet that the sound of your footsteps would scare you to death."

"It's on the edge of a residential area," she said. "I think it's a good spot."

"So do I," he said. "I was going to suggest we go to a restaurant, but I'm not hungry."

"Neither am I. I suppose it was the ice cream. I ate some peanuts, too."

"Let's pick up something interesting at one of those gourmet take-out shops on the square and eat it when we get home. What do you say?"

He bought crab cakes, leek soup, biscuits, asparagus, corn on the cob and a green salad. "Anything else you'd like?" he asked her. "We could have some of those big shrimp.

"A pound of shrimp," he said to the clerk.

"How can we eat all that?" she asked him.

"I don't believe in being hungry when it isn't necessary."

They reached Queenstown shortly after eight o'clock.

"Would you like to eat at my place?" he asked. He loved her smile and the way in which she used it to reinforce her contentment with him.

"Sounds good to me. I'll go home, walk through the alley and knock on your back door."

Always hiding their relationship. He hated it, but he didn't want to make her uncomfortable, so he smiled. "Don't take too long."

By the time she knocked on his door, he'd set the table,

put out the food and had the leek soup warming. "I wish I'd thought to get a flower for you," he said. "We have candles and some really good white burgundy to go with this wonderful food, and flowers are all that's missing."

They had nearly finished the meal when she said, "With you here, Reid, nothing is missing. Absolutely nothing."

He stopped eating, dropped his fork on the side of his plate and said, "You're my soul mate, the only true love I've ever known. There are times when what I feel for you nearly overwhelms me."

"Darling… Oh, Reid, you don't know how deeply you've touched me."

He stood, but at that moment the doorbell rang. "Damn the lousy timing! Who the hell can that be?"

He opened the door, and his heart plummeted to the pit of his belly. "What the… What are you doing here?"

"May I come in?" She pushed her hair away from her face, let her bottom lip drop slightly and looked at him from slightly lowered lashes. "I came all the way from Baltimore just to see you."

"I'll bet you did. Same old Myrna." He laughed, realized that he enjoyed it and let the laughter pour out of him. "Looks as if you've had some experience at selling your…self. You've been reading the *Maryland Journal,* too. Well, babe, there's nothing you can do for me." He slammed the door shut, leaned against it and let himself breathe.

"Who was that woman?"

"My ex-wife. This is the first time I've seen or heard from her since she told me that poverty wasn't her style. The news of my contracts with Reginald English and my consultancy with Marks and Connerly was reported in the *Maryland Journal,* and she wasted no time getting here."

"What for? Isn't your divorce final?"

"It's been final for almost seven years, but this is her style. She plans to lie herself back into my life, but there isn't a chance of that. Not if she was the last woman alive on this earth."

"Oh, I believe you."

"Yes, and what a moment for her to barge in." He couldn't get back into the mood that Myrna had interrupted. That was a time different from any he had ever experienced, and he knew that a minute later he would have sunk to his knees and asked Kendra Rutherford to be his wife and the mother of his children. He gazed down at her, and her forlorn expression told him that she knew it, too.

"It was wonderful," she said, "but it's getting late, and I'm tired. I think I'll be going."

She didn't succeed in hiding her disappointment, and as desperately as he longed to, he couldn't give her the reassurance she needed. The very sight of Myrna had destroyed any tenderness that had resided in him.

"I'll take you home." He held her hand as they walked through the alley to her house. "This was a terrible time for her to show up," he said as they stood at Kendra's back door. "All of my anger and distaste for her resurfaced, ruining my mood and my disposition."

She focused on the bit of floor between them. "I know, and I sure hope you get over it soon. When you came back to me, it was like having a bucket of cold water dashed into my face. It's over between you, so please let it lie, Reid."

"I'll try. I won't give her the power to blot out my happiness."

He bent to kiss her, and while she put her arms around him, she didn't part her lips, for she was no better at pretending than he. "I love you," he whispered, and left her.

It didn't surprise him that when he arrived in the lobby of the building in which he lived, Myrna waited for him. If she had been less tenacious, he probably would not have married her. "What do you want with me?" he roared, anger billowing from him like smoke from a chimney.

"Can't we talk? I've been looking for you for the longest time. I wanted you to know how sorry I was, and that I made the biggest mistake of my life."

"Yes, it was, wasn't it? Whose Jaguar are you driving around in these days? And where's all that gold and those diamonds I bought you? You never used to leave the house without them. What happened? Did you pawn it? It's interesting that you didn't find me until I was out of the ditch, until you read that I had a multimillion-dollar contract. Well, you listen to this. You have spent the last one of my pennies that you will ever spend. You are wasting your time, and I don't intend to allow you to waste mine."

She sidled up to him and put her hands on his chest. "You don't mean it. There's no way you could forget how I used to tie you into knots in bed."

He allowed himself a laugh that had the sound of a snarl. "What a joke! You're not even in the league with some women, and remove your hands. It would give me

the greatest pleasure to slap you, so don't tempt me."
He brushed her aside and went into his apartment wondering what he'd ever seen in her.

He didn't need her back in his life, and he wondered
if her arrival bore a relationship to the timing of his
upcoming case against Brown and Worley. Somehow,
he doubted it, but it paid to be forewarned. Suddenly,
something akin to fear sent an electric-like charge
shooting through him. Where did Myrna live? She had
probably seen him go out of the building with Kendra,
and she knew that he didn't go far, and she had waited
to see whether he would return home that night. Damn
her! He threw off his clothes on the way to the shower.
She'd eaten holes in him when his world fell apart, but
she had no power over him now. The knowledge made
his whole being glow, and as he showered he whistled,
"When the Saints Go Marching In," dried off and slid
his naked body between the sheets.

Kendra sat on the side of her bed musing over her
relationship with Reid. Maybe it wasn't meant for her
to have a man like Reid: a loving, caring man willing
to share life with her on an equal footing, a brilliant man
with whom she could express herself fully and freely
without being accused either of being highfalutin' or of
"talking down." Just when she thought he would get
down to business, his ex-wife torpedoed his mood and
the occasion.

She got ready for bed, but she knew she wouldn't
sleep. After wrestling with the sheets for half an hour,
she sat up and dialed Reid's number. "You mean you

were asleep?" she asked when she detected grogginess in his voice.

"Yes. I guess I was. Why? Can't you sleep?"

"Not so far."

"I'm sorry, sweetheart. Myrna busted up a precious evening. Promise me you won't let her turn you against me."

"She couldn't do that, but she can cause strain in our relationship. She did that tonight. I want her to go back to wherever she came from, but I have a feeling she'll be around for a while."

"Not with any encouragement from me, she won't. I don't want her or any woman but you, and I want you to write that down. Do you love me?"

"Oh, yes."

"Then no one can get between us. What are you doing in the morning?"

"I think I'll go to church. Something tells me I'm going to need all the support I can get." They talked awhile longer, but in spite of his reassurances, daybreak found her trying to get the first minute of sleep. She promised herself to go to bed as soon as she returned from church. However, Reid had other plans for them.

She had been asleep less than an hour that Sunday afternoon when he called her. "How about riding over to Caution Point with me this afternoon to the building I designed for Marcus? He's practically dancing a jig because the local paper wrote that the building adds to the city's beauty and personality."

"I thought you said it was a factory."

"That's true," Reid said, "I didn't design the exterior

to resemble a factory, but a golf clubhouse, or some such thing."

She walked down the alley and entered Reid's apartment by the door leading to his garden. "I'm parked in the garage," he told her, "so we can take the elevator down and get the car there. It's very convenient when the weather's bad."

Or, she thought, when she didn't want to be seen leaving or entering his building. But when the elevator door opened, Myrna stepped off. "Oh, there you are," she said, ignoring Kendra. "I was just going to ask if you wanted to come up to my place for coffee and some of those cranberry popovers I always made for you that you loved so much."

"I'm sure that if I ate one of them or anything else you cooked, I'd be sick to the stomach within minutes. Excuse us." He took Kendra's hand, brushed past his former wife and closed the elevator door. "I see she's planning to be a pain in the ass."

"Why didn't you introduce us?"

"Because she would have converted that into a moment of triumph. She never passes up an opportunity to advertise herself."

In Caution Point, Marcus met them at the factory. "Hello, Kendra. I'm so glad to see you again," he said. "Reid has made me something of a celebrity in Caution Point. Would you believe one woman asked me if I would rent her the north end of the building for her daughter's wedding reception?"

"Did you?"

"I was tempted, but Amanda said that if I did that

I'd have to rent it to every person who asked or I'd make enemies. And a businessman doesn't need enemies. Do you have time to stop by the house? Amanda's made a slew of apple turnovers, and those things just melt in my mouth."

As Kendra had suspected, Amanda had prepared more than apple turnovers, and invited them to a wonderful late-afternoon meal.

"My mother is the best cook in the world," Amy said to Kendra. "Everything she cooks is good. I'm not going to learn to cook, because then we wouldn't eat her cooking. We'd eat mine."

"I don't think we have to worry about that for a few years yet," Marcus said to his daughter, his eyes beaming with obvious love.

Kendra couldn't help remembering her first impression of that family as a unit where a very deep love abided. When she and Reid were en route home, she told him as much. "It's true," he said. "She gave Marcus and his daughter so much love that he fell head over heels for her. He practically worships her. They have three children, one of his, one of hers and one of theirs, but no one would guess that all of those children didn't come from Amanda and that Marcus isn't their father."

"She told me that she was forty when she met Marcus, and I found that very encouraging."

"Say some prayers," Reid said, and she wondered what he meant, though she didn't want to ask. "Our day will come, and soon, I hope."

So do I, she thought, and decided to move the subject away from herself. "That building looks like a beautiful, oversized country cottage," she said of Marcus's factory. "Yet he said it's everything he's ever wanted in a factory."

"I'm glad he's so pleased. It does enhance its neighborhood, but I wasn't thinking of that when I designed it."

She saw Myrna as soon as they turned onto Albemarle Heights. "Look at that," she said to Reid. "It looks as if she's pitched camp right here on Albemarle Heights."

"Who?"

"Myrna. Isn't that her in that pink miniskirt?"

"Yeah. That's Myrna. I wouldn't put anything past that woman if she thinks she can worm something out of me. I wonder where she's staying." He parked in front of the apartment building, cut the motor and waited. "Myrna eventually shows her hand. She's up to something, and I want to know what it is."

Don't bother to get angry, she told herself, although anyone well acquainted with her would have known from her deep breathing and narrowed eyes that she was fuming. Myrna walked directly to the car.

"I see you're back," she said. "I was wondering when you could go over our divorce papers with me. There seems to be something irregular."

He got out of the car, walked around and opened the passenger door for Kenya. "Your papers are identical to mine, and there is nothing irregular in my papers. If you'd like, I'll have the district court judge review my papers and let you know if they contain any irregularities. Are you still Myrna Pickett?" She nodded, but Kendra could see that she'd become less assured. "The judge will mail you the result. What is your address?"

"Uh…right here… Same as yours. I sublet apartment 5R."

His eyes narrowed, and she thought his cheeks began swelling. "Don't ever knock on my door again," he said, "and if you're smarter than you used to be, you'll stay away from me."

"There's not one thing irregular about my divorce papers," he said to Kendra. "She thought she'd trick me into going to her apartment."

"I'll look them over and send her a letter if you wish."

"If she persists, I'll ask you to look at them."

"If she persists with this annoying behavior, you can get a restraining order. In fact, you should indict her for harassment."

"I'd hate to do that. I'd rather find some other way of calling her off. She's pathetic. Besides, a court case at this point would call the attention of Brown and Worley to my presence here. They know I'm here, but in a trial of that sort, I'd have to lay out all my business. Brown and Worley are not yet aware of some of my crucial plans, and I want them to get some surprises."

"When will that airline terminal in Caution Point open?"

"Not until next year. The builders have completed the structure, but the interior fittings will take a while."

"I can't wait to see it."

"Does that mean you'll go to the opening with me?"

"Of course I will, if you ask me. I may call you later. I have to study a couple of cases that are on my docket for tomorrow morning. Thanks for the pleasant afternoon and the visit with the Hicksons."

"Any time I spend with you is precious time," he said.

At that moment, she glanced toward the front door and saw that Myrna sat with legs crossed in the lobby waiting for Reid. *Oh, what the hell?* she said to herself. *Let him handle her.*

Reid followed Kendra's gaze, saw his ex-wife waiting for him in the lobby of the apartment house, got back into his car and drove into the garage. Aware that she couldn't see the elevator from where she sat in the lobby, he managed to circumvent her, went into his apartment and flopped into the chair nearest to the door. *Please, God, don't let her make me lose my temper. When I think of the pain that woman caused me...*

He jumped up and raced to the phone, thinking that Kendra was his caller. "Hey, man," he said to Philip. "What's up?"

"Where's that ebullience you've had since things developed with you and Kendra?"

"Don't ask me, man. I opened my door a few nights ago, and who's standing there but the Wicked Witch of the North. And the worst of it is that she sublet an apartment in the building I live in. She wants back in, and it will never happen."

"You mean your ex-wife? Get rid of her! She'll ruin your relationship with Kendra. Found an office yet?"

"Nothing's going to interfere with my relationship with Kendra if I can help it, but Myrna will definitely try. I've found an office in Edenton, about twenty-five minutes from here by car, but I'll work out of my apartment until I can renovate it and furnish it. How's everybody there?"

"Fine. This is the best time of the year here."

They spoke for a short time and promised to stay in touch.

In spite of his considerable efforts to avoid her, Myrna managed to appear whenever Kendra was in his apartment or when she was with him in the vicinity of the building in which he lived. He concluded that Myrna spent her days and half of her nights monitoring his comings and goings. He also concluded that Kendra was near the breaking point, for they had no privacy; whenever they were alone in his apartment, Myrna rang the doorbell. If he didn't answer it, she achieved her goal of disturbing them nonetheless. When they were in Kendra's house, the telephone would ring, and when Kendra answered, the caller would hang up.

"I think I'll go visit Claudine," Kendra said one evening, when she'd become exasperated.

"I know it's wearing on you," he told her. "It's still too cool to go to Cape May, but if you can take Friday off, maybe we could spend a long weekend down at the estate. It's beautiful there this time of year."

"I'd like that. It's not a solution by any means, but at least we can enjoy being together."

"Myrna's like a leech," he told Philip that Thursday night as they sat together at the edge of the pool. "She has no pride. She'll suffer any insult in order to get back into my good graces. She's insufferable, and she's going to force me to indict her for harassment."

"You should have done that already." Philip held up his left hand, palm out. "I know you think it's unseemly to mistreat a woman who was once your wife, but you're not required to be a gentleman with anyone who behaves as your ex does. If you'd marry Kendra, your problem would be solved."

"Yeah, I've thought about that. Indeed, I was within minutes of asking her when Myrna knocked on my door that first time. Seeing that treacherous woman destroyed my mood. In fact, it ruined what had been a perfect evening."

Philip let his toes dangle in the pool. "Are you ever going to ask Kendra to marry you?"

"I'm a cautious man, Philip. I've learned that nothing is certain but death. I have a fantastic contract and consultancy. The consultancy alone would take care of me and a family for several years, if I didn't get foolish with money. But I haven't seen one penny of this sudden wealth. I want Kendra to know that I'm solvent, able to give her the home she wants and where she wants it."

"You were solvent as an assistant architect with Marks and Connerly. Surely, you are not going back to the three-car-garage style?"

"No. I couldn't stand myself if I did. Besides, Kendra wouldn't tolerate such conspicuous consumption."

"I didn't think so." Philip dove into the pool, swam its length and got out on the other end where Kendra was talking with Arnold, his father.

"I was just telling Kendra that she isn't her usual ebullient self," Arnold said to Philip.

Philip patted her hand. "Go slowly, Kendra. Reid was just telling me of his problems with his ex, and he's worried mostly about how it affects you."

"I'm thinking of putting in a request for my vacation. What I need is a long respite from this. It's getting to me."

"It's only as bad as you let it be," Philip said. "She won't get Reid, and she can only achieve her other goal if you let her. She doesn't plague you with anonymous phone calls because she wants Reid. She does that to drive a wedge between you."

"Right," Arnold said, "and this is the wrong time to take a vacation unless you and Reid take a vacation together. And he can't, because he's assuming new responsibilities just now. We saw him close-up day in and day out for six years, Kendra, and I'll tell you he's a man worth any woman's investment. That's what his ex-wife learned after she walked out on him, and it's why she's tucked in her pride and is trying to get him back."

Philip's smile seemed almost sorrowful when he said, "It isn't for nothing that he's my best friend, Kendra. He's my best male friend, the closest friend I've had in my thirty-eight years. That ought to tell you something. He loves you, and I can see that you love him. Myrna left him when he was in trouble and needed her desperately. He needs you with him now. I won't say more."

"But you shouldn't forget, either," Arnold cautioned, "that you're a prize for any man, and it won't hurt to find subtle ways of reminding him. I'm telling you what I would tell my daughter. You're loving well, but don't forget to love wisely."

"Thanks, Arnold. I appreciate your concern." She looked at Philip. "You were blessed to grow up with such a wonderful father."

"Reid's sitting over there alone, which means he's in deep thought. I'm going over there." She discarded her first inclination, which was to swim the length of the pool, decided that she didn't want wet hair and strolled along the side of the pool, slow and leisurely, to give him time to enjoy the sight of her walking toward him bedecked in the tiniest of bikinis.

He stood as she neared him. "You know how to give a guy the sweats," he said, exposing his white teeth in a wicked smile. "Why don't I get us a couple of margaritas and let's drink them in your room?" The smile had been replaced by an intense gaze that she recognized as a reflection of raw need. And as he stared, desire blazed hotter and hotter in his eyes.

She heard the awkward, scared tumble of her heartbeat. "Oh, darling," she said, leaning against him. "Do we really need the margaritas?"

He sucked in his breath, apparently unable to answer, and merely grasped her hand and headed for her room. She pushed the door open, and he picked her up, stepped in and kicked the door shut. "Shouldn't we lock it?" she asked him.

"Nobody's coming in here tonight," he said, and set her on her feet, threw back the bedcovers and stood staring at her. "It's been so long since I was inside you that I…I need you so badly, and I'm afraid I'll mess things up. It may not work for you the first time, but trust me, I'll make it right later."

"I don't want finesse, love, and I don't need skill. All I want is to climb that mountain where you always carry me and to come alive in your arms." She let her hands slide down to his swimming briefs and inch toward the target but not touch it. He dragged her swimming top over her head, pitched it aside and locked her body to his. She parted her lips and he plunged into her, twirling and dipping, kissing her as if he'd been starved for the taste of her.

She put his left hand on her breast. "I need to feel your mouth on me."

He bent his head, sucked her nipple into his mouth, pulling and feasting like a hungry man. She sank her hands into his briefs and pressed his buttocks to her, wiggling against him for the friction she needed.

He stopped kissing her and gazed down at her, his eyes pools of brown heat. "Do you want me?"

She squeezed his buttocks. "You know I do."

He picked her up, placed her on the bed, and rolled the bikini bottoms over her hips. She lifted her body toward him, unable to control it, and he tumbled onto the bed.

"Woman, you do something to me." He locked an arm around her shoulder and brushed kisses on her forehead, eyes and cheeks before he inserted his tongue between her lips and began stroking and pinching her nipple. She didn't want all of that; she wanted him inside her.

"Get in me, honey," she moaned. "I'm just as starved for you as you are for me."

But that seemed to heighten his determination to do it his way. Her body stiffened when his tongue began swirling around in her navel, for she knew what would come next. He parted her legs and let her feel the tip of his tongue.

"Oh, Reid," she screamed as his marauding tongue began to knock her senses into disarray. He stilled her swaying hips with his hands and let his educated tongue drive her to within a minute of climax.

"I can't stand it," she moaned. "Please, honey, let me have it."

"I will." He licked his way up her body, handed her a condom, put his head on her breast and whispered, "Can you take me in now?"

She pulled up her knees, put the condom on him, buried him into her, and he began to move. Almost at once, her thighs started trembling, heat pelted the bottom of her feet, the squeezing and pumping in her vagina took possession of her and she sank into a vortex of ecstasy.

"Are you all right?" he asked her.

"Yes. Oh, yes."

"Oh, baby!" he shouted, and as zonked on him as she was, she could nevertheless feel his complete surrender as he collapsed in her arms.

He didn't know how much time had passed, and he still couldn't harness his strength. Slowly, he raised himself up and looked down at the woman who had the power to bring him to his knees.

"Kendra," he said, startled. "Why are you so…so solemn, sweetheart? I was sure you had an orgasm. What's wrong?"

"I don't know. It's just… I don't believe that shacking up makes sense, and even if it did, it's not suitable for a female judge in a small town. But we can't even be together in peace once in a while. I have a house, and you have an apartment, but we have to go out of town if we want to make love. And then, we always have to be so careful not to get me pregnant."

"Do you want to get pregnant?"

"No. I want to have children, and I think you would make a wonderful father for them. If I could have that without getting pregnant, I wouldn't hesitate for a second."

He couldn't help laughing. When Kendra got testy, she didn't force you to imagine it. She put it right there in your face.

"I know it isn't easy, but if you'll have confidence in me, we should be over this by autumn. I want to spend my life with you, I refuse to ask you for a commitment until I have something to offer you. Right now I have only promises. And as long as I'm charged with negligent behavior as a result of that collapsed building, I don't consider it appropriate to ask you to marry me."

"So if you lose the case, I can go to hell? Is that it?"

"Of course not, but wouldn't it be the end of my career? By opening this case, I'm taking a chance."

"I don't want to hear that. You are going to win it. Oh, Reid. I'm so happy when we're together like this."

"You're the one who said we shouldn't be seen consorting before that trial, and it makes sense. It's only a little while longer, sweetheart." She bit his lip gently, and he felt himself harden again within her.

"Any more where that came from?" he asked her. She nodded, and he drove them to ecstasy.

"You light up my life," he told her later. "I'm going

downstairs and get those margaritas and some sand-wiches. Sex makes me hungry."

"I thought you said you were starved for me," she said and flipped over in the bed. "Hurry back, and be sure and get plenty of sandwiches. I've got some more work for you to do."

"Yeah? I'll make fast tracks." He knew his face was one big grin. Nothing made a guy feel bigger than to know that his woman wanted him. He was going to double his prayers for success with that trial. God help him if he lost.

Chapter 11

She had hardly been able to bear the joy of being with Reid, of having his loving arms envelop her as if she were the most precious being in the world. Her heart beat as if it wanted to dance out of her chest. If only she could be with him always!

She rolled out of bed and headed for the shower, singing as she went. For the first time in her life, she'd spent an entire night wrapped in the arms of a man she loved. As the water cascaded over her body, she had a sudden feeling that she might drown. But even after she stumbled out of the shower, a sense of apprehension plagued her. She couldn't understand why, after such a precious night with Reid, she felt threatened and un-characteristically insecure.

Never one to bathe herself in sadness, she lectured

herself. "You're being silly, girl. Button it up. You've got a man who adores you and about whom you're nuts. What more could you, a forty-year-old spinster, want?"

She stopped suddenly, midway on the stairs. Wasn't that the problem? She was forty, a big-shot judge whom people admired and respected, but who else was she? She didn't really have Reid, and maybe he would never truly be hers. And although she had a lovely house, she didn't have a home: no children ran up and down the stairs and around the house calling for mama, and Reid did not slide into her bed every night and fold her into his arms. Worse, maybe he never would. She willed herself to continue down the stairs, walk into the breakfast room and smile.

It soothed her only a little that Reid rose from the table, went to meet her, put both arms around her and greeted her with a kiss. She held him to her with such strength and enthusiasm that he stepped back and regarded her with raised eyebrows.

"Are you all right?"

"Super," she lied. "I couldn't be better." She smiled at the others who had already begun eating. "Good morning, everybody. Looks as if we're going to have a great day."

Both Arnold and Philip eyed her quizzically, but she ignored their skepticism and did her best to change whatever impression she'd given them, smiling when she didn't want to and laughing at remarks that weren't clever or witty.

She made it through most of the day, but her pretense had begun to wear on her.

"Would you like to go for a ride?" Reid asked her in the midafternoon, in what she perceived as concern for her.

She caught herself just before shrugging her shoulders, for she knew that indicating disinterest would exacerbate his worries about her odd behavior. "It's too hot to take the horses out, and considering that long trip back, a car ride doesn't seem attractive right now."

His gaze seemed to penetrate to her very depths, a strobe invading the distant darkness. "Something isn't right," he said, "and it's been that way all day. It seems to me that, after last night, you should be bubbling with happiness. But you're not—you're miserable. I've never seen you this way."

Kendra knew that her behavior had to cause Reid anxiety, for he was, if anything, a very perceptive man, and she wanted to comfort him. She leaned against him and rested her head against his chest, murmuring, "Don't worry, darling. I'm just tired. One thing is certain. I love you more than ever."

He clasped her to him and stroked her head, shoulders and back, but the twitch in his jaw, the unfamiliar, steel-like clutch of his fingers on her left shoulder and his jagged breathing belied the calm that he sought to express. Tension still gripped him.

"I…think I'll take a nap," she told him. "By dinnertime, I should be fit as a fiddle."

He walked with her toward her room. "That may be a good idea." At her room door, he said, "Kiss me, sweetheart, and don't pour it on thick."

How could she tell him that, even after a night of

loving, she needed the real thing, not a sample? She sucked his tongue into her mouth and prepared herself to enjoy her rising passion and to enjoy the sudden bulge of his sex against her belly, but he broke the kiss.

"Let's postpone that until after dinner, sweetheart. Since you don't want to go riding, I'd like to help Philip with something, and this seems like a good time. Okay?"

She kissed his cheek. "Of course. I'll see you around six-thirty."

Although she tossed in bed for nearly three hours, she was not able to sleep for one minute. Tired and exasperated, she dressed and decided to stroll around the estate. Perhaps if she exhausted herself physically, she would fall asleep that night. She left the house through the kitchen, stepped out on the deck and took a deep breath of the late-afternoon air. A soft breeze pushed her hair away from her face, and the perfume of roses from Doris's garden filled the air.

She walked toward the fields, thinking that with not a single human being or animal in sight, it was as if she were the lone individual in a world of green trees, flowering plants and abundant crops. It hadn't occurred to her that the property would be deserted on a Saturday afternoon when the workers had time off. As she passed one of the barns, she picked up a stick and continued toward the river.

The ocean, lakes, rivers and streams always gave her a feeling of serenity and peace. Anticipating a few minutes of calm and peace by the river, she quickened her steps. After half an hour, the distance to the river seemed much farther than when she had ridden there by horseback with Reid. An hour elapsed, and she stopped walking and leaned against the stick that she had picked up by the barn.

Perhaps the river was just beyond that little thicket, so she struck out in that direction. However, she soon discovered she hadn't entered a small thicket, but a forest. Worse still, darkness encroached. What was she to do?

"I've been phoning Kendra for the last half hour to let her know we're having pre-dinner drinks," Doris told Reid, "but she doesn't answer. She can't be in the shower that long unless she's trying to turn herself into a prune. And that phone in her room rings loud enough to wake the dead. Maybe you'd better go up and see if she's all right. I didn't like the way she acted this morning."

Neither had Reid. "I'll run up and see if she's awake." When she didn't answer his persistent knock, he opened the door and went in.

"Kendra!" After calling her several times and determining that she was not in the room, Reid ran down the stairs and into the family room where Philip, his father and Max sat with Doris drinking wine, beer, a margarita or lemonade, according to their choice.

"Kendra isn't in her room." He didn't bother to minimize his concern. "Did any of you see her?"

No one had. "Maybe she went for a walk," he said as alarm settled over him. "Philip, do you mind if I take Casey Jones and canvass the place for her?"

"That's a good idea. I'll saddle Mountain, and we'll go in different directions."

"Right," Max said. "Count me in."

He appreciated their help, but knowing that he had it didn't ease his disquiet. He didn't know what he'd do if he lost Kendra.

They rode out past the strawberry patches to the grazing land and stopped. "Let's check back at this point every fifteen minutes," Philip said.

"All right. She loves the water," Reid told them. "Maybe she went to the river." He headed for the stream beyond the thicket, and his heart plummeted when he didn't see her there. He rode Casey Jones up and down the riverbank for several miles in each direction, didn't see her and headed back to the checkpoint, praying that he'd see her there with either Max or Philip.

"I went all the way down to the ravine," Philip said. "I can't understand it."

"She wasn't on Bunker Road, either," Max said, running his fingers through the few strands of blond hair left on his head.

"She must have gotten lost." He looked around as dusk settled in and told himself not to panic. "It's almost dark. You two go back to the house and eat your supper. I have to find her."

"You're not serious?" Philip snorted.

"We go back when you do," Max said. "I sure hope she didn't wander into the woods."

"Right," Reid said, "and she could have if she was looking for the river." He turned Casey Jones around and headed for the woods. Reid remembered that Casey hated traveling after dark, so he lit the way with his flashlight. When he reached the edge of the woods, he called her name.

"Kendra. Kendra, where are you? Answer me, Kendra." If only he'd thought to bring a foghorn. "Kendra!"

He pulled his horse to a stop. Either he heard his name, or he had begun to hallucinate.

"Reid!" This time, he knew he heard it.

"Kendra. Keep calling me. Keep on yelling. I'll find you, sweetheart." He turned Casey Jones in the direction from which the sound of her voice came and eased the horse along slowly so that the horse's hooves would not drown out her voice.

"Reid!" The sound was closer now, close enough that he could hear the fright and unease that it communicated, and he had to force himself to go slowly.

If I can't see her, maybe she can see me, he thought, and aimed the flashlight around, lighting a semicircle, hoping that she would see it and gain comfort from it.

"Reid!" Her voice was so close now.

"Are you all right? Don't move."

"Where are you?" she screamed. "I can't find you."

He realized that she was behind him, turned and directed the flashlight to the trunk of a tree, and mercifully the light caught her walking away from him. He jumped down from his horse and rushed toward her.

"Kendra! Baby, are you all right?"

She turned, ran to him, and he grabbed her, locked her in his arms and sobbed into her hair. "Kendra.

Sweetheart! I thought I'd lost you." He held her and rocked her as tears cascaded down his cheeks. He didn't know how long he stood, deep in the dark woods, holding her in his arms. It could have been a few minutes or half an hour.

"Reid," she said, her voice barely a whisper. "Oh, Reid, I was so scared. All these strange noises, and I was afraid of wild animals."

"I know you were, and for good reason. Let's get out of here."

He didn't tell her that the rustling leaves, the sounds of breaking sticks and the strange conversations of the night animals would have unnerved him if he'd been lost. He took her hand and, with the flashlight to guide him, found his way back to Casey Jones, whose snort amounted to a message that, although he'd waited, he hadn't done so with patience.

Reid put Kendra in the saddle and mounted behind her. He didn't worry about finding his way out of the woods, for Casey Jones always knew the way home. A sense of brotherly love and deep gratitude pervaded him when he reached the checkpoint and saw Max and Philip waiting.

"She lost her way," he said, knowing that both men would accept the simple truth without prodding for reasons.

Philip took out his cell phone and called Doris. "Kendra was lost in the woods. Reid found her, and we'll be home in a few minutes." Arnold had alerted two of the workers who awaited them at the barn to relieve them of the burden of grooming their horses.

"Thank God, you're safe," Doris said to Kendra, but even as Kendra acknowledged the end of the danger, she stood before them rubbing and wringing her hands as if in despair. Doris draped her arm across Kendra's shoulders. "Do you want time to freshen up before supper? I'll bet a drink wouldn't hurt you a bit, either."

"Thanks, Doris. I would like to freshen up. It won't take but a few minutes."

"I'll go up with you," Reid said. "I need to wash up, too." When he emerged from his room twenty minutes later, he saw her standing outside her room door wearing a yellow sundress, and she would never know how happy the sight of her made him.

"You look so pretty," he said, "but right now you'd look pretty to me wearing a tow sack. I died many times since the sun went down this evening."

"I'm sorry I caused you so much worry, Reid. I only wanted to sit by the river for a few minutes."

"It's all right. I want to hold you so badly, but I don't trust myself to touch you because they're waiting for us."

She walked ahead of him, almost unable to believe that she was at last in a modern, well-lit house, and that she no longer feared ravishment or injury by a wild animal or a poisonous insect. She had always hated the darkness. At dusk, an automatic switch turned on a light in her foyer, and she slept with a night-light in her bedroom and bathroom. Since early childhood, darkness had been her nemesis.

At the foot of the stairs, she stopped and waited for Reid. "I was scared," she told him, "but I knew you wouldn't rest until you found me, and knowing that comforted me."

He took her hand and squeezed it, communicating to her the tenderness he felt, a silent symbol of what he felt in his heart.

Very little alcohol was consumed in the Dickerson household, so it startled Kendra to see Philip drink two margaritas before supper.

"Philip hasn't settled down yet," Arnold told Kendra. "You scared the insides out of him and all the rest of us."

"I won't wander off like that again," she said, "unless I tell someone where I'm going. I wanted to sit by the river, and I thought I remembered the way."

"You're here with us now," Arnold said, "and that's what matters."

Philip raised his glass. "Yes, indeed. That's behind us now, thank God."

At dinner, no one seemed to have a hearty appetite. It was as if their fears for Kendra's safety had depleted the energy needed for consuming and digesting food. Kendra suspected that hunger would attack her later, so she forced herself to eat. As he finished toying with dessert, eating little of it, Reid looked at her with a question in his eyes that she could not misunderstand.

She stood. "I'm wrung out. I think I'll call it a night."

"Wait for me," Reid said.

"What time are you leaving tomorrow?" Philip asked Reid.

"Shortly after twelve or thereabouts," he replied, his tone suggesting the vagueness of his words. But anyone familiar with Reid knew that his thoughts were not on Philip's question, but on Kendra.

"There are a couple of bottles of white burgundy open over there," Philip said, pointing to the bar. "Take one with you."

Reid's face bore a half smile. How refreshing to be back among friends who neither postured nor pretended with each other! "Thanks, friend," he said, effectively admitting that sleep would not be his first order of business. He wrapped the bottle in a white towel, picked up two wineglasses and said, "Good night, all."

"I'm not leaving you tonight," he said to Kendra when they reached her door. "Not unless you put me out, and then I'll go kicking and screaming."

She opened the door, took his arm and walked in. "If you leave me, I'll have a very hard time forgiving you."

Eventually, he would demand to know why she had wandered off alone without telling him or anyone else where she intended to go, but she knew he wouldn't do that tonight. She opened her arms to him and hours later when, still locked inside her, he remembered the wine; it had reached room temperature and was too warm to drink.

"Come back any time," Philip told Reid as they prepared to leave just before one o'clock Sunday afternoon. "I confess it gets dull here when we don't have guests. Claudine will be here next weekend."

"I was surprised that you didn't have plans with her this weekend," Reid said.

"We would have been together either here or at her place, but she had an opportunity to attend a retreat for teachers of handicapped children. She has two handicapped kids in one of her classes, so I encouraged her to go."

"So it's still on," Reid said.

Philip stuffed his hands into his pockets and grinned. "Indeed it is."

Reid embraced his friends and headed back to Queenstown, but one question haunted him. "Are you going to tell me what made you so morose all day yesterday and why you needed to be alone? I figure you had to sort out things because you didn't invite me to go with you. I need the answer to this, Kendra."

She remained silent for a while, evidently formulating her answer, for she knew he would weigh every word she said. "I went to sleep happier than I had ever been, feeling that I had in you the love I've always needed and dreamed of but which, until now, always eluded me.

"I had it in the palm of my hand, and I was so happy that I could hardly contain my feelings. And then thoughts about the facts of our lives—yours and mine— intruded, crowding out all else. I thought of unsettled problems that can split us up, and I saw this wonderful love slipping through my fingers.

"Yes, I saw a fifty-fifty chance that what you and I are facing can wreck us, and as I've done for years, I tried to think, to reason and analyze my way out of our entanglements. But the more I reasoned, the more I despaired. You know the rest."

He drew in a deep breath and blew it out slowly. "And after last night, do you still believe anything can separate us?"

She leaned her head against the headrest, closed her eyes, and he could hardly breathe while he waited for her answer. "I know that nothing can make me stop loving you, but that's all I do know."

He slowed down and tried to shake off the words that had come to him like a blow on the head. *Better be careful here,* he told himself.

"It'll take me a while to digest that," he told her. "It's what you didn't say and what you probably are not going to say that's bothering me."

Kendra arose early Monday morning, went to her bedroom window to gaze at the Albemarle Sound and inhaled the fresh salty air. It seemed that each time she reached a new high with Reid, a letdown followed. When they had arrived home the previous evening after their weekend at Dickerson Estates, Reid didn't suggest that they prolong the evening. She wouldn't say he was withdrawn, but he was more pensive than she'd ever seen him. While she stood at the window, still wearing the teddy in which she slept, a burst of wind reminded her of her isolation in the dark woods adjoining the Dickerson Estates and of that minute when she was at last safe in Reid's arms.

"I can't let him out of my life," she said aloud. "Because of him, I'm a different woman, ripe with life and living. He's everything to me. I'll find a way. I have to."

She dressed, drank a cup of coffee and headed for work. As she turned the corner into Albemarle Heights, she nearly collided with Myrna.

"You're not driving today?" Myrna asked her.

"I don't drive to work," Kendra told her, aware that the woman knew who she was, what she did and where she worked. "Have a great day." She didn't want to walk along with Myrna, so she crossed the street, hoping that the woman wouldn't have the temerity to cross with her.

"'Morning, ma'am," Carl Running Moon Howard said as she walked into her chambers. "Have I got a dilly for *you!* A group called CFSL, Citizens for the Sacred Lands, have managed to bring suit against Brown and Worley, and it's on your docket for next Monday."

She gripped the back of her desk chair. "What did you say?" He repeated it.

"But doesn't the county clerk know that I moved out of Albemarle Gates?"

"Yes, ma'am, but Brown and Worley said you moved because of some problem with the house's structure, and that it was amicably settled. Their lawyer accepted you as trial judge without reservation."

"Thanks. Let me see the papers on it."

The case could tie up the court for weeks, and Reid would wait that much longer to clear his name. Life could be rough. As soon as she walked into her house after work that day, she called Reid. "Where are you?" she asked him.

"Home. I walked into my apartment ten minutes ago."

"I have some news that will interest you," she said.

"Good or bad."

"Time will tell. Right now, it's probably more good than bad. Where can we get together?"

"I can always walk over there."

"Good. See you in a few minutes." She made coffee, put some frozen hot cross buns in the oven and waited. As soon as she sat down and began to read the case of CFSL against Brown and Worley, she heard his knock and got up slowly, wondering how he would greet her.

He stared down at her for a minute, then locked her to his sweet and wonderful body and let his tongue find its home inside her mouth. It was she who broke the kiss. She took his hand and walked with him into the kitchen.

"Want some coffee?"

"Don't I always? I was about to make a cup of instant when the phone rang. What's the news?"

She poured the coffee into mugs, added milk to Reid's cup, removed the hot cross buns from the oven and put a plate of them on the table, all the while gaining time in which to frame her thoughts. She sat down, sipped the coffee, which she discovered that she didn't want, reached across the table and caressed his jaw.

"A citizen's group is suing Brown and Worley to stop them from building on those sacred lands across from the park. The case comes to court next Monday."

"Sounds good to me. What could be bad about it?"

"I don't know yet. I'm the judge."

"But how? You had a settlement with them over your house."

"Their lawyer told the county clerk that it was an amicable settlement, that I dealt fairly and that I was acceptable as judge for the case. Frankly, I'd rather not have anything to do with it."

"How long do you think the case will last?"

"That depends on the number of witnesses, and how long it takes to get together a jury. I'm concerned that this case will cause yours to be postponed."

"I certainly hope not. So much is riding on the outcome. I want it to be over as soon as possible."

"So do I." She passed the plate of hot cross buns to him.

"If you have any more buns for yourself," he said, "I'd like to take these home with me. I'll be up in Edenton all day tomorrow, and they'll come in handy."

"You'll be working there every day now?"

He nodded. "I'm my own man again with my own business and my own office. I have to find an office assistant, someone who'll serve as secretary, office assistant and girl Friday."

She cocked an eye and regarded him with a measure of skepticism. "Be sure that's all she serves as."

His features arranged themselves into a bright smile, displaying his charm and the sultriness that could make her heart palpitate. Then the smile disappeared. "At first I thought you were joking, but you haven't smiled. You're serious, aren't you?"

"If I appear serious, I'm serious. As I was on my way to work this morning, I encountered Myrna. She wanted to talk, but I got rid of her by crossing to the other side of the street."

"It wouldn't surprise me if she tried to make friends with you. Myrna's devious. I'd hoped that she'd given up and left Queenstown."

"As long as you're unattached, she'll think she has a chance, and she'll stay right here."

"She must believe in miracles," Reid said.

They talked for more than an hour, and at times she thought the tension between them would rise to a boiling point. He would stop talking in midsentence and stare at her not remembering what he had intended to say; his gaze would seem permanently focused on her breasts, and he would actually shake his body to free himself from their grip on him. Once, his eyes narrowed when she dampened her lips, though she hadn't done it as an act of seduction.

"I'd invite you to dinner," he said at last, "but after eating three of these buns, I won't be hungry for another hour and a half." He stood, leaned over her and bathed her lips with his tongue. She parted them and took him in, though she knew he hadn't intended to give her that pleasure. She wrapped six buns and walked with him to her back door.

"Let me know when you get over your annoyance with me. I'm getting tired of it," she told him.

"I imagine you are. I'll call you when I get in tomorrow," he said. "Tonight, I want to look over the contract Jack sent me." He kissed her quickly on the mouth and left.

When he gets ready, he'll tell me what the problem is, she told herself. *Who am I kidding? I know what I told him as we were driving home Sunday, and he's trying to protect himself from probable pain. But what's done is done. If he thought it inappropriate for me to judge CFSL versus Brown and Worley, shouldn't he question the propriety of my judging his case against anybody? There is no way I can be unbiased in that case against him, because my future depends on it.*

She made a shrimp salad sandwich, ate it and returned to her study of the case that she knew could attract national attention. She had no sympathy for Brown and Worley because they had deliberately bought the properties long held to be Native American gravesites, properties that were vacant only because other developers had shied away from them. Thus, it behooved her to know everything about the case in order to avoid leaning toward the Native Americans' cause.

On the morning that the trial was to begin, a day after completion of jury selection, the lawyer for the defense asked to see her alone in her chambers before the session began, but she refused, sending word that she would see both attorneys ten minutes before court convened. The defense lawyer had a reputation for toughness, but he'd better not let her see it; he'd find that she had the upper hand.

The lawyer for the citizens presented records for burials predating the American Revolution and witness after witness who related oral histories of the burials of their ancestors in that site and beneath Albemarle Gates. Most shed silent tears as they spoke, and she noticed that many in the audience also cried. Brown and Worley presented what appeared on the surface to be an airtight case, pointing to the need for housing at a fair price and for the continued development of a town once thought to be dying.

"Have you reached a verdict?" she asked jury fore-woman Reba Hollings—the second friend she'd made in Queenstown—on the sixth day of the trial.

"We have, Your Honor, and we find that the defendants, Brown and Worley, conspired to use and abuse land fraudulently obtained and to which they had no entitlement, that they owe restitution to individuals with families interred beneath Albemarle Gates, and that they have no right to build on any other sacred burial grounds."

She polled the jury, received no dissent. To Brown and Worley, she said, "Will the defendants please rise. You are hereby ordered to desist from building anything on a sacred Native American burial site anywhere within the area under this court's jurisdiction and to pay five thousand dollars to each descendant of an individual buried beneath Albemarle Gates."

She clapped her hands over her ears at the uproar from those in the audience. So loud was it that she thought her head would split. They rose as one, applauding, yelling and shouting her name. She wondered how they would have reacted if she had imposed ten thousand per person instead of five as she had originally planned to do. But when she remembered that thousands of people in the area had ancestors buried beneath Albemarle Gates, she had lowered the amount to five thousand dollars.

I pray it doesn't bankrupt them, she said to herself, *for Reid is surely going to charge them with defamation of character.*

"What's next on the docket?" she asked Carl Running Moon.

"Same old things, ma'am," he said as he rifled through papers on his desk. "Paternity suits, divorce, theft and more theft, wife abuse. Say, what's this?"

He removed a sheaf of papers from the bundle in his hand and studied them. "Looks like Brown and Worley will be back with us in two weeks."

Chapter 12

Kendra made her way to her chambers, exhausted and wishing for one of Philip's margaritas. She hadn't even hoped that the jury would bring in a verdict after one day's deliberation. Nor had she envisaged a recommendation for restitution, though she had hoped for that and believed it to be just.

"Congratulations, ma'am," Carl Running Moon said after she sat down at her desk. "These are for you from your staff." He handed her a vase of white roses. "We're all mighty pleased at the result of the trial and real proud of you. You stuck it to those guys. Almost half of this town has somebody buried under Albemarle Gates. The money won't compensate for the fact that we can't visit our loved ones and perform our ceremonies and rituals, but it will put bread in the mouths of many and help the local economy."

"I didn't think of that," she told him. "I levied those fines because I believed them to be just."

"Well, you're a hero, and your fame will spread far. This is the kind of justice we've been trying to get."

When she left the courthouse, she noticed the honking of horns, Old Glory waving from the hoods of a number of cars and small groups of people standing on the street talking and gesticulating. She put on her sunglasses and prayed that no one would recognize her.

As she entered her house, she heard the phone and raced to answer it.

"Hello."

"Judge Rutherford, I'm Minnie Canyon. Thank you on behalf of the Ossewendas of Wisconsin and all of my Native American brothers and sisters everywhere. You've set a great precedent, and we plan to make you an honorary Ossewenda. I hope you will come here for the ceremony."

"I'm honored, Ms. Canyon. Thank you so much. I only did what I knew was right."

Before an hour had passed, she received half a dozen calls from individuals who identified themselves as Native Americans, African-Americans and plain Americans in several states rejoicing in the outcome of the trial. "I had no idea this trial would generate such interest," she told one caller. "I am glad that so many people are pleased, and I thank you for your good wishes."

At last she answered the phone and heard Reid's voice. "Congratulations. I was listening to the radio as I drove home, and the announcer actually *sang* the verdict and the sentence. I'm proud of you, sweetheart. It would have been so easy to give them token punishment, but they will feel that deep in the pocket, where it hurts."

"Thank you, Reid. Your opinion of me matters more than that of any other person. I've had congratulatory calls from all over. Three tribes are making me an honorary member, and I'm going to the ceremonies, too, if it doesn't interfere with my work."

"I'm sure they'll arrange it to suit you. How about dinner at my place? We could go to a restaurant, if you'd rather eat out."

"Are you going to cook?" she asked him. "You've never eaten my cooking at my house except snacks or something sweet that goes with coffee. I'll fix dinner. Bring some white wine."

"A woman after my own heart. See you at seven-thirty."

"Don't I even get a kiss? You're getting stingy."

"You think so? Well, I sure as hell don't *feel* stingy." He made the sound of a kiss. "I'll fix that at seven thirty-one."

She had committed herself to giving Reid a decent meal, so she'd better get busy. She rummaged around in her deep freezer and found Atlantic salmon, shrimp and scallops. Her refrigerator vegetable crisper revealed asparagus and lettuce. She had lemons, eggs and sugar, and some tomatoes on the windowsill. If she had any potatoes, she could make a decent meal.

At ten minutes past seven, she stepped out of the shower, patted herself dry and went to her closet. "What the hell!" she said aloud. "I'm going for broke. I'm not letting him get away with trying his cool stuff on me." She put on her red bikini panties and stepped into her red silk jumpsuit, its halter top and plunging neckline guaranteed to activate the libido of a healthy man. The last time she'd worn it, she'd nearly gotten in to serious trouble. If she got into the same kind of trouble with Reid, the jumpsuit would have done its job. She combed her hair down, attached some long gold hoops to her ears, and sprayed perfume in strategic places. If he thought he'd see the judge when she opened the door, he was in for an awakening.

As she'd expected, the bell rang precisely at seven-thirty. When she opened the door, he gasped, and she let her grin tell him that he'd reacted as she'd hoped and planned. He picked her up and walked into the house with his arms around her and his tongue in her mouth.

When at last he released her, she asked him, "Don't you want any supper? Keep this up and the food won't be fit to eat when you finally get it."

He handed her a bag containing two bottles of white wine. "I'm taking whatever you give me any way you give it."

If that wasn't a loaded comment, she'd never heard one. "Have a seat in the dining room," she said, glad that she had planned for them to eat there and not in the tiny breakfast room, for he wore a suit, a dress shirt and tie. "You look very spiffy. Don't tell me you dress that way for work."

"Thanks for the compliment. I did when I worked at Marks and Connerly, but I had on Dockers, a T-shirt, and sandals all day today. I plan to keep a suit, shirt, tie, shoes and socks at my office to change into when I have appointments."

I'd have gotten what I want tonight without putting on this Sherman tank, her name for the sexy jumpsuit. *As it is, I can't lose.*

She served the first course, a mousse of scallops in a sauce of tomatoes, shallots, wine and dill, said grace and glanced up as if to get Reid's reaction. "If the remainder of the meal is anything like this mousse," he said, "I may never leave here."

"Thanks. I made a menu out of what I had in the house. Next time, I'll plan it properly."

He devoured the salmon that she'd baked in foil with lemon, herbed butter and paprika; the tiny steamed potatoes rolled in butter, lemon juice and minced parsley; steamed asparagus, a lettuce and red onion salad, followed by Gorgonzola cheese with crackers and then a lemon cognac soufflé.

"This is wonderful wine," she said as if she hoped to start a conversation, but his focus was on the food, and he'd forgotten the obligatory polite conversation.

"It is," he said. "This is one of my favorite cheeses. It's better with red wine."

"Really?" She got up, went to the kitchen and got a bottle of red wine. He watched her walk and thought his eyes would pop out. She knew she'd get to him in that getup, but she needn't have gone to the trouble; he was starved for her.

"We aim to please," she said, putting the wine on the table.

He poured wine into the glass she brought and raised it to her. "And please, you definitely do. Don't tell me you made a dessert," he said when she brought in the soufflé.

After consuming two helpings of the dessert, he got up, removed his jacket, kissed her on the mouth and said, "Go in the living room and play something cool, loud enough for me to hear it."

"But what about the neighbors?"

"Hang the neighbors. This is *my* night."

Reid cleared the dining-room table, put the dishes in the dishwasher, cleaned the pots, made the place as neat as he could and looked at his watch. Seventeen minutes. He figured she hadn't had time to cool off, but if she had, he knew how to heat her up.

In the downstairs bathroom—more of a half bath, since it didn't have a tub—he rinsed his mouth, freshened his breath, straightened his tie and rolled down his sleeves. *With this woman, a guy needs everything going for him or he can forget it.*

He slipped on his jacket, got two wineglasses and the second bottle of white wine and made his way to the living room. He stopped short at the sight of her bending over the CD player with her assets on display and her voluptuous body sending out signals like a powerful wireless. He told himself to slow down. He'd been keyed up ever since the door had opened and he'd gotten a look at her cleavage from a neckline that plunged almost to her navel.

"Hi," he said.

She straightened up and smiled in a way that suggested she hadn't seen him for a long time. He poured two glasses of wine and put one to her lips, and she sipped the wine without taking her gaze from his. Feeling is if he was about to be carried away, he drank the wine that she held to his lips, and its dazzling effects settled in his belly.

It isn't the wine, he told himself. *I'm getting drunk on her.* He took the wine from her hand and placed both glasses on the coffee table. "I want to dance with you." She raised her arms and placed her hands against his shoulders. "I want us to dance to our own music," he said as she moved against him while Luther Vandross sang "Here and Now."

He stopped dancing. "I'm in deep with you, Kendra. I believe you love me, but you're sending me all kinds of messages tonight. I…I feel as if I may not be able to contain what I'm feeling right now."

"As long as you love me, truly love me," she said, "I'll be happy."

And he didn't doubt that she would be the one who decided whether he truly loved her.

"You're so firmly planted in here," he said, pointing to his chest, "that I can't imagine my life without you."

She stepped closer, traced his left cheek with the palm of her right hand, pressed her lips to his and then parted them, sending a shock wave throughout his body. He plunged into her, aware that she meant him to hold back nothing. She sucked his tongue into her mouth, and he could feel her getting hotter as she began to move against him. He sampled every crevice of her mouth with his tongue until her breath started coming in short spurts, and she grabbed his hand and shoved it into the neckline of her dress.

He looked down at her exposed breast, and swallowed the liquid that had accumulated in his mouth. Lord, how he loved it! He sucked the nipple into his mouth, picked her up and carried her up the stairs to her bedroom while he suckled her. He got her out of the jumpsuit, threw back the covers and put her in bed.

"Let me help," she said, watching him undress.

"It wouldn't do for you to touch me right now, sweetheart. I'm starved to death for you, and the sight of you lying there in that scrap of red cloth isn't making me simmer down."

She reached over and stroked his penis. "Hmmm," she said, licking her lips.

"Like what you see?" he asked her, not trying to keep the grin off his face.

"Like it, and can't wait to get it."

He kicked off his shoes, didn't bother to pull off his socks and stood staring down at the treasure before him. She opened her arms in a gesture as old as women.

"Come here to me." He nearly fell into her embrace as she spread her legs in a familiar welcome. He put his arms around her and kissed her eyes and her forehead, praying that he wouldn't erupt.

"Honey, I don't need the finesse tonight. I just want to feel you moving inside me." She reached down to fondle him, but he moved his hips, thwarting her effort.

"You're not ready, and I don't want to hurt you," he said.

She held her breast. "Kiss me. You won't hurt me. You can't. I want…" He found her vulva with his fingers and let them work their magic until he knew she was ready for him. She took him in her hand, stroked and caressed him until he shouted aloud.

"Stop it, baby, or it'll be over."

She raised her body and took him in. *Home.* No other word described the feeling he got when he slid into her. Pure heaven was his. He rode her fast and furiously.

"Do you feel it coming? Am I in the right place? I can't last much longer the way you're swelling around me. Oh, Kendra!" And then he could feel her clutching and squeezing him. Screams poured out of her.

"I love you so much," she said.

He wanted to tell her how much he loved her and what she meant to him, but the words wouldn't come. He managed to breathe as he gave himself to her, gave himself as never before. "I'm yours. Only yours." With those words pounding in his head, he came apart in her arms.

She seemed weightless and lifeless in his arms, as if the experience had drained her, yet he knew her now, and understood that, after a quick recovery, she would be ready for more.

"How do you feel?" he asked her. "That was rather short. I know you had an orgasm, but was it complete?"

Her arms tightened around him. "It was wonderful. Why? Are you tired?"

He couldn't hold back the laugh. "No indeed, but I could use a bite of something."

"I know. Lovemaking always makes you hungry. There are some buttermilk biscuits with ham wrapped in aluminum foil in the oven. I'm sure they're still warm."

"Did you plan them for dinner and forget to serve them?"

"No. I planned them for you, 'cause I knew you'd get hungry."

He stared down at her, wishing he understood women, any woman. "How did you know we would make love?"

She locked her hands behind her head and purred as any sated feline would. "Because I planned it." He stared at her with what he supposed was a quizzical expression. "You don't think you're the only person who can get hungry, do you?" she said.

With no answer for that, he rolled out of bed, went to the kitchen, put the ham biscuits and wine on a tray and got back in bed. "You'd better have some of this, too," he told her. "You can't make love on an empty stomach. At least, I can't."

At a quarter to four the next morning, he sat on the side of her bed tying his shoes. She tightened her robe, poured the last of the wine into a glass and handed it to him. "I forgot to tell you something. My clerk said that Brown and Worley are on the court's docket for Monday after next."

He hardly believed his ears. "You forgot to tell me *that?* You've been with me nine hours, and you haven't remembered to tell me until now?"

"I don't know who the plaintiff is."

"And you didn't go to the trouble to find out?"

"I didn't want to appear overly interested."

"That's a weak excuse. Since you didn't know the answer, you could ask, and especially since you just judged a case against them. I wish you had waited and told me tomorrow. This isn't the ending I'd wish for to one of the most wonderful evenings of my life. I'll call you."

It hurt, and she suspected that the pain would deepen with the passing days. She hadn't asked Carl Running Moon for the name of the plaintiff in the Brown and Worley case because she knew. She walked into her chambers the next morning, found the file on her desk—Maguire versus Brown and Worley—and telephoned Reid.

"Hello, Kendra."

Well, she thought, *if he's feeling frost now, he'll probably freeze when he hears what I have to say.* "Hi. In the Brown and Worley case two weeks hence, you are the plaintiff."

"I know. My lawyer told me a few minutes ago."

"Reid, I'm going to recuse myself from that case."

"What did you say?"

"It would be improper for me to judge that case, Reid, and that's a matter that has worried me ever since we met. I am incapable of impartiality concerning something so important to you."

"I don't believe what I'm hearing."

"Please, Reid. I could be disbarred for judging your case, and besides, I have to live with myself."

"Why would you be disbarred? Nobody here in Queenstown knows about us but us."

"Myrna knows, and so does that architectural examiner…uh…Helligman. But if no one else knew, I know, and I have to respect myself. I'm sorry, Reid."

"Do what you have to do. I'll be seeing you."

She hung up and telephoned the county clerk. She would do most anything for Reid except compromise her integrity. He hadn't understood, and he'd walked. It hurt like hell, but it wouldn't kill her. She got through the day as best she could, fighting to focus upon the trials and to stave off images of Reid smiling, grinning, hot with desire and in the grip of orgasm.

She got home later than usual, for she had no reason to rush. Reid wouldn't call. The red light flashing on her answering machine didn't fool her, either. After checking, she returned her sister's call.

"How's it going?" she asked Claudine.

"Great, but I see things aren't so good with you. When did you ever ask me 'How's it going?' What's wrong?"

After Kendra's recitation, Claudine said, "He's upset because he has so much at stake. Too bad he can't see it your way. If I were you, I'd find ways to help him behind the scene."

"Oh, I plan to observe the trial, and I hope his lawyer will accept whatever suggestions I may have."

"That's the spirit. Years from now, you'll look back on this as a mere ripple in a pond."

"Please God you're right. I'm paying for his ex-wife's folly, but I'll get through this. Are you spending the weekend with Philip?"

"I'm going down Thursday night. I've applied for a teaching position in Princess Anne, and they want to interview me."

She let out a gasp. "Does this mean what I hope it means?"

"You know Philip can't move. His life is there. I'm sure I'll get the job. That man has so much clout that evidence of it continually shocks me. Kendra, everybody seems to love Philip. I haven't met anybody, from the local postal clerk to the mayor, who doesn't seem to admire him. Last Saturday, I went with him to a reception at the Naval Academy in Annapolis. He doesn't seem to know what a big shot he is."

"And, honey, let's hope he never learns."

"I think we'll probably get married around Christmastime. Doris is planning to barbecue two grown pigs. You and Reid had better get it together, because he'll be best man and you'll be maid of honor."

But they didn't get it together. On the Monday morning when the trial opened with the Honorable Judge Weddington presiding, Reid met Kendra in the courthouse lobby, nodded and kept walking. He had a good lawyer; she knew and had worked with Dean Barker, and now she shook his hand.

"I'd been hoping that you would try the case, Kendra, but I hear you recused yourself and stepped down. Mind if I ask why?"

"Reid is a personal friend, and I want to see him win."

"I see. Well, I'll take any hints you can give me. We have a pretty tight case, but the jury will be impressed with the fact that he lost this case earlier."

"I'll be taking notes, Dean." She took a seat in the rear of the court so as not to be conspicuous. Her belly twisted into a knot when Brown and Worley entered the court with Fred Emerson between them. Among unscrupulous lawyers, Emerson stood out.

Immediately, she sent Dean a note. "Reid's ex-wife is in town. Ask her to testify. She wants him back, so she won't lie."

Dean opened with a history of Reid's accomplishments and noted his deal with Reginald English and his consultancy with Mark and Connerly. "If it pleases the court, I'd like to read and file a registered architectural examiner's affidavit on the condition of Judge Kendra Rutherford's house and other cases in which structural damage was discovered in Brown and Worley's buildings."

In spite of that evidence, Kendra sensed that Dean did not have the jurors with him, and when Emerson began his attack on behalf of Brown and Worley, she got busy and asked for a meeting with Dean and Reid.

"Three of those jurors were witnesses for Brown and Worley in their case against CFSL a couple of weeks back," she said. "Have them thrown out. Reid, you should have Marks and Connerly—especially Jack Marks—testify on your behalf, also Philip and Arnold Dickerson, especially Philip. And Myrna? What happened to her?"

"She flew the coop as soon as Dean called her. Myrna couldn't pass muster if Emerson decided to expose her as a person without honor. She's gone for good," Reid said. Kendra tried not to show her delight, but the grin that brightened Reid's eyes told her that her solemnity hadn't fooled him.

Dean opened his cell phone and called Jack Marks. "This is Dean Barker, Reid Maguire's attorney. Would you be willing to testify on his behalf at the Brown and Worley trial that's now in progress?" He listened for a

minute. "Thanks. We hadn't thought we'd need witnesses, but the defense is playing hardball, so I have to
shore up our fences. Tomorrow morning. Many thanks.
Reid? All right, I'll tell him." He thanked the man and
hung up. "Reid, he wants you to call him."

"Another thing," Kendra said. "There's no law that
says you can't read Helligman's affidavit to the jury
again. Imprint it in their minds. Don't ask permission.
Just do it." She noticed how Reid observed her professional demeanor, all the while nodding in agreement.
"If I think of anything else, I'll let you know."

"Reid," she said as they left the lawyer's office, "have
you thought of writing out some relevant questions for
Dean to ask you? I mean questions about that building
that collapsed. You *are* going to take the stand, aren't
you? You'll make an immense impression, especially if
you wear what you wore to my house the night I fixed
dinner for you."

His eyes blazed hot with the fire of desire, and she
let her own eyes answer his in kind. "I'm going to take
your advice about this and everything else. I have to call
Philip, but I'll be in touch later."

She watched him as he headed for his car, his masculine swagger proclaiming who he was. Whether or
not he knew it, his sense of self did not depend on the
outcome of the trial; he didn't need the validation that
a victory would give him. And she hoped he would
realize that he had recovered his self-image and his
status as an architect without Brown and Worley having
been found guilty of incompetence.

"I'll look forward to it, Reid," she told him, and she

would. She'd had enough of sleepless nights and soggy pillows.

"You're helping me in spite of…of my ungraciousness," Reid said when he called her. "Why?"

"What a pity you feel you have to ask. I want you to win, and I don't love you less just because you were pigheaded."

"I suppose that's about as kindly a way as you could describe it. Trust me, I've paid for my pigheadedness a thousand times. You're one hell of a woman, Kendra. When this is over—"

She interrupted him. "Let's focus on winning this case, Reid. We can't afford to miss a single trick. Emerson is not a nice man, but he's a very clever lawyer, and after losing the case against CFSL, he doesn't plan on losing this one. Did you speak with Philip or Arnold?"

"Philip and Arnold will be here tomorrow around eleven. I'd like to see Emerson tie up with either of them."

As it happened, Jack Marks's testimony practically sealed the case in Reid's favor, for he testified that he had accepted a contract worth one hundred million dollars only after Reid had agreed to be the architect, working for him as a consultant. "I don't have an architect capable of designing that kind of building," he said, "but for Reid Maguire, it's little more than a chicken scratch. He can design anything, and he certainly didn't put any structural flaws in that simple building that Brown and Worley erected in Baltimore. Reid showed me the plans. I couldn't find a flaw in them."

When Emerson began his cross-examination, after his

first question, Marks eyed him scornfully and said, "Man, if you're going to be a lawyer for architects, learn something about architecture. That's a ridiculous question."

She hardly recognized Philip when he took the stand, for she hadn't previously seen him dressed in business attire, and the effect was stunning.

"A level-four hurricane severely damaged my barns and stables, but only a few shingles came off the two-story dormitory that Reid designed," Philip told the court. "He also served as engineer for the building which has eleven bachelor apartments, a recreation room, lounge, dining room and professional kitchen. The exterior resembles an elegant clubhouse. Reid Maguire doesn't do shoddy work, not even when it comes to grooming a horse."

When Reid strode to the witness stand, she'd never been so proud. *What a gorgeous man!* she said to herself. Dean Barker fed Reid questions guaranteed to make him shine, and shine he did.

"So you think a man like you can take on a prestigious firm like Brown and Worley, do you?" Emerson said to Reid as he began the cross-examination. *That question means he knows he's lost the case,* Kendra said to herself, leaned back and crossed her knees.

A grin lit up Reid's face. "That can't be a serious question. They're sloppy builders, and the court has as proof the sworn opinion of one of the best architectural examiners anywhere. Imagine leaks in a house completed less than six months earlier…" And so it went, as lawyer and witness showed their mutual antagonism.

The next morning, both sides summed up and the

case went to the jury. Kendra didn't go to court that day or the next for although she believed Barker had won the case, she'd learned never to second-guess a jury. At three-thirty on the second day of the jury's deliberation, a banging on her front door startled her, and she peeped out of a second-floor window, saw Reid standing there and raced down the stairs. As she reached the door, fear gripped her, fear that he might have lost. When he banged again, she slipped the door chain, turned the lock and opened the door.

He picked her up, twirled her around and around and then, as if becoming suddenly sober, he set her on her feet, wrapped her in his arms and whispered, "We won. You and I. We won, baby. I have my reputation and six million, a million for each year. They're probably too broke to pay it, because you stuck it to them when they lost to CFSL.

"Kendra, love of my life, it's over. Let's go down to the estate this weekend and celebrate."

"Honey, we can celebrate right here. There's no reason now why we can't be seen together. Where are Philip and Arnold?"

"They went back right after Philip testified. Feel like making us some coffee?"

"And after you get your caffeine fix, we'll toast this occasion with some wine," she said. She made the coffee and gave it to him in a mug. "Did Philip tell you that he and Claudine are planning to get married?"

"He said he hoped they would marry by the time school opens. Did she tell him she'd marry him?"

"I guess so. She told me she's planning to marry

between Thanksgiving and Christmas, so Philip can relax. When Claudine makes up her mind, she records her decision in stone."

He took several sips of coffee, put the cup down and asked her, "What about us? I've missed you terribly these past two weeks. That last night we were together poleaxed me. Kendra, I didn't know I could be so happy."

"You were not alone. I'd waited all my life for that evening, and—"

"I know. In a way, I'm glad it happened as it did, because we both had a chance to stand back and think about this relationship. And I like what I learned about you. Since you wear that robe at work, being pregnant shouldn't be a problem, should it?"

"Being…what? What do you mean? I'm not pregnant."

"I know, but don't you want a family?"

"Yes, of course I do," she said, her voice quavering.

"Then we'd better get started on that." He stood, pushed the chair aside and knelt before her. "I love you with all my heart, and I'll always put you and our children first in my life, before my work and before me. Will you marry me?" His eyes beseeched her.

She reached toward him with arms open, spread her knees and clasped him to her body. "Oh, yes. I will. I'll be honored to be your wife, Reid Maguire." She kissed the tears that clung to his lashes. "I love you so much."

"I know," he said. "You taught me the meaning of love."

National bestselling author
FRANCINE CRAFT

The Way You Make Me Feel

The diva who had amnesia...

Suffering from amnesia, singer Stevie Simms
finds refuge in Damien Steele's home. As they
become lovers, Damien's frozen heart thaws
and Steve starts to recover. But someone is
trying to kill Stevie—if only she could
remember who!

*Available the first week of March,
wherever books are sold.*

www.kimanipress.com   KPFC0090307

BESTSELLING AUTHOR

AMOS ROBYN

Promise ME

After taking a break from a demanding career and a controlling
fiancé, Cara Williams was ready to return to her niche in the
computer field. It looked like clear sailing—until AJ Gray came
on the scene. As the powerful president of Captial Computer
Consulting, AJ offered Cara the expertise she needed—even as his
kisses triggered her worst fears and her deepest desires.

Coming the first week of March,
wherever books are sold.

ARABESQUE®

www.kimanipress.com

KPRA0070307

An emotional story of family and forgiveness…

National bestselling author

PHILLIP THOMAS DUCK

PLAYING WITH
DESTINY

As brothers, Colin and Courtney Sheffield know
their lives will always be connected. But their mistakes,
and those of their absent father before them, have tangled
them in a web of bitterness and regret neither can shake.

As painful secrets threaten to shatter their futures,
both must deal with the emotional complexities
of true brotherhood.

"Duck writes with a voice that is unique,
entertaining and compelling."
—Robert Fleming, author of *Havoc After Dark*

*Available the first week of March,
wherever books are sold.*

sepia™

www.kimanipress.com

KPPTD0390307

A dramatic story about cultural identity, acceptance and being true to oneself.

The Edification of Sonya Crane

JD Guilford

When Sonya Crane transfers to a predominantly black high school, she finds that pretending to be biracial makes it easier for her to fit in and gives her the kind of recognition and friendships that she's never had before. That is, until popular girl Tandy Herman threatens to disclose her secret....

Look for it in March!

Second chance for romance…

When
Valentines
Collide

Award-winning author
ADRIANNE
*B*YRD

Therapists Chante and Michael Valentine agree to a "sex-
therapy" retreat to save their marriage. At first the seminar
revives their passion—but their second chance at love is
threatened when a devastating secret is revealed.

"Byrd proves again that she's a wonderful storyteller."
—*Romantic Times BOOKreviews* on *The Beautiful Ones*

Available the first week of February,
wherever books are sold.

KIMANI™
ROMANCE

www.kimanipress.com

KPAB0050207